Falling Apart Together
J.B. Lee

J.B. Lee

Book Cover, Chapter Header Images, and Scene Break Images by Lauren Gnapi with Elemental Opal

Edited by Caitlin Lengerich

Contents

Author's Note

Thank you for taking a chance on *Falling Apart Together*!

This book has heavy content which was inspired by personal experience. The main character's mother is diagnosed with cancer, and while her exact diagnosis and parts of this story are written for a fictional character, there are parts that I used from my experience with my own mother's cancer diagnosis. I took the grief I've had built up since losing my mom to her battle to stoke the flames of that particular storyline.

However, this book does not solely focus on the grief. There is happiness and spice—lots of spice. For those who like to know when the spice happens, there is a dicktionary located at the back of the book.

As much as I'd love for you to read this book and fall in love with these characters, your mental health matters. This book has the following topics, and if you don't feel like you can read this please do not hesitate to put it down and find something more lighthearted.

Content Warnings:
Cancer and death of a parent
Estranged parental relationships
Depressive episode
Hyperemesis Gravidarum (HG) briefly mentioned
Explicit sexual content

Playlist

These were songs either mentioned within the story, or songs I listened to while writing. Feel free to find the album on Spotify.

"Flowers" by Miley Cyrus

"I Can't Help Falling in Love with You" by Elvis

"I Will Always Love You" by Whitney Houston

"I've Got You Babe" by Sonny and Cher

"Like My Mother Does" by Lauren Alaina

"I Won't Back Down" by Tom Petty

"You Belong With Me" by Taylor Swift

"I'm Gonna Love You Through It" by Martina McBride

"The Show Must Go On" by Queen

"Big Bottom" by Spinal Tap

"Amazing Grace" by Chris Tomlin

"Forever Like That" by Ben Rector

"Steep" by Jordyn

"U Can't Touch This" by MC Hammer

"All the Small Things" by Blink-182

"(God Must Have Spent) A Little More Time on You" by NSYNC

"I Will Always Love You" by Vitamin String Quartet

Dicktionary

For those who like to know where the spice is:

To my mom, I hope I'm making you proud, even though I write a little bit of spice.

Prologue
Sherri

1 *week after diagnosis*

It's been one week since the doctors told me there's no cure.

I've been trying to cope with the news while also trying to remain strong for Paul and Tessa. One would think I'd have a reprieve at work, but Graham is there and he keeps telling me the same thing Paul does, "It's okay if you aren't okay. This is scary stuff, Sherri, you don't have to be strong if you aren't feeling strong." They're right, of course. But I don't want them to know just how scared I am.

Today was my last official day at the middle school, and I decided to come out to the lake afterwards to really let myself feel all the feelings without fear of making anyone else lose it too. I'm sitting on the dock, looking out at the water, with empty envelopes and the journal that Tessa bought me in my lap. The breeze on this early March afternoon has me pulling my jacket tighter around my thinning frame.

The maple trees are still mostly bare, while the pine trees are holding strong to their needles. The water laps against the dock as I sit crying at the realization of what my diagnosis means.

"Why me?" I take in a shuddering breath. "I'm not ready to die. I had dreams for Paul and I. Tessa still has a life full of milestones that I'm going to miss," I sob into the afternoon sky. I know I won't get a response, but saying my thoughts out loud feels therapeutic in a way.

The first letter I write is to Paul. I need him to know that it'll be okay to move on and find someone to make him happy again. He's still young, and fine as hell, if I do say so myself. He shouldn't spend the rest of his life alone just because I'll no longer be here. Once I've gotten that one written, I set it aside. I let the tears continue to fall as I sit contemplating who I'm going to write next.

Grabbing the journal and my pen again, I begin my letter to my sweet Tessa. I know she's going to struggle with this. But I also know that Paul and Graham won't let her drown in her sorrow. They'll be strong when she doesn't feel the strength within herself.

I look down as I pick up the envelopes. I plan on adding a sticky note to each so Paul knows when it's time to open them, and after sitting here for what was probably two hours, I'm finally ready to head back home.

Chapter 1

Tessa

"Ugh. I can't believe we're going to Glenda's on Valentine's Day," Nell complains as we walk in the door of the local karaoke bar. The smell of stale alcohol hits my nose as soon as my foot hits the sticky bar floor.

I roll my eyes as I wave at the table our friends have gathered at. "Nell, you're the one who made us promise we would come here for karaoke bi-weekly once we met Felix and you found out he could sing. It's not my fault this week happened to fall on your favorite holiday." I finish my sentence as we get to the table and I give out hugs to our friends before placing a quick kiss on Bennett's cheek.

"Hey, T, I got you a strawberry margarita," Bennett says in greeting. I give a smile that doesn't reach my eyes. I hate tequila, but we've only gone out a few times so he doesn't know that.

Blair, Vanessa, and Nell watch me as I pick up the glass and sniff the drink. "Thanks, I'm not really a tequila girl, though." In past relationships I would have sucked it up and drank the damn thing, but the girls have told me I need to start speaking up for what I want, and tequila is not it.

He frowns and a cute crease forms in the middle of his brow. "I'm sorry, I didn't know. What would you like instead?" he asks, reaching for the glass and taking a sip, claiming it for himself.

"Anything with vodka and I'm golden!" I reply, smiling—this time a full one. He taps my hand before walking over to the bar to get me a new drink and I shamelessly watch his ass. I faintly hear the conversation going on at the table as I observe Bennett and the bartender, his neat blond hair reaching just slightly above his ears, his brown eyes sparkling as he laughs at something she says. I should feel jealous, but the obvious pang doesn't hit.

As he turns to walk back to the table, my attention shifts to the conversation my friends were having. "What song did you sign up for tonight, Blair?" I ask, knowing full well that this is her favorite activity: singing in front of a ton of people.

Blair's bright blue eyes widen as a devilish smile crosses her face. "Well, it's Valentine's Day and that sorry, piece-of-shit ex of mine posted on his stories that he'd be here tonight. So, I'm singing 'Flowers' by Miley Cyrus."

We all let out a laugh as she shimmies in her bright pink sequin dress. I look around the crowded bar to see if I can see said piece of shit—Dalton. My eyes roam the room, but I don't spot him. I glance at the stage as a guy sings a song by Elvis, and a few girls stand by with hearts in their eyes.

Bennett sets my drink down in front of me and asks the group, "Did T tell you about our cooking class date the other day?" There's nothing but humor in his eyes.

They collectively shake their heads, but Jace is the only one actually verbalizing the "no." Bennett looks at me as I narrow my eyes at him and slightly shake my head, laughing.

"Go ahead, tell them," I say, chuckling. "It probably sounds funnier coming from a third party anyway." I roll my eyes.

He puts an arm around my shoulder and pulls me in, kissing my forehead before jumping into the story. "So, we went to a cooking class over the weekend and the meal we were learning to make was chicken Alfredo, which doesn't sound difficult, right?" They all look at me and I continue shaking my head, aware of where the story is going. "Everything was going great. The instructor had homemade pasta made for us when we arrived so that was taken care of, we were just in charge of making the chicken and following his instructions on making the Alfredo sauce."

Nell and Vanessa's eyes both go wide as they realize where this is going. The three of us lived together for a bit, so they are well aware of my lack of culinary skills when it comes to anything but breakfast food.

"Well, the instructions called for two cloves of garlic." At that I hear Felix gasp as he too realizes where the story is headed.

"No. You didn't," Felix says, looking at me with pity and amusement in his brown eyes.

"In my defense," I argue, "everyone says you can never have too much garlic when cooking. Plus, if I'm being honest, I don't know what two cloves of garlic is equivalent to when it's minced, and I've only ever cooked with minced garlic." The table erupts with laughter, including my own.

"Exactly how many cloves of garlic did you add?" Blair leans across the table, staring into my soul.

I cover my face before I mumble out, "Five." The gasps I hear from everyone confirm what I found out when we tried the sauce: too much garlic. Thankfully, the emcee picked that moment to call Felix up to the stage for his turn at karaoke.

We turn our attention to the stage as he saunters up there. "This one's for you, babe," he says, blowing a kiss and grinning at Nell. Her face turns a shade darker from the attention everyone is giving her. I start laughing as the opening notes of Whitney Houston's "I Will Always Love You" begins.

I drink two more vodka sodas as a few more singers take their turn, and before I know it, the emcee is back on the microphone, drawing my attention away from my conversation.

"Okay, okay. Let's put our hands together for the last singers of the night. Nell and Tessa, come on up here." I turn to Nell whose eyes go wide—she was in the bathroom when I signed us up. She also isn't privy to the song choice. I grab her hand and pull her as Jace gives her a slight push from his chair. Felix lets out a loud "Whoop, that's my baby!" as we make our way to the stage.

I take the microphones from the emcee, handing one to Nell and keeping one for myself. I stand facing her, smiling as the music starts to play. Her face immediately lights up and she starts laughing as Sonny and Cher's "I Got You Babe" blares through the speaker. She grabs my hand as the words start on the screen and takes the first verse, singing while looking at me.

As the song comes to an end, people are standing, clapping for us, and we both take dramatic bows. We hand the emcee our mics and walk back to the table, waving and blowing kisses to the crowd as if they are here solely for our performance.

Chapter 2

Tessa

I'm sitting on the couch working on a sketch for a client while Lizzo, my roommate's cat, kneads my thigh. I keep getting frustrated because I want the couple on the cover of this book to look more in love, but I'm having a hard time conveying that in their gaze. As I reach for another piece of week-old Valentine's Day chocolate, my phone buzzes with a text.

Dad:

> *Hey Bug, can we FaceTime tonight instead of calling?*

Me:

> *Yeah, sure. Everything okay?*

Dad:

> *We just want to FaceTime tonight.*

I drop the chocolate I had just picked up back in the box and stare at my phone. I absentmindedly bring my thumb to my mouth and chew on my nail. Our phone call isn't for another thirty minutes, which makes my mind wander.

We've talked on the phone every night since I moved, because I honestly can't go a day without talking to my parents. But we video chat once a week—on Sundays. It's Friday.

Why would they want to chat tonight?

I moved away from home fourteen years ago for school and didn't go back. I love my parents, but I didn't want to live my whole life in Middleburg. Our weekly video calls started a few years after I left home, after my dad had a dream that I fell and broke my arm and didn't tell them. Looking around my open-concept living room, I can't help but let my mind drift to all the reasons they might want to switch it up this weekend.

Curling and uncurling my legs beneath me, I check the time. Why is time moving so slow? As if willing it to happen, my phone starts ringing, and my mom's face fills the screen.

"Hey, Mom. Hey, Dad!" I say, trying to hide the sudden rush of anxiety from my face. I'm not sure I can hide it from my voice, though. I watch my phone as my dad's face appears next to my mom and they place the phone down in front of them.

"Hey, Tessa-bug," my dad greets me, with a tight-lipped smile on his sun-kissed face. Years of working in the yard without sunblock showing.

My heart picks up speed as I take in the red rim around my mom's soft brown eyes. "Hey, sweetheart," she says.

"What's wrong, Mom? Did something happen at school today?" I ask. I don't want to upset her anymore, but the anxiety swimming in my brain and the hammering of my heart at seeing her upset isn't going to allow me to drag this out.

My dad starts to fidget with the corner of the pillow he's holding in his lap. He's not looking at the phone, nor is he looking at my mom. His eyes are trained on the beige pillow he's messing with.

What feels like minutes pass by without anyone saying anything. Lizzo curls up in my lap and dozes off to sleep and I watch my mom as her eyes struggle to hold tears back.

"Okay, will one of you tell me what the hell is going on? You asked to FaceTime tonight." I pause. "I can tell you've been crying, Mom. And, Dad, you look like you're going to take apart that pillow at any moment. Frankly, you're scaring me," I finally get out with as little yelling as my nerves will let me. After saying it, I hold my breath as I wait for the shoe to drop. It has to drop.

My mom lets out a sob and puts her face in her hands. My dad's hand goes up as he rubs soothing circles on her back. His bright blue eyes look at me through the phone, tears are forming in the corners. My eyes start watering at the sight.

I don't think I've ever seen my dad cry.

"Tess, this is news we would much rather tell you in person." He swallows and then continues. "But considering we were just there for the new year, and you don't have a visit home planned any time soon, we just didn't think we should wait," my dad says, his voice breaking through the sorrow-filled silence.

I sit upright on my couch, too afraid to say anything. Almost too afraid to even breathe. I just sit, blinking at the screen, fighting back the tears that want to fall. The shoe is most definitely about to drop.

"Honey," my mom says, collecting herself, "do you remember the appointment I had with my doctor a few weeks ago? The one I made because of the pain in my chest. How I was so sure it was just caused by stress?" She continues without letting me so much as nod. I don't like where this is going. "They wanted to do some tests, and they . . ." She stops, looks at my dad who is sitting there, laser focused on his hands, and takes a deep breath. "They found multiple masses during those scans and they referred me to an oncologist. I had that initial appointment this past Wednesday."

Time stands still. I'm unable to hear, but I see her mouth still moving. I can't breathe. Everything stops. This is not happening.

I had forgotten to ask about that appointment a few weeks ago. How could I forget to ask her about an appointment she had? Why didn't she tell me about the tests they needed to run?

I have to stop my mind from the endless spiral it's about to go down. "What do you mean they found multiple masses? What did the oncologist say?" I cut her off, tears threatening to spill out of my eyes—the brown eyes I got from her. I put words to the thoughts swimming around in my brain. "How could they think that's what they saw? You're healthy!" I practically scream, tears falling freely now.

My dad, clearly startled by my outburst, sits up fully and puts his hands on his knees. My mom just sits there with sorrow etched on her features. Taking a steadying breath she replies, "The oncologist said they believe it's stage four cancer with how many masses they found in my lungs. I'm scheduled to get a full body scan on Monday to see if it's spread further than just the initial location. However, he isn't very hopeful." She looks over at her husband, my dad, whose face has grown ashen and has also stopped trying to keep the tears at bay.

"After they get the results from those scans we can figure out a plan of attack. I'm not going down without a fight," she says, determination in her voice.

"I'm coming home," I choke out through tears. "I've been working remote anyways. I'll email my boss tonight, and I'll tell Nell to start looking for someone to rent out my room. I want to be there to help in any way that I can." I leave no room for negotiation in my words.

"Tessa, that's not why we're telling you. You have a life in Richmond; you've been seeing that Ben guy. We don't want you to uproot yourself to come back home. I will take care of your mother like I have for the last thirty years," my dad responds, but I'm not listening. I already pulled out my laptop to start looking into moving truck rentals. It's time to pack up the life I've created for myself the past ten years and go back to Middleburg.

I won't let my parents go through this alone.

Chapter 3

Graham

Sherri didn't come to work again today—that's three days in a row. She doesn't always tell me when she won't be in, but since we're the only two seventh grade English teachers at Middleburg Middle School we like to get together on Fridays to plan for the following week. Sherri has been my mentor since I first started at the school, and over the years we've become really good friends. So, typically, if she'll be out on a Friday, she gives me a heads-up.

I grew up down the street from Sherri, her husband, Paul, and their daughter, Tessa. And while I didn't spend a lot of time at their house, they were familiar with who I was—the lanky little dark-haired boy who was infatuated with their daughter. I was always trying to tag along with Tessa and her friends when they were outside, or asking if she wanted to come over and jump on my trampoline, ride bikes, or play basketball with me and my brother. Honestly, I would do anything to be near her.

The older we got the harder it was for me to keep my feelings for her a secret. We weren't little kids anymore and I couldn't just ask her to come play, so instead, we would sit at our computers for hours talking to each other through instant messaging. But as we grew up, I could never tell if she was talking to me because she liked being my friend, or if there was possibly more.

Tessa wasn't just nice though, she was smart, funny, and the prettiest girl I'd ever seen. Especially when we got to high school. She always wore her long golden-brown hair in curls down her back, and her stunning cocoa-brown eyes always had a sparkle in them. The joy in her heart escaped, radiating warmth and kindness, causing everyone to gravitate towards her.

Tessa moved to Richmond a few years after we graduated high school and only comes home for short visits during the holidays now. I've caught glimpses of her a time or two in the past few years, and those glimpses confirm that she still manages to take my breath away.

I moved back into my childhood home when my parents decided to downsize to a townhome. So, now, I'm back to living down the street from Sherri.

The school day ended a few hours ago and I'm sitting at my kitchen table with my laptop open looking over the lesson plans I wrote for next week. I intend to send them to Sherri in case she hasn't had time to plan anything. My tuxedo cat, Jay Catsby, weaves between my legs, purring, reminding me it's dinner time. Before I get up to feed him, my laptop pings letting me know that I have a new email. I reach down, scratching Jay Catsby behind the ear before opening it.

To: <u>GRLink@mcps</u>.edu
From: <u>SEGunter@mcps</u>.edu
Subject: Absence

Graham,

I'm sorry I didn't let you know I would be out the last few days. My appointment didn't go as expected the other day. If you'd like to come over this weekend we can talk. I should be back to work on Tuesday—I have another appointment on Monday. I requested Ms. Appleby for my substitute. If you don't mind helping her with plans for the day, I would really appreciate it. We're still working on *Hoot*, so there shouldn't be too much for her to do, but you know that.

Again, I'm sorry I didn't let you know I wouldn't be there sooner. Just stop by tomorrow or Sunday evening and we can talk. Paul found a new recipe for his zucchini he'd like to try. See you soon, honey.

Have a good evening,

Sherri

So, her doctor appointment wasn't nothing after all. I have noticed her lack of appetite during lunch lately, and her energy is almost completely depleted by the end of the day. I just assumed it was the regular stress of teaching at this time of year, but now, something in my gut tells me her news is going to be bad.

To: <u>SEGunter@mcps.edu</u>
From: <u>GRLink@mcps.ed</u>
Subject: Re: Absence
Attachment: Lesson Plans Week of February 26

Sherri,

Don't even worry about Monday. I sat down and worked out lesson plans for next week and was about to email them to you. In fact, I'll attach them to this email.

I can come by for dinner tomorrow. Tell Paul I look forward to this new zucchini recipe!

See you tomorrow,

Graham

Chapter 4

Graham

I hate showing up at someone's house empty-handed, so as I wait at the door, I shift the pie I made between my hands. Since I started working at the middle school with Sherri nine years ago, I've come over on many occasions to spend time with her and Paul. So, I don't know why I'm so nervous this time.

"Graham! Welcome, welcome, come on in! Sherri's in the kitchen making some iced tea." Paul answers the door with a smile on his face.

"Good evening, Paul," I say to the man I've come to view as a second father. I reach up to give him a one-arm hug before offering him the apple pie. "I brought dessert."

His smile grows as he pulls the aluminum foil up to take a peek. "Apple? You spoil me, Graham. You know this is my favorite."

I smile in return because I do know.

We walk into the house and just like every time before, my gaze instantly goes to the pictures of Tessa on the wall. The foyer has pictures of her from infancy into late toddlerhood, and when you turn the corner into the living room, the pictures document her as she continued to grow.

"Sherri! Graham is here, and he brought apple pie!" Paul calls. "He's going to make me fat if he does this every time he comes over!" he continues as he walks out of the room, leaving me alone in the living room.

It's been a few weeks since I've been over and I notice a new picture on the mantle. My eyes focus on it like it's the only thing in the room, so I walk over to get a better look. It's a picture of Tessa sitting under a tree, head tilted slightly, as she laughs at something someone said. Her full lips are the color of red wine, and she's wearing a cream turtleneck sweater and dark-blue skinny jeans, with her legs tucked to the side, her feet out of the image. Her long hair slightly covers her face, but I can still see the sparkle in her brown eyes. I haven't heard her laugh in years, but I immediately hear the melody in my mind just by looking at the picture.

Fuck, she's still as gorgeous as ever.

Lost in the picture, I'm startled by a hand on my shoulder. "Oh, I'm sorry. I didn't mean to scare you," she says with a chuckle. "Paul took that picture of her when we were visiting over New Years. She took us for a picnic at a park she loves to visit. We just got around to having it printed," she adds, pointing to the picture she caught me admiring.

I smile at the older woman as I turn to greet her with a hug. "Hello, Sherri, how are you doing?" I ask, as I take in her uncharacteristically disheveled appearance. I know from her email that she has some news, but besides her worn-down look, I can't decipher any clues as to what's going on.

"Dinner is ready, if you're good to sit down and eat," she says, giving me a tight squeeze before releasing me from the embrace.

As we eat dinner the conversation is normal, bouncing between discussing Paul's job at the police department, and what's new with my brother and his family. Sherri asks about my niece and nephew, while I ask about the recipe Paul used for this zucchini dish.

During dessert, I tell Sherri about the school gossip that she missed in her absence and inform her that she was right about the art teacher, Daphne Plumb, having a new partner.

"How did you find out?" she asks, laughing.

"Well, I passed by while Kyle was asking her to dinner, to which she said 'I don't think my partner would like that very much,' and then she walked away," I say, right after I wipe pie crumbs from my mouth.

After we've finished eating, Paul looks at Sherri and she gives him a slight nod. He stands up and collects the dishes.

"Let's go sit in the living room, honey." Sherri pats my hand and then stands up.

When we've gotten comfortable in the living room, Sherri wastes no time jumping into her news. My mind starts bouncing around as I listen and try to keep up with everything she's telling me. By the time she's done, Paul has joined us and is sitting next to Sherri, holding her hand as tears silently fall from her eyes.

Seeing her cry suddenly takes me back to my second year teaching. My brother, Grant, and his wife, Lisa, had just gotten the news that my niece, Corinne, their two-year-old daughter, was diagnosed with autism. Her speech had been delayed and the doctors were concerned she wouldn't ever talk.

My brother confided in me the fears that they had, and it broke my heart. I didn't know what to do since I didn't have kids myself and I wasn't close with our parents. So, with my brother's permission, I went to the only parent figure I had: Sherri.

She immediately went into Mama Bear mode, giving me all sorts of games I could play with her to teach her sign language and titles of books I should read to better understand the diagnosis itself.

Her eyes had glistened with unshed tears as she said, *"My cousin is mute and the best thing her parents did when they found out was learn to communicate with sign language. You are a wonderful uncle, wanting to be this involved in how to support the possibility of that being your niece's future. We will get you through this, and you will help get your brother through this. I'm here for you."*

My eyes mist over as I look around the living room before I fix my sight on Sherri and Paul as I repeat those words she said to me all those years ago: "We will get through this." I swallow as I reach for the hand Paul isn't holding. "I'm here for you. Whatever you need."

I have no idea how I can help, all I know is I will do whatever I can.

Chapter 5

Tessa

"Thanks for meeting me," I say as I hug Bennett.

"Of course, it sounded pretty serious," he says as we sit down with our coffees.

I take a minute before jumping into the reason I asked him to meet me so I can look around Cogan's Cafe. It's a small coffee shop around the corner from the library where Nell and I met. The atmosphere is cozy, with a few tables but mostly small couches placed strategically around the small space, allowing for you to feel at home.

I take in a deep breath and let the aroma of fresh-ly-brewed coffee and homemade baked goods fill my nostrils. My eyes find Bennett's before I begin to speak. My heart quickens at the fear of how he might take what I'm about to tell him. "I received some not-so-great news about my mom and I've decided to move home, at least for the time being, to be with her and my dad." I watch his face as his eyebrows pinch together and his thin lips curve down into a slight frown.

He nods his head and looks down at his coffee cup. "Do you want to talk about it?" he asks as he looks up at me through his ridiculously long and beautiful eyelashes. I sigh with relief that he doesn't seem angry.

"I don't know. I just got the call Friday night, so I'm still processing everything." I pick up my coffee to take a sip, but don't fully bring it to my mouth before adding, "But I know we're still in the process of getting to know each other as more than friends, so I wanted to let you know that I think we should pause this. At least until I move back."

"I get it. I mean, it sucks, because I like you, and I've been enjoying our dates, but I do get it." His brown eyes don't leave mine.

We talk about the book cover I'm working on as we finish our coffees. Considering we met at a conference for artists who specialize in digital drawing and traditional drawing, I know his interest in my current project isn't just for show. Once we finish our coffees, I give him a hug and promise to text him to let him know when I've made it to Middleburg safely.

I let out a shaky breath as I put the last box in the moving truck. I pull the door down and put the lock in place before turning to head back into the house I've lived in for the last ten years.

It's Sunday morning. As soon as I got off the phone with my parents Friday night, I ran into Nell's room with a tear-streaked face and we made a plan of action. We rented a U-Haul, asked around for moving boxes, and spent all day Saturday crying and packing up my things in preparation for me to head back to Middleburg.

Nell, my best friend and roommate for the last decade, is standing in the kitchen with her hip leaning against the granite countertop when I walk back in. I met Nell two weeks after I graduated college, at the library. I was living in a hotel as I figured out my next steps, and I needed to get out of my room for a change of scenery, so I set up at the library. I was sitting at a desk with my cheek resting on my hand when this beautiful goddess of a woman approached me. She was tall and thin, with the most beautiful russet, reddish-brown skin I'd ever seen, her coily, raven-black hair held back with a floral silk headband.

"Do you mind if I sit there?" she asked, pointing to the chair sitting across from me, placing her things down before actually giving me a chance to respond. "I'm Janelle—Nell, for short. What's your name?"

"I'm Tessa," I answered, quickly moving my belongings to make room for her. Her take-charge attitude drew me in instantly, and I knew I had to be her friend. A few weeks later, I moved into one of the guest rooms in the house she had recently purchased. What started out as temporary—until I could find a steady job and a place of my own—turned permanent pretty quick.

Looking at her standing in our kitchen—*her* kitchen—breaks my heart. Nell was my first friend when I moved here and leaving her to go back home is going to be tough. Not that her fiancé, Felix, seems all that broken up about it. He loves me, but he was definitely glad when he found out he'll be able to move back in. He was living with us for a while when we were all just friends, but once he and Nell got together he moved out because he felt he was making things awkward for me in my own home. I tried to reassure them I didn't mind, but he insisted.

I pick Lizzo up off the counter and nuzzle my face into her calico fur. "I'm really going to miss you guys," I say, trying to keep my voice steady.

"I know, we'll miss you too! But hey, it isn't forever. You take care of what you need to and you come right back home. I'll kick Felix back out," Nell says, pulling me into a hug. Felix, however, gives a "humph" from the dining room table.

"I appreciate that, but you two are going to finally sit down and set a date for that wedding. And now that I'm not going to be here, you can fill all the extra rooms with beautiful babies," I say, trying to lighten the mood. It works a little seeing as they both laugh.

I turn around to survey the open-concept space and everything in it that I'm leaving behind. As I make a full circle my eyes catch on the clock.

"Shit, I have to go," I curse. Giving Lizzo one more kiss on her head, I place her on her favorite perch on the counter and turn toward Felix. "I know you're going to miss me most of all," I tease, pulling him into a hug.

"Yeah, yeah. We both know that a three-hour drive isn't going to keep you gone forever. Plus, you're gonna have to come back to help with the wedding dress shopping and whatever else it is that the maid of honor does with the bride," Felix says, his tight hug revealing more than his words are. He's going to miss having me around.

Nell grabs my hand and walks with me to the driveway. As we walk I choke out, "What if we lose her, Nell? How will I be able to be happy if I lose my mom?"

She stops me and pulls me into a tight embrace. "Hey. Hey! Listen, she's going to go into that appointment and they will find that it's not as bad as they thought. She will fight this. Your mom is resilient, just like you."

I let out a horrendously loud sob as she rubs her hand over my back.

As I pull back from the hug she says, "I'm gonna miss you, Tessa-bug. Who else is going to sit up all night with me watching crappy reality TV shows and eating too much junk food?"

"Felix," we both say at the same time, laughing, breaking me out of the negative thoughts.

I look back at the house and Felix standing at the front door before hopping into the front seat of the U-Haul. It'll take about three hours to get home, and I promised myself I would be there in time for her scans on Monday morning. I'll be damned if I miss it. I steal one last glance at 335 Shrive Lane as I pull out of the driveway and take a right as I head toward the past.

Chapter 6

Tessa

It's a little after six when I finally pull into the driveway of my childhood home. My dad is sitting on a wicker chair with a glass of what I'm assuming is iced tea in his hand. He sets his drink down and stands up as I put the truck in park and climb out of the driver's seat. I run straight into his outstretched arms and immediately start crying.

"How's she really doing, Daddy?" I ask through sobs.

My dad squeezes me tightly and kisses the top of my head. "She's tired, Tessa-bug. She's nervous about her scans tomorrow. Then it'll be another week or two before we get the results back. So, unfortunately, that's more time for her to worry herself sick." He inhales and loosens his grip from my shoulders. "And she's scared, baby girl. That's the hardest part for me. I've known your mom for the best part of my life, and I don't think I've ever seen her this scared. She's trying to hide it, but I can tell."

I squeeze my eyes shut to try to stop the tears from falling. She is the strongest woman I know; I can't picture her being scared. "Then we'll have to be brave for her," I say, trying to force a smile on my face as we turn to walk into the house.

Walking into the living room, I come to a sudden stop as I see my mom taking a nap on her recliner and notice the subtle changes I couldn't pick up on over a FaceTime call. I suck in a deep breath, noticing the weight loss on her face and arms, as the reality of my mom's news starts to hit me and I can't help but wonder if I will ever be happy again if we lose her.

My mother isn't a tall woman, nor is she what others would consider thin—I take after her in both ways. While I'm slightly taller than her five-foot-three-inch frame, we probably weigh about the same. Being overweight, by doctors' standards, never bothered me because it never seemed to bother my mom. She wore her curves with confidence and pride, saying, "*God gave me these voluptuous curves for a reason. Why would I ever hate what He created?*" So, I held on to that same mentality. Sure, I work out and I eat healthy—most of the time—but I don't let my weight keep me from being anything but awesome.

I walk over to the recliner and pull the blanket off the back of the chair next to her and cover her up—she looks so peaceful. My dad turns the TV off and motions his head towards the kitchen. "We saved some chicken and dumplings for you. We weren't sure if you were planning on stopping to get some dinner on the way or not," he says, taking a food container out of the microwave.

"Thanks." I take the dish from his hand and get a fork out of the drawer. I sit down at the island and watch my dad pour a glass of lemonade. "I did a little research on stage four cancer. Even if they don't find anything else—" I choke on my words, unable to voice my thoughts. Maybe if I don't speak it, it won't be true. "There's no cure, is there? I mean, that's what I've read." I stare blankly at my dad as I move my food around, not quite sure if I'm even hungry. "Everything I've read says that chemotherapy and radiation will just help keep it from progressing, but there's no undoing what's already there. Especially if there are multiple masses. And they won't be able to do surgery to remove them all, will they?" Tears well up in my eyes again.

My dad leans down and places his forearms on the island and hangs his head, his bald head shining under the light. "No, honey. From what I've been reading, and based on what the doctor said at our visit last week, there's no cure." He lifts his left hand and runs it down his face. He glances up at me, tears brimming his bright blue eyes.

I put the lid back on the chicken and dumplings and set it aside. I don't understand how this could be happening. My mom is only fifty-two. She's still young; she's healthy in all the ways that matter, so how did she get lung cancer?

"Do you need any help bringing anything inside tonight?" My dad's voice breaks through my thoughts.

"No, I just planned on bringing in my laptop case and one of the bags of clothes. I'll deal with all the other stuff tomorrow after her appointment." My mind drifts to my dad, and the pain he must be feeling.

My parents were high school sweethearts—not Prom King and Queen, but that didn't matter. Their love story was always my favorite. My dad was failing English sophomore year of high school and the teacher asked my mom if she could tutor him. He always said that he would have pretended to fail if it meant he got to meet and spend time with her. They got married right after graduating. My grandmother on my dad's side swore her son "*must have knocked that poor girl up*," but that wasn't the case. They just couldn't fathom life without the other. Two years later, they had me. They tried for a few years after I was born to have another baby, but for some reason she just never got pregnant again. But that didn't change the love they had for each other, or for me.

How was he going to handle life once she was gone?

"Did you hear me? Tessa?" my dad asks, putting his hand on my shoulder. "I know it's still early, but with your mom being so tired, we will probably call it a night shortly. The appointment is at nine, we'll leave here at eight fifteen."

Chapter 7

Graham

I'm bringing groceries inside when I see her walk out of her parents' house. My breath catches and I watch as she walks down the path. Her curly brown hair is tossed up in a messy bun, her leggings hug her thick thighs, and the hoodie she's wearing gives just enough of her figure away.

I feel like I'm dreaming.

My eyes bounce from her to the moving truck sitting in the driveway. A U-Haul? Surely if Paul and Sherri planned on moving to Richmond, that would've been mentioned at dinner last night.

I stand at the back of my SUV, staring at Tessa Gunter like some creep. When I see the boxes and furniture in the back of the truck my heart starts slamming in my chest. She grabs a duffle and a smaller bag that, from this distance, looks like it could be for a computer, before shutting the door again.

She's taking things out.

Paul and Sherri aren't moving away, she's moving back.

I catch a glimpse of jerky movements out of the corner of my eye and realize she's caught me staring and is now waving at me.

"Hey, Graham!" she shouts across the road.

Fuck, I guess I wasn't being as stealthy as I thought. "Hey, Tessa! Good to see you!" I shout back as I grab the remaining groceries out of my trunk and walk inside, ending any conversation before it can start, like an asshole.

I set the groceries on the counter and slide to the floor, grabbing Jay Catsby. "Why did I all but run away just because she said hi? What am I, a teenager who doesn't know how to interact with the opposite sex?" I stare at my cat as if he's got the answers, but he just rubs his head against my hand, purring in response.

I lean my head back against the cabinet and exhale. I can't believe she's moving home. I mean, obviously, I can—she wants to be here for her mom. But that means she's finally going to be around again. Well, not necessarily around me, but I can hold onto hope that we can rekindle some kind of friendship.

Setting Jay Catsby down, I stand up and start putting the groceries away. I grab an apple from the bag and wash it off. Taking a bite, I absently stare out my back window, looking at the backyard. Memories of my childhood come flooding back.

My older brother Grant and I would spend hours on the trampoline that used to be out there, talking about the plans we had for our future. The future I talked about always included Tessa and he would tease me relentlessly, but I didn't care. Once Tessa moved away, Grant used to joke that unless I followed her, she would come back married to someone else. Just the thought had knots forming in my stomach. I know I never had a claim on her, hell, I never even told her I liked her, but the image of her with someone else didn't settle well with me.

I understand, it's very hypocritical of me. After all, I didn't stay single after she left, in fact I was close to getting engaged once. But I think I realized that I would be settling for Amber if we stayed together, and I couldn't do that to her. When I ended things, she slapped me, not that I blame her, and told me I wasted three years of her life. I guess she wasn't exactly wrong.

I've only had flings since I realized I would never find someone else whose smile melted me to my core. Tessa is the only person who has given me that butterfly feeling in my stomach that is talked about in movies and books. Other girls, Amber included, just made me feel a little less lonely.

I've grown accustomed to the fact that I won't get married and have a family like my brother. Hell, my self-proclaimed lifelong bachelorhood has kept my parents off my back, which is a plus in my book.

George and Betsy Link couldn't be more disappointed that I haven't settled down and started a family yet. Grant was married with two kids by the time he was twenty-three. Yet, here I am, a full decade older than he was and my crowning accomplishment, besides my job, is my cat. My parents decided I wasn't worth arguing with when they realized I was serious about not getting married, which ended with them no longer speaking to me. So, when they decided to move and I asked what they were doing with the house, they sold it to me with the expectation that I don't come visit until I've found myself a wife. My parents have this barbaric idea that a man must marry or he isn't worth anything. So, to them, my decision to not get married means I don't respect them or their opinions.

My phone buzzing pulls me back to the present. "Are your ears burning?" I ask in place of a greeting.

"Uh, no. Why would they be burning?" Grant asks in response.

I chuckle at his clear confusion. "No reason, what's up?" I ask before taking another bite out of the apple in my hand.

I hear faint voices on his end of the phone before he answers. "I was just calling to see if you wanted to go to the park with me and the kids one day after work this week? They keep asking to see Uncle Graham, and Lisa would really appreciate it if I could get them out of the house for a few hours."

It's been a few weeks since I've seen Grant and the kids, but I doubt they're asking to see me. They're both just about in middle school, which also makes me question if they'd truly enjoy spending time at the park with me and their dad. "Sure, what day are you thinking?" I ask, putting him on speaker phone and pulling up my calendar.

Chapter 8

Tessa

Morning got here quicker than I'd have liked it to. I'm extremely nervous about the appointment, even though today is just a scan. I keep trying to tell myself it's just routine, to make sure there's nothing else wrong with her.

They won't find anything else.

They *can't* find anything else.

"Hey, Mama," I say, walking into the kitchen. I lean down to give her a hug and kiss her cheek. "You feeling okay?"

"Oh, Tessa, I'm so sorry I was sleeping when you got in last night," she says, ignoring my question.

I let her non-answer slide as my dad walks in and notices her full plate of breakfast. "Not hungry this morning, Sher?" he asks my mom, concern etched on his face.

She looks down at her plate and then up at my dad with a faint smile. "It's just my nerves. I'll be fine after they finish the scans, and you can take us out for a big brunch." She stands up, taking her plate of sausage, scrambled eggs, and toast to the trash.

"Hey! I would have eaten that," I say with a frown as I watch her dump her untouched breakfast.

"Oh, I'm sorry, dear. I'm just not thinking this morning." She pats my arm as she walks to the sink with the empty plate. "Grab something to-go if you plan on coming with us, we have to head out in a minute."

We pull up to the doctor's office and my stomach decides to do somersaults. My mom leads the way as we head inside, and we don't wait for very long before they call her back.

We all stand to head back to the room when she turns to my dad and me and says, "I'd like to go back alone." She turns and follows the nurse as my dad and I slump back down in our seats.

My dad sits beside me and grabs a magazine off the table in front of us, and I pull out the sketchbook I keep in my bag. He warned me the scans can take a while; I just assumed we'd be in the back with her while they happened. As the minutes pass by, I try to focus on the design my client described for her upcoming novel but my mind keeps wandering to my mom.

Thinking about how hard life will be if we lose her—all the happiness I've ever known will be cut in half. I take a deep breath and repeat my mantra again.

They won't find anything.

They *can't* find anything.

An hour passes and I've got a rough outline of the cover: a woman sitting in a chair at the front of an empty room, staring at a closed casket, when my mom walks out. She has a tight smile on her face as she walks over and waits at the checkout counter.

"—follow-up once the results come in." I catch the end of the receptionist's sentence as I walk up and grab my mom's hand. It's been a while since I've held it, but it feels right. She gives me a gentle squeeze, then responds to the receptionist.

"Thank you, I'll be waiting for that call."

Back in the car, I buckle my seatbelt and absentmindedly start biting my thumbnail as a somber silence fills the space. My dad is the first to break, turning to my mom to ask, "So, honey, what did you have in mind for brunch? Zigglers?"

"Oh, Paul," she responds with a sigh. "My stomach is still in knots. I think I'd like to just go home. I'll drink some ginger ale, relax on the recliner, and enjoy the day with Tessa." She must not feel well; she never turns down a trip to Zigglers—it's her favorite brunch spot. My dad must have the same thought because he glances at me in the rearview mirror and gives me a knowing look.

On the ride home, my eyes are looking out the window but my mind isn't focused on what we're passing. Instead, I'm thinking about my mom. She didn't touch her breakfast and now she's turning down Zigglers? My mind wanders back to how she looked this morning, standing in the kitchen. Her skin is sagging a bit more on her arms, and her pants are slightly looser than she normally wears. I can't help but wonder if she's losing weight because of the stress, or if there's more than just the cancer.

Chapter 9

Graham

After work today I head straight to the park to meet with Grant, Ethan, and Corinne, instead of going home. I arrive before them, so I take a seat at a bench facing the parking lot. I feel like I look less like a creep just hanging out in a park if I'm not facing the playground while kids play.

As I wait for my brother, I pull my collar up around my neck and bury my hands deeper into my jacket's pockets. Why Grant chose to come to the park when it's thirty fucking degrees is beyond me. It's times like this where I wish I didn't get rid of all social media. But after spending my first three years of teaching fielding requests from students and parents alike, I decided just to delete everything. Unfortunately, it means no mindless scrolling on days like today.

After what feels like twenty-five minutes of sitting in this terrible weather, Grant finally shows up. Ethan and Corinne get out of the car and immediately run straight for me. I stand up and hug my niece and nephew tightly, then shake my brother's hand in that manly way that shows we're too cool to hug. "Uncle Graham, Daddy said you really wanted to come to the park with us! Does that mean you will come swing with me?" my ten-year-old niece asks, smiling up at me.

While I can't quite imagine the logistics of me, a six-foot-tall man who weighs over two hundred pounds, swinging on a swing, I can't say no to her. "Oh he did, did he?" I say, taking her hand and looking at my brother. Of course he told them I wanted to come spend my free time at the park. "Lead the way, Cori."

Corinne and I start towards the swings, while Ethan takes his basketball and walks toward the basketball court on the other side of the playground. At the age of eleven, he definitely thinks he's too cool for the park. Grant gives me a sly grin and follows after his son.

Noticing the two of us walking towards the swings, a mother, or maybe a nanny, yells to twin girls, "Regina! Rebecca! You've been on the swings the whole time we've been here! Let someone else have a turn!" Reluctantly they get up from the swings and run to the monkey bars. How they plan on doing those with gloves on, I have no idea.

Sitting on the swing, I turn my attention to Corinne and ask, "So, how was school today? Anything exciting happen?"

Corinne looks at me with the biggest smile and shiny brown eyes. She nods her head. "Mikey Anders got in trouble for calling the new girl, Tricia Sting, Tricia Stinks. Even though I sat next to her in class and she doesn't smell at all." She takes a breath and then adds, "But Mikey is always calling people names and being mean."

"I hope this Mikey kid doesn't ever call you names, or is mean to you," I say with a tinge of anger in my voice. I don't even want to think about someone bullying my niece. I deal with twelve-year-olds all day and I know all too well how mean they can be, and the damage it can do to the ones being bullied. Especially someone like Corinne, who might not fully understand what's happening.

She quickly shakes her head. "No! He's never mean to me. In fact, he's asked me to be his girlfriend a bunch. But Mommy and Daddy say I'm too young to have a boyfriend. So, I told him we can only be friends."

I look at her thoughtfully and then shift my sights to my brother and his oldest. "Anything else on your mind, kiddo?" I return my gaze to her, giving her my full attention.

Her face lights up like a Christmas tree. "Yes! But, I'm not supposed to say." She bites her lip as she looks over at her dad. I give her a small nod, letting her know she can share whatever it is with me. "Mommy is having another baby!" she all but shouts. "And Ethan is *not* happy about it. He said, *'We don't need another baby. We already have Cori!'* But Mommy and Daddy just kept hugging and laughing. Then Mommy looked at Daddy and said, *'Don't even think about telling anyone yet,'* so you have to promise you won't say anything!"

I just continue sitting here with a stunned expression on my face. I didn't realize they were trying for another one. Not that it would have been my business. And it's not like they're too old to be having another, it's just that there's going to be a huge age gap between Ethan, Corinne, and this new baby. But the more I think about it, the more it makes sense. Grant has always wanted a large family. I can't help the smile that comes to my face as I think about how excited he must be.

We sit on the swings in a comfortable silence for a little while longer. Corinne pumping her legs making herself go as high as she can, me slowly moving myself back and forth with my feet firmly planted on the ground. While we swing, I look over at Ethan and Grant playing basketball. Both have abandoned their jackets and have their long sleeves rolled up. The sight of it makes a shiver run through my body.

I look out at the trees and then back at my niece, a sad smile forming on my face. I love my niece and nephew, and I'll no doubt love this new addition too, but I can't help but think if I'm being too stubborn with not trying to find happiness for myself.

I check my watch and realize it's getting late so I stand up from the swings. "Okay, Cori, I have to get home to feed Jay Catsby some dinner. Let's make our way over to your dad so I can chat with him for a bit before I leave." She stops swinging without complaint and reaches for the hand I have outstretched for her.

When we reach Grant and Ethan I tilt my head to motion for Grant to come talk. Corinne runs over to her brother and tries to grab the ball from him. We stand there watching the two of them run around before Grant breaks the silence.

"So, did you enjoy swinging?" He glances at me without shifting his face.

"I did. I learned some pretty interesting things. Like, this Mikey kid is a little bully. If he ever once says something unkind towards Corinne—"

He cuts me off. "Don't worry about Mikey. He's harmless, at least, for the most part. His twin is in most of Corinne's inclusion classes because he's got his own issues." This time he turns his full gaze to me. "Did she say anything else?"

I shake my head. I'm not about to rat out a ten-year-old. If he wants me to know there's another baby on the way, he can tell me himself.

"Oh come on, she didn't say *anything* else?" he practically shouts, causing Ethan and Corinne to stop playing and turn their attention to us.

"Nope. Is there something she was supposed to tell me?" I suppress the grin trying to take root.

He takes in a deep breath and shakes his head. "Well I'll be damned. She actually listened."

I lift an eyebrow in question and he grunts, "Nevermind. Get out of here; go feed your cat."

I pat my big brother on the shoulder, call out a farewell to the kids running around the basketball court, and head to my car. As I walk to my car, I pull my jacket closer and contemplate the choices I've made in life.

Chapter 10

Tessa

The week following my mom's appointment flies by. I spend the Monday after unloading most of the U-Haul, and since the house isn't big enough for everything I brought back, I spent Tuesday morning unloading the rest in a storage unit I rented.

I walk around each day, cleaning an already clean house, and have completed two book covers—receiving glowing reviews from the happy authors. I workout for about an hour each day, trying to release this built-up nervous energy that seems to be growing, as my mom awaits the phone call from the doctor.

The call comes on Thursday while she's at work. My dad and I are sitting at the table eating lunch when she calls.

"Hey, Sher—" my dad answers. "Calm down, honey, it'll be okay." I can only hear half the conversation as my dad stands up and paces the length of the kitchen. "Well, what exactly did they say?"

He stops at the refrigerator and looks at the calendar hanging on the door. He nods his head in agreement to something she must be saying on the other end. "Well, if that's when they can get you in, that's what we'll do." He grabs a pen and writes something down on the calendar. "I'll see you when you get home. I love you, too."

I pick up my plate before heading to the sink. "What did she say?" I ask as I glance at the calendar.

He takes in a deep breath before he answers. "The results came back sooner than expected. Her doctor wants to see her tomorrow morning, at nine."

I'm no doctor, nor do I have any real experience with them, but I would think that when the doctor wants to see you so soon after getting results, the news can't be good. I spend the rest of the day walking anxiously around the house, trying to find things to do to calm my mind.

By the time my mom gets home from work I've completed my daily workout, vacuumed the whole house, cleaned the dishes that were in the sink, emptied the refrigerator of the leftovers I knew wouldn't get eaten, and dusted. I wish I could say all that cleaning and working out had helped release my nervous energy, but I'd be lying.

"Woah! You really cleaned up here, Tessa!" my mom exclaims as she pulls me into a hug. "You even dusted? I know how much you hate dusting." She laughs, taking a look at the mantle.

"I did. I didn't know what to do today and I couldn't focus on my current drawing. My client is going to be so pissed." I laugh. "I would have started dinner, but I didn't know what you'd be in the mood for." I say the last part as I look at my mom. She hasn't eaten much since,

I'm assuming, Sunday night, before I got in. Maybe even before then.

She nibbles on her breakfast each morning before leaving for work, and at dinner she eats a few bites then just moves her food around her plate. I think she assumes my dad and I won't notice if it's not in the same spot it was at the beginning of the meal. I have to trust her when she says she eats her lunch at school, because I'm not there to witness it myself, but I've been tempted to show up at lunchtime to bring her something.

"I'm not really in the mood to eat right now. Why don't you and your dad go get some take-out? I think I want to just take a bath and relax a bit before bed. Maybe bring me back a cup of soup from Arlynes," she says, making my suspensions grow.

She's not eating. That can't be a good sign.

I'm really hoping this appointment tomorrow can shed some light on things.

My dad and I decide to grab sandwiches from Arlynes. That way, we can bring some soup like Mom asked. We sit in the diner—our dinner mostly tense silence.

My mind is spiraling with all the possible outcomes from tomorrow's appointment. The doctor could say they didn't find any more masses—they are just located in the lungs. That's the best case scenario. And then, we can plan a course of action so she can fight this thing. Or, the doctor could say they found that her body is riddled with tumors and there's absolutely nothing they can possibly do and that we should start saying our goodbyes.

I let out a muffled sob as I try to hide the fears that have sprouted in my head. What am I going to do if that's the news we get? If the doctors tell us that she doesn't have much time left, then I'm down to my last few happy days. The sunshine in my life will be gone.

I look over at my dad who has his head hanging low over his plate. Tears are streaking down his sun-kissed cheeks. I reach over and squeeze his hand, the only form of support I can muster right now.

When we get home, we find my mom is already asleep, without having eaten dinner. I give my dad a worried glance and then give him a hug before heading to bed.

"Goodnight, Dad. I'll see you in the morning."

"Goodnight, sweetie," he says as he rubs his hand over the back of his neck and lets out a defeated-sounding sigh.

My alarm wakes me from my restless sleep. I think about turning it off and rolling over to go back to sleep until I remember where I am and why I'm here. My mom has her appointment today to go over her scans and hopefully figure out a plan of action. So, even though I'm exhausted, I climb out of bed to start my day.

After taking a shower and blow-drying my hair, I check the temperature for the day and then look in my closet for something to wear. I hate the cold and the high is only supposed to be forty-two degrees. So, I grab a pair of thick jeans, a turquoise sweater, and a pair of black boots. Once I'm dressed and presentable, I walk to the kitchen where I hear a hushed discussion between my parents.

Trying not to eavesdrop I make as much noise as possible as I enter, but I still hear my dad finish his comment. "Sherri, I know you're nervous about your appointment, but, baby, you need to eat something." I look at his face and see his eyes pleading with her.

Tears form in the corners of her brown eyes as she whispers, "I can't, Paul. Every time I eat, I feel like I'm going to be sick. I can't explain why. I just feel sick to my stomach."

Hearing her comment makes my heart pick up and my stomach knot as a feeling of unease creeps through me. "It's okay, Mom. I can grab something small for you to eat on the way there, maybe a protein bar?" I say, grabbing a peanut butter bar out of the cabinet, eyes on my dad. He nods in defeat.

About twenty minutes later, we pull into the parking lot of the doctors office. As my dad puts the truck in park, I slowly take my hand away from my mouth. Looking down at my thumb in disgust, I realize at some point during the drive I started chewing on my nail again. Reaching for the door handle, I glance in the front seat and notice the protein bar sitting unopened in the cupholder. I quickly blink to stop the tears threatening to fall.

My mom goes to check in while my dad and I take a seat in the waiting area. Bouncing my leg anxiously, I watch her talk to the receptionist. Once she's sitting in the seat between my dad and I, I grab her hand and give it a squeeze. "No matter what we learn today, you've got Dad and I. Always."

She squeezes my hand back and grabs my dad's with her other. "I know I do, sweetie. And you have no idea what it means to me to have you back home with me for this." She quickly blinks as tears form in the corners of her eyes.

When they call her back, Dr. Trice greets my parents and introduces herself to me. She informs me that she's been an oncologist for twenty-three years and plans to take the best care of my mom, which eases just the smallest amount of anxiety I have.

"Before I read over your results, have there been any changes since the last time we saw each other?" she asks, her gaze bouncing between my parents.

My mom shakes her head at the same time my dad rushes out, "She's lost her appetite; she barely eats. And I know you weighed her when you brought us back, so I know you can tell she's probably lost weight since her last appointment."

Nodding her head, Dr. Trice looks at my mom. "Sherri, is there any reason you shook your head no?" She doesn't sound accusatory, just curious.

She sucks in a breath. "Because, for me, my appetite hasn't really changed much. I've been slowly losing my appetite for a while, but it's only gotten worse with the stress of these appointments. My nerves aren't letting me eat."

I can tell that's not what she really believes, but I just sit there, watching.

"I see. Well, are you ready to hear the results from your scans from earlier this week?" she asks, glancing down at her notes and then back up at my mom.

We all nod.

"Well, I want to start by saying what we already knew: your lungs are teeming with various-sized tumors. Unfortunately, these new scans didn't come back with anything positive. And I can say, with ninety-eight percent certainty, that your loss of appetite is not just from nerves." She takes a breath before continuing, watching my parents for signs that they need a minute. Her twenty-three years of experience are shining in this moment. This is a woman who has had to deliver devastating news countless times. "The scans from Monday show that the cancer has spread into seven organs—"

Like when my parents first told me the news, my ears stop working. I watch as she talks but no sound is penetrating my ear drums. I take multiple breaths, trying to calm myself.

Seven.

She said my mom has tumors in *seven* different organs. Tears fall down my cheeks. I don't even try to stop them. I watch as my mom crumbles into my dad's embrace. I wonder if she's able to hear the rest of what the doctor has been saying, or, if like me, her ears stopped working. I turn my attention back to Dr. Trice and try to focus so I can hear what she's saying.

"—likely that the cancer didn't start in your lungs. You said at our first appointment you've never smoked, so it's safe to speculate that it started in one of the other organs but didn't manifest in symptoms until it spread, causing the chest pain." My hearing snaps back suddenly. "Unfortunately, there's no way to tell where it started."

My dad holds my mom, his hands rubbing up and down her arms. "Okay. So, what does this mean? What can we do? I was doing some research on Google, so I know it's not the most accurate, but I saw that there are treatment options for cancer that has progressed to stage four. It's not a cure, but it can keep it from potentially getting worse—because there's always worse." He adds the last bit with a bit of force. As if his best friend having cancer throughout her whole body isn't the worst thing that could happen.

"You are correct; there is no cure, based on how far it has progressed. But, there are some options I feel comfortable trying." I sit in the chair, zoned out as the doctor goes over what few options she has. I close my eyes, praying that when I open them I will wake up in my bed in Richmond and this whole thing will have been a nightmare.

My mom finally speaks up and it brings me back to my harsh reality. "What . . . What is my life expectancy? With and without the treatments?" She sounds so brave asking, and I'm so focused on hearing the answer.

Dr. Trice moves her chin slightly—clearly one of her least favorite questions. "There's no telling, exactly. But I would guess, without the treatments, maybe a few weeks, months if we're lucky. With the treatments, it might buy you a few extra months, maybe a year." She hands me a box of tissues when she notices I've resorted to rubbing my snotty nose on my sleeve.

Before leaving the doctor's office, a course of treatment is settled on. She'll go once, every other week for chemotherapy. The day before her treatment she'll have blood work done to make sure her levels are stable enough for her body to handle it.

The doctor told us, when chemo starts next week, we could expect nausea, vomiting, more loss of appetite, fatigue, mouth sores, and overall pain. But the side effect that upset my mom the most was the potential hair loss—she doesn't want to scare or worry her students by potentially becoming bald. My dad assures her she can always buy wigs—ones with fun colors and styles.

When we get home, my parents go to their room to talk privately. I think it's to finish the conversation they started on the way home: my dad's thoughts on my mom continuing to work. I understand her desire to continue to work, but I also agree with my dad, she doesn't need the additional stress on her body.

To keep my mind off everything that happened this morning at the appointment, I throw myself into work. I put my headphones in, turn on my music, and just hone in on this design. Hours pass before I finally have a product I'm happy to turn in to my client, so I send over a few pictures before wandering out to the living room.

My mom is reclined on her chair watching some Lifetime movie, and my dad sits at the kitchen island with his head resting in his hands. I sit on the couch next to her, just wanting to be in her presence.

I watch her as she watches the TV and I'm thrown into a memory of my childhood. I really wanted to play Barbies, but I didn't want to play alone, so my mom helped me carry all of my dolls and accessories out to the living room. I didn't have a dream house, so we created a house using all sorts of household supplies to create separate rooms. We laid on the floor for hours, making up stories for our Barbies. I feel a tear slide down my cheek as I grasp the severity of my mom's diagnosis.

My mom finally breaks the silence, making me jump. "You know, I think I knew I was getting sick a while back. I kept having these weird feelings, but I could never describe exactly what it felt like so I didn't think I needed to go see a doctor." She pauses. "Paul, do you remember me mentioning those moments before? You told me to make an appointment, but I didn't listen." She raises her voice a little to get my dad's attention.

My dad walks into the living room and crouches down next to the recliner. "I remember, Sher. But there's no use getting worked up over something in the past—we can't change it."

I watch as he rubs his hand over her arm and leans in for a kiss. I can see the love between them, and the pain that is now marking both of their faces.

They have a year left together, if they're lucky.

My throat constricts and I decide I need air and to move my body.

"I'm going to get changed and get my weights. I think I'm going to go workout for a bit in the front yard," I say to no one in particular as I stand up and head to my room.

Once I'm in my room, I let the tears fall freely. I pull on a pair of bright pink leggings, a black T-shirt, and pull a gray hoodie over the T-shirt because, well, it's still forty-two degrees outside. I throw my curly hair up into a messy bun, put on a pair of tennis shoes, grab my weights, and head outside, hoping that, if I get my body moving, I'll be able to forget how useless I am with what's to come.

Chapter 11

Graham

Sherri and I were sitting in her classroom eating lunch yesterday when she got the call. Well, I was eating, she was absentmindedly poking around her food with her fork. I stepped outside so she could have privacy, and when I returned she informed me her results from Monday's scans were back—sooner than expected. They wanted to see her in the office tomorrow to go over what was found.

She sat at her desk and started weeping. "Graham, I'm so scared. I know what they're going to say—there's no cure. I'm going to die. How can I just leave Paul and Tessa? I haven't had enough time with them. I'm not ready," she said through her tears.

I was quickly by her side, helping her stand as I pulled her into a hug. "Hey, hey, we will get through this. I wasn't lying before, and I didn't change my mind. Whatever you, Paul, and Tessa need, I'm here. You've been there for me, so I'm going to be here for you," I said, rubbing circles on her back as she cried into my chest. I took in a steadying breath to keep my voice from breaking; I didn't want to let her know how scared I felt too. I could be here emotionally for her, but depending on this news, there's not really anything I can actually do.

"Have you told them about your fears?" I asked as I heard her sobs start to calm.

She shook her head in my chest and put her hand to her face. "No. I'm not ready for them to see me this scared. Not yet." She stepped back, looking at the clock, and grabbed a tissue. "Shit, lunch is almost over and I'm a blubbering mess over here. Do you think it's okay if I just assign them two chapters to read and have them write their thoughts in their journal? Then I can let them have a free period for the rest of the class? I don't think I have it in me to teach the rest of the day."

"Sherri, you can do whatever you want. If Dr. Kingsley comes in to observe you, just try to explain that you got some bad news and needed a day. I'm sure he'll understand," I said, handing her another tissue.

Now, it's Friday afternoon and, according to Ms. Appleby, her classes were unruly today. But that's not a problem she needs to deal with. I glance over at the Gunter house and stop breathing as I see Tessa working out. She's currently doing walking lunges across the yard, holding some type of weights. I'm mesmerized and find myself staring.

I'm well aware of how bad it would be if someone saw me. I know that I one thousand percent look like a creeper, but the way those damn hot pink leggings are hugging her thighs, and how good her ass looks as she lunges away from me . . . I can feel myself growing hard in my slacks.

She suddenly stops and I hold my breath, thinking she can feel my gaze on her. Instead of looking around, she puts her weights down and takes off the hoodie she's wearing. The black T-shirt underneath slides up as it sticks to the hoodie, allowing me to get a glimpse of her soft curves. My dick pulses in excitement. I sit in the car for a few more moments, caught up in watching Tessa as she picks her weights back up and starts doing squats with her back facing me. Fuck, that's it, I need to get inside now.

I make it in, feed Jay Catsby, and decide I'm in desperate need of a shower. I get my clothes off as quickly as I can as I start the shower. Without even waiting for the water to heat up, I hop inside, hoping the cold water will help with my raging hard-on. Unfortunately, my mind keeps flashing images of Tessa doing those lunges then squatting down and pushing her ass in my direction.

As the water heats up, the images go to the soft curves of her stomach that peeked out under her shirt and my dick throbs in response. I get a handful of conditioner and fist my cock. As I pump my hand up and down, I start undressing her in my mind. First, she loses the hoodie, then she's slowly taking that black T-shirt off, leaving her gorgeous stomach on display. In my mind, she's wearing a cute, hot pink sports bra that matches her leggings, but there's no padding, so I can see her hardened nipples through the fabric.

Just the thought of her in a sports bra and those leggings makes me feel close to coming. Suddenly, I'm picturing her on her knees in front of me, taking my cock in her mouth. I lean forward and put one hand on the wall as I continue pumping my hand faster and faster. I squeeze a little harder, adding more pressure as I picture her messy bun bobbing up and down as I fuck her mouth. I envision her stealing a glance at me through her eyelashes as she takes me deeper into her mouth. With that image, my body tenses and I start to feel my cock pulse. I can tell I'm about to come. The tension keeps building until, finally, I release my load on the side of the shower. I hang my head down by the arm that's holding me up against the wall.

Fuck, how I wish that wasn't just a fantasy.

Taking the shower head off, I rinse the wall, making a mental note to actually wash it later. I finish my shower only to find myself with a hard dick once more before getting out.

Sitting down at the kitchen table, I rest my head in my hands. How can I think about Tessa like that when she's going through so much shit right now? I'm over here, blowing a load just from thinking about her mouth on my cock, while she's over there dealing with whatever shitty news the doctor told them today. As I think about how much of an asshole I have to be for that to be my life, my phone pings with a text message.

Sherri Gunter:

> *Hey Graham, I think you should come over tomorrow for lunch and I can fill you in on what the doctors said.*

Without hesitating, I respond.

Me:

> *Of course! What time and should I bring anything?*

Chapter 12

Tessa

The next morning, the aroma of coffee wakes me up. For a minute, I question whether I fell asleep on the couch with how strong the smell is. I open my eyes and slowly peek around the cream-colored room. I notice on my desk, by the door, is a coffee mug with a note attached. Seeing the note makes me jump out of bed.

TESSA,

I TOOK YOUR MOM OUT FOR A LITTLE BIT—GET HER AWAY SO SHE'S NOT THINKING TOO MUCH. I THINK SHE JUST NEEDS SOME FRESH AIR. SHE INVITED GRAHAM OVER FOR LUNCH, SO WE'LL BE BACK BEFORE NOON, WHEN HE SHOULD GET THERE. TRY TO RELAX YOURSELF; YESTERDAY WAS HARD ON ALL OF US.

LOVE,

DAD

The note makes my heart sting a little. It's good he's getting her out of the house, but part of me feels sad they didn't ask if I wanted to come. I'd love to be able to make more memories with them. I pick up the coffee and take a big sniff of the smoky dark roast my parents love to drink. But before taking a sip, I open my laptop and pull up my email. I'm waiting for a response from my client about the design I turned in. I'm really hoping she likes it.

> To: *Tessa.E.Gunter@designs4you.com*
> From: *GraceWarner@email.com*
> Re: Design for Dearly Departed cover
> Tessa!
> I love it! I can tell from the design that you actually read the book and understood what I was going for with the themes of it! It's better than I could have even imagined! The way she's got her head in her hands while she's sitting in front of the casket, it's truly beautiful! Thank you, thank you, thank you!
> Sincerely,
> Grace Warner

I'm able to take a full breath after reading her email.

I'm so glad that she loved it. I really did read the book and was absolutely moved by it. Considering the recent events in my life, it really resonated with me.

I take a generous sip of my coffee and send her a quick reply before looking for my next assignment.

About an hour goes by before I suddenly remember that my dad said that Mom invited Graham over for lunch. Fuck. I knew she had built a close relationship with him since he started working with her nine years ago, but for some reason I didn't think their relationship would extend to him coming to the house. Although, I don't know why that wouldn't occur to me since he lives right down the road. Hell, my dad has talked about how he comes over to watch various sports games with him.

I don't really know why I'm so surprised by this news, but for some reason I am. And suddenly I have butterflies thinking about seeing my childhood friend again.

Now that I've come to terms with our lunch guest, I start to have a mini panic attack. It's been a very long time since I've seen Graham or had a conversation with him. When my mom first started talking about him and work I tried to stalk him on social media—like anyone in my generation would. It wasn't hard at first because we were social media friends for a few years. But then he randomly deleted it all.

In high school, he was on the smaller side. Not too skinny, but he definitely had room to fill out. His light brown hair was always shaggy, and I remember he had a gorgeous pair of hazel eyes.

Since moving back, I've seen him from a distance, and from what I can tell, he did indeed fill out. I haven't gotten to see how much he's bulked up, but gone are the days where I would be able to joke with him about being a string bean.

I wouldn't say I had a crush on him per se, but I definitely found myself thinking about him from time to time. Especially with the way my parents dote on him. As I anxiously pace in front of my closet trying to decide what to wear, I find that I've ended up with my damn thumb back between my teeth. It takes me a solid twenty minutes to pick out an outfit for a casual lunch with my parents and an old friend, but hey, at least I finally found something and won't be eating in my pajamas.

By the time my parents are back from their outing, I've gotten dressed in a pair of black skinny jeans and a sea-foam green top that hugs my curves. I'm also wearing a thick pair of socks that I got around Christmas, so they have little reindeer on them.

I'm not sure if Graham wanted any particular food for lunch, but I decided I'd risk cooking anyways. As horrible as it sounds, I choose to make one of my dad's favorites—a spinach Alfredo pasta—instead of one of my mom's favorite dishes because he at least will have the appetite for it. This time I stick to the recipe in the cookbook. I can't risk another cooking class disaster when feeding someone I haven't seen in a while. I also make some chicken broth and heat up bread for everyone.

"Are you sure that's safe to eat?" my mom jokes as she peeks at the food I'm removing from the stove, clearly remembering my story of the failed cooking date.

I shake my head, laughing. "I hope so. It doesn't taste as bad as the Alfredo I made with Bennett. So hopefully it doesn't make anyone feel sick."

"I'm only teasing." She pats my shoulder and walks back toward her room.

A knock comes from the front of the house and my dad answers the door. Seconds later, he's ushering Graham in the kitchen. "Sherri, he did it again! Fresh baked goods—apple fritters this time!" my dad says, holding a glass container up like a trophy, or a prized fish.

My eyes catch Graham's as he walks into the kitchen and I feel like the world has slowed down. He's definitely put on some muscle and is officially *not* a string bean. He's what I would describe as brawny. You can tell he's strong, but not in the way a bodybuilder is. He looks really good in his black sweater and blue jeans, and his brown hair is no longer long and shaggy on top like it used to be. Now he wears it in a short and tousled look. He also has long stubble along his jaw. I'm not sure if he couldn't grow facial hair in high school, or just chose not to, but this is definitely a good look. And for some reason, I can't stop staring, and I'm afraid I might start drooling at any moment.

He stops across from me at the island. "Hey, Tessa, it's been a while. How've you been?" A lazy smile spreads across his face. My knees suddenly feel weak.

I force myself to swallow without it being too obvious that I'm clearing excess saliva from my mouth. "I'm good." I take a brief moment and add, "All things considered. How about you? I hear you teach English with my mom?" I smile what I hope looks like a genuine smile and isn't creepy.

With the mention of my mom, she walks out from the back room. "Good to see you, Graham," she says, pulling him into a hug. His thick arms wrap around her and I can tell his muscles are straining even under the sleeves of his sweater. I have never felt more envious of someone receiving a hug as I do right now.

His smile grows while he embraces my mom. "You too, Sherri," he says, releasing her as she pulls back. He turns back to me. "I do. Seventh grade is pretty great now that I'm not on the student side," he says with a chuckle. "Is there anything I can do?" he asks, motioning toward the kitchen and the food I have sitting on the counter.

"Thanks, but no. If everyone is ready to eat, though, we can—everything is ready," I say, picking up plates and walking them to the table. I have to keep busy or I might actually attempt to climb him in front of my parents. Who even am I right now? Not even Bennett elicited this kind of reaction out of me.

Chapter 13

Graham

I knew she was going to be here, but the sight of her still takes me by surprise and leaves me breathless. She's wearing her beautiful dark brown curls pulled back in a half ponytail to keep from falling in her face, a sea-foam green top that clings to her curves in the best way possible, and a pair of black skinny jeans that show off her ass, making my dick react. Gorgeous as ever.

I sit at the table across from Tessa, with Paul and Sherri on either side of me. I can't take my eyes off her as she moves the food to the table, setting it in a way that gives everyone equal access. Then, she walks back to the kitchen one last time to grab a bowl of something she set in front of Sherri—her movements so graceful. My eyes roam over her body once more before she takes a seat and I smile as I notice she has on the cutest reindeer socks.

"I hope you like spinach Alfredo. If not, I suppose there's more chicken broth in there I could get you," Tessa says, breaking me from my trance.

"Oh, spinach Alfredo sounds delicious. Thank you," I say, picking up my empty plate and reaching for the spoon in the pasta.

Once everyone has food in front of them, Paul breaks the silence by talking about the basketball game he's looking forward to seeing. Sherri sits quietly, sipping at her soup, watching Paul with sad eyes, and Tessa's observing her mom intently as she eats her lunch. I carry on the conversation with Paul, trying to include Sherri and Tessa as much as possible, but I get the feeling they have other things on their minds.

"I went to one of their games last year in Richmond, it got pretty intense and they went into overtime," I say as Paul talks about his favorite team. Tessa's eyes meet mine at the mention of Richmond.

"You were in Richmond last year? I wish I would have known, I could have shown you around," she says with a small smile on her face.

My eyes are fixed on her smile, her slightly crooked teeth, and her plump bottom lip. I cough when I register that I've been staring too long. "I went with my brother and nephew. It was Ethan's first NBA game."

She nods her head in understanding before taking a bite of the last of her meal.

When lunch is done, Paul helps Tessa clean up the mess as Sherri grabs my arm and leads me to the living room. "I can help clean up," I try to say, looking back toward the kitchen, trying to get a glimpse of Tessa.

"You could, but then I wouldn't be able to fill you in on what happened at my appointment yesterday, now would I?" Sherri pats my arm before gesturing to the couch as she takes a seat on the recliner.

I sit down and lean forward so my forearms are resting on top of my knees, giving Sherri my full attention. "Okay. What did they say?" I ask, not sure I'm ready to know the answer.

She lets out a shaky breath and tears immediately form in her eyes. I can tell by that alone I'm not going to like what she's going to say. "Well, the good news is, they don't think it started in my lungs." She tries to laugh but fails. "The bad news is, they found tumors in my stomach, spleen, liver, pancreas, kidneys, and my lower intestine."

I take in my own shaky breath. Seven. That was seven organs she just named. I reach forward and grab her knee, letting my head fall briefly to try to fight the tears I can feel brimming my eyes. "What does—What does the doctor say as far as treatments and everything?" I ask, trying to keep my voice steady.

As Sherri fills me in on the treatment plan the doctor suggested, Tessa and Paul enter the room. Paul pulls a chair over, to sit next to Sherri, and starts stroking her arm. My body tenses as I feel Tessa sit on the opposite end of the couch.

"Paul and I have discussed it at length. He doesn't think—and I agree with him—that it's in my best interest to continue teaching. The doctor said the side effects of the chemo will leave me with very little energy. And due to that, I don't think I'll be much fun as a teacher to those students." She's now sobbing into her hands.

The selfish part of me wants to protest and tell her she'll be fine—the students need her. *I* need her. She's been my biggest supporter at that school since the moment I walked into the front door on my first day. But I can't be selfish, not when it comes to this. "I understand why you're making this decision. I'll help your replacement as much as I can, and I'll fill you in on all the goings-on around the school," I say, pressing against the corners of my eyes.

We talk for another hour before Sherri announces she needs to take a nap. I say my goodbyes as I stand to leave.

Tessa walks with me to the front porch and she sits down on one of the rocking chairs. "Sit," she says, motioning to the chair next to her.

I sit down and immediately rest my head against the back of the chair. "How are you hanging in there?" I turn my head to face her.

Her lips are pursed; her shoulders rise and fall with her deep breathing. "I'm scared. My mom is my best friend. She's my role model, my sun, my light, my happiness. How can I go on without her? How will my dad go on without her?" She turns her head toward me, her eyes shining with unshed tears.

I shake my head, unsure of the words to say. Reaching over, I grab her hand, offering the only piece of solace I can. We sit there for what feels like eternity, but just holding hands in the silence is one of the best moments of my life.

Back at home that evening, I lay on the couch with Jay Catsby kneading my stomach. The pain and fear I saw in Sherri's eyes as she told me the doctor's prognosis has me rubbing at my chest trying to ease the pain in my heart. If I'm this broken up about it and Sherri has only been in my life consistently for the past nine years, I can't even fathom the pain Paul and Tessa must feel.

I grab my phone and pull up the calendar. The moment Sherri gave me the dates of her treatments I knew I wanted to be able to do something for her. Even if I can't go to them, I will make a point to stop by after work. Her first treatment is on Wednesday morning. While I would love to be there, it's too late for me to try to take time off of work. Not to mention, I want the first treatment to just be the three of them. So, I close out of the calendar app and look up different things that help cancer patients during chemo to see if there's anything I can do or get her.

Chapter 14

Tessa

Relaxing in a bath Saturday night, I replay the day in my head. I let out a sigh of relief when I think about finally finishing another art piece and finding my next assignment. The drawing helped a little today to keep my mind off the news. I smile as I think about the image I drew of the woman holding her little boy, waving at the ship sailing away.

My mind drifts to Graham next, and how good he looks now. He was attractive in high school, but now it's magnified. His broad shoulders, thick thighs, the beard he has—I've always been a sucker for a nice beard. The thought of what the scratch of it against my skin would feel like when being intimate sends a shiver through my body.

I lean my head back and slowly lower my hand between my legs as I think about the smile on his face, the way it made the corner of his eyes crinkle. The sound of his laugh at something that was said at the table.

Thinking of the way his sweater hugged his shoulders has me slipping two fingers inside my center and letting out a soft moan. The way his pants squeezed around his ass makes me close my eyes and bite my lip. I've never thought of Graham this way before, but there was definitely something about him today that got me hot and bothered. He was so caring in the way he talked to my parents, and in the way he held my hand as I silently cried on the porch.

I grasp my breast with my left hand and tug on my nipple, rolling it firmly between my fingers as I find my rhythm with the fingers pumping in my center while my thumb massages my clit. I envision Graham walking into the bathroom and sitting on the side of the tub. Just the thought of him coming in and seeing me makes me let out another soft moan. I lower my left hand to my thigh as I picture Graham reaching in to touch me—the warmth of his hand as he slowly caresses my knee.

I don't know if I was imagining it or not at lunch, but it definitely felt like he kept looking at me—his hazel eyes staring at me. Just thinking about it makes my body tense and my vision blur as I come undone. Fuck, if just thinking about that while getting myself off isn't proof that I haven't gotten laid in forever, then I don't know what would be.

As I drain the water and get my toothbrush ready, I can't help but think if I really was imagining the side glances and the small smiles. I know he had a crush on me growing up—I'm pretty sure everyone and their mom knew. But I'd be stupid to think that crush is still there. Hell, he might even have a girlfriend. Shit. He probably has a girlfriend. I can't believe I just masturbated while thinking of someone else's boyfriend.

As I'm climbing into bed, I look over at the picture of my mom, dad, and me on my nightstand. Nell took it when my parents were visiting one Christmas. We're sitting next to the Christmas tree with our matching pajamas, holding our stockings. I close my eyes as a tear slips down my cheek. My best friend more than likely won't be around at Christmas time. That fact hits me, causing the tears to fall in earnest, knowing last Christmas was my last happy Christmas.

Monday, I meet my mom at school at the end of the day to help her start packing up her personal belongings from her classroom. Her last official day is on Friday, but she's leaving early tomorrow to get her blood work done and port placed. Wednesday she has her chemo, then Thursday and Friday she might not feel well enough to have a full day of work.

I walk into her classroom and pause when I see Graham standing on a ladder, reaching into a shelf. I silently stare as he grabs something and hands it to my mom who's standing at the bottom of the ladder with a box at her feet. I don't interrupt as they continue a conversation too low for me to hear, but watching them together causes an ache in my chest.

I moved away—I wasn't here to watch this friendship blossom. I haven't been here to come volunteer in her class, and now I won't ever get that opportunity. I missed out on so much living three hours away, and only seeing her in person every few months.

"Oh, Tessa, great, you're here!" my mom says, catching me before my thoughts could escalate.

I walk over to where she's standing next to the ladder. "Of course, I said I would come help. What do you need me to do?" I ask, bumping my hip against hers.

"I actually got called into a meeting with the principal, but I've told Graham all the things that need to be removed from the top shelves, if you don't mind putting them in boxes as he passes them down?" She squeezes my arm gently before she grabs a notebook off her desk and heads to the door.

I nod and answer, even though she's already walked away. "Aye, aye, captain."

Graham and I work in comfortable silence for a few minutes before he talks. "How are you enjoying being back? Besides the stress of all the bad news?" He climbs down from the ladder and moves it so he can get into the next shelf.

"Honestly, it's not bad so far. I've been working on sketches while Mom and Dad work, and I get a workout in then too. And then I sit in the living room with Mom when she gets home. We've gotten in the habit of playing board games and watching TV." I respond with a half-truth. I don't want to admit that it's hard seeing her skip meals and cough until she's red in the face.

I watch as he carefully maneuvers the items in the cabinet before pulling anything out to hand to me. "And you're doing okay given the circumstances of what brought you home?" he asks, looking down at me from his perch. His hazel eyes are assessing me, making it feel like he can read what I'm not saying.

I angle my body toward the door to check to see if my mom has returned yet, and to be able to see when she walks in. Letting out a dejected sigh, I decide to tell him the truth. "It's hard, and I know it's only going to get harder once her treatments start. She's up all hours of the night coughing, and she's not eating. I know all of this is the new normal for her, but seeing her in this pain is just . . . hard."

He shakes his head. "I can only imagine how difficult it is. I'm sorry. If it gets to be too much, let me know." Before he gets a chance to say anything else, my mom comes walking in the door, coughing.

"Are you guys ready to take this stuff to the car?" she asks, putting a smile on her face once the cough has subsided.

Wednesday morning, I wake up and prepare myself for a long day at the treatment center. I have no idea what to expect, so I went to the store the other day and picked up a few things for her. I got her a few different books, trashy magazines, some yarn and knitting needles—I know she used to knit, but I'm not sure if she still does. I also got some cards, a few different coloring books—some that are very clearly for children, with characters from various TV shows and movies, and a few that are more elaborate—and the last thing I bought her was a journal. She might decide she wants to write down her thoughts and feelings that she isn't ready to verbalize with anyone yet.

As I'm stuffing all the entertainment items I bought in a large bag, my dad walks in with a small bag of snacks and different flavored drinks. We both want to be prepared for whatever she will need. The last thing I grab before walking out the door is a throw blanket and a small pillow from my bed. I will be damned if she isn't comfortable during her first treatment.

Walking down the hall of the treatment center, I find myself looking around at the families gathered around and the patients who are either arriving for their treatment, or leaving. I give a small smile to an elderly woman who's sitting in a chair near a water fountain.

This facility is set up so each patient has their own little space for a recliner chair and the machine they will be attached to for the visit. Across from the recliner, just outside of the space, are two seats for family or friends. The space has two thin, brown walls separating itself from the space next to it, and there's a large window that makes up the outer wall that overlooks a small pond. The recliner is positioned so the patient has their back to one brown wall, facing the other wall. It allows for the person receiving treatment the option to face the window, or any guests that are with them.

A nurse directs my mom to the chair and pulls a curtain I didn't notice, closed, so she can remove her shirt and change into a gown that allows for the port to be accessed. My dad walks in to be with her as they hook her up to the medication. There's a small part of me that's thankful they kept me out. I don't know if I could emotionally handle watching her get attached. We'll see how well I handle seeing her once it's ready and they open the curtain.

I take a seat while I wait and rummage through the items I brought. On the way here, my mom said she'd like to color first, so as I wait, I take out the coloring books along with markers, crayons, and colored pencils. I, myself, am partial to colored pencils, but I don't know what she will be interested in using.

The curtain is pulled open, and as the nurse walks out I hear her say, "If you need anything, there's a button connected to the machine. Just press it and someone will be with you shortly." She smiles and then walks away.

My dad pushes the small trash can closer to my mom—we read that chemo can make patients nauseous very quickly. She has her gown on, covering all the wires, which makes me release a breath, and she's got the blanket I brought covering her legs. I stand up to move the table tray in front of her with her coloring options on top. "Are you still in a coloring mood?" I ask before walking away, just in case she says no.

She looks up at me and smiles. "Yes, I think I would like to color. Goodness! Look at all these choices!" she says, moving the books around before stopping on one of the children's coloring books with various animals. I watch as she stacks the remaining books, setting them aside, and then reaches for both the crayons and the markers.

The hour goes by rather quickly with my mom only feeling nauseous twice. She reached for the trash can, but the feeling subsided as soon as it was in her lap. The nurse comes back and closes the curtain again to undo all of the wires. I do my best to keep my mind from thinking about how much that hour-long session drained the glow from her face.

We aren't even home for twenty minutes before my mom says she wants to take a nap. After watching her slink into her room, I head to mine so I can work on my newest commission. I'm lying on the floor with my sketchbook in front of me and my laptop next to me, so I can easily refer to my notes, when my dad startles me with a knock.

"Hey, Tessa-bug, sorry, I didn't mean to scare you. I'm thinking about ordering in. What would you like?" He leans on the doorjamb with his arms crossed.

I stick my thumbnail in my mouth as I think. "How about you order Leroy's? You can get me a Combo 13. I haven't had that in forever," I respond with saliva gathering in my mouth just thinking about the garlic knots that come with it.

He nods once. "Sounds good." He starts to shut the door, but before he closes it he adds, "Oh, I think Graham plans on stopping by after he gets home from work to visit with your mom." After dropping that news, he turns and walks away.

With the news of seeing Graham again, my heart starts to race and I immediately feel a heat pool between my legs. I stand up and look in the mirror to make sure I look presentable. I fix my hair into a bun and look at my navy blue leggings and pale pink top. I can't change back into my clothes from earlier because my dad has seen that I've officially donned clothes for the workout I was planning to do, and he would definitely be suspicious if I changed back. This will have to do.

Chapter 15

Graham

When I get home from work, I catch a glimpse of my fat tuxedo cat trotting into the kitchen, no doubt waiting impatiently by his food bowl. I duck into my room and grab the bag of goodies I bought for Sherri then walk into the kitchen. After feeding Jay Catsby, I grab the frozen items from the freezer.

I wasn't sure what to get someone going through chemo, so I got almost everything the Internet suggested—from books to a playlist on Spotify I made her. I also got her a few things to keep her comfortable, including a pair of very cozy-looking green slippers that made me think of St. Patrick's Day, and some electrolyte popsicles to keep her hydrated, because I read chemo can make people dehydrated. I also bought her a very large bag that had books all over the side. I arrange and rearrange all of the items into the bag before heading to her house.

I've never felt more nervous knocking on this front door than I do right now. I know I saw Tessa the other day, but the possibility of seeing her again while I'm visiting with Sherri makes my heart skip. Paul opens the door and gives me a perplexed look. "Boy, what in the world is in that bag? It can't be full of those tasty treats you usually bring over, or can it . . ." he asks, trying to take a peek inside the bag.

I respond with a chuckle, "Sorry, no apple treats today. But I did come bearing gifts for Sherri. Is she still in the mood to see me?" I add the last part as I mentally scold myself for not texting to make sure she still wanted company.

"Yeah, yeah. Come on in. She's in the living room." He leads me out of the foyer.

When I walk into the living room, I inhale deeply. Sherri is right where Paul said she would be, on the recliner, but I wasn't prepared for the sight before me. Even though today was only her first day of treatment, I can tell it's going to be a long road for her. Her pretty round face, that reminds me of an older version of Tessa, is leaning over a trash can as she violently throws up.

Paul immediately runs to her side as I stand there paralyzed, unsure what I'm supposed to do. "Hey, Graham, do you mind running into the kitchen and grabbing a towel from the counter and getting it wet, please?" Paul asks from his wife's side as he holds her hair back and rubs soothing circles on her back.

Without wasting a minute, I set the bag down and jog to the kitchen. I instantly see the towels Paul mentioned and grab the top one. While letting the water run over the cloth, I allow myself a minute to glance around and I get a brief look at Tessa in the enclosed back patio with headphones in, working out. I set that image aside for later and return to the living room.

Sherri grabs the towel from my hand with a small smile on her face. "Thank you, honey. I'm so sorry you had to see that. Please, have a seat." She wipes at her mouth and sets the cloth on the table next to her.

Before taking a seat, I walk to the living room entrance, grab the bag I brought over, and then move to take a seat on the couch. Paul grabs the trash can and walks out of the room with a sad smile on his face. We sit in silence for a few moments as Sherri fiddles with the blanket on her lap and takes a small sip of water. "So, are you going to tell me what's in that bag, or do you want me to guess?" She motions to the bag with a laugh.

"Right," I say, leaning down to pick the bag up on the couch next to me. "Well, I went a little crazy at the store, unsure of what you would want and need. So, I grabbed a little bit of everything." I pull out a handful of items and hand them over to her.

As she looks through each item, the smile on her face gets wider and wider. "You know you didn't have to get me anything," she says, coughing between words. Giving her a moment to get another sip of water, I hand her another stack of items.

"Yeah, well, I didn't think you'd be all that interested in my original plan," I say with a half-grin.

This piques her interest and she hands me the items to put back in the bag. "What was the original plan? And if I want that, do I get to keep all the other goodies you got me too?" She coughs again, this time taking a bit longer to get it under control.

"I was thinking about bringing you a couple of stacks of ungraded papers and letting you grade them for me. But that didn't seem as fun as all this other stuff."

She's now coughing through a laugh.

"You know," she starts, before coughing, followed by a rather large gulp of water, "that wouldn't have been a horrible gift. I didn't even think to bring my students' papers home to grade so I could get it out of the way for my replacement." Reclining her chair back she asks, "How were my classes the rest of yesterday and today?"

I ponder her question for a moment, unsure what to tell her and what to leave out. "Ms. Appleby didn't have any complaints about them, and I didn't hear any loud noises coming from across the hall. So, I'm going to take a guess and say they were well-behaved."

She nods as I talk and then inhales slowly. "They hired my replacement. I checked my email this morning before my treatment. I knew they were interviewing already, but getting the news that they offered the position to someone already was unexpected."

I give a small nod in assent. "I met her today. She's a recent graduate from UVA—they asked me to be her mentor. They said, *'Mrs. Gunter was your mentor so we feel it would benefit Miss Gooding for you to work with her as she adjusts to this new responsibility.'* Honestly, it doesn't sound like I have much of a choice, but I know it's just her and me in the seventh grade English department, so it makes sense."

Sherri watches me as I talk and puts her hand up, indicating she'd like to talk. "They didn't give me any specifics, but you said she's a recent grad, and her last name is Gooding?" I nod in response. "Does her first name happen to be Farrah?" she asks, looking hopeful.

It takes me a minute as I recall what her first name was. I've honestly stuck to calling her Miss Gooding because I've been feeling salty that she's replacing my work mom. "Yes, I do believe her first name is Farrah. How did you know?" I ask, curious.

A smile lights up her face, one that has me thinking about Tessa. "She's going to be a wonderful replacement. I taught her way back when she was in seventh grade. She was actually in my class the year before you started teaching, so she would have been in eighth grade your first year." She looks off into the distance, like she's remembering something she hasn't thought about in a while. Shaking her head and returning to the present, she adds, "In fact, she probably remembers seeing you in the hall when you first started."

We sit for a while longer, talking about all the things I got her, and I share a few stories of things that happened at school. As I'm talking, she ends up nodding off to sleep so I head into the kitchen and sit at the table next to Paul as he looks at something on his computer. He holds his finger up at me, indicating he'd be a minute.

Talking about how Farrah was in eighth grade when I first started teaching makes me feel old. But it also reminds me of my first few years of teaching. I didn't start right out of college like most people. I graduated college at twenty-one and decided I wanted to travel a bit before working. I traveled around the States and when I came back home my parents bitched, saying, *"You need to get your shit together because you are an adult now,"* and *"You need to be serious about finding a job because jobs just don't fall into people's laps."*

I got hired for the first job I applied for.

When I walked into the office on my first day of training, I saw Mrs. Gunter and immediately felt relieved. I remembered that she taught there when I was a kid, but for some reason the thought didn't occur to me that she would still be teaching there. I walked up to her to reintroduce myself and she instantly pulled me in for a hug and said, "Oh, Graham, of course I remember you!"

Upon hearing I was the new English teacher being added to her grade level, she enthusiastically offered to be my mentor. She even walked me to my new classroom so I could put down some things before heading to our first meeting of the school year. I spent that whole first week basically attached to Sherri's hip. Since she was a veteran teacher, her classroom was already set up, so any down time we were given to prepare our classrooms, she helped me set mine up.

"Why do I never see you in the neighborhood anymore?" she asked when helping me hang up a few posters on the wall.

I contemplated telling her the truth, or just giving her the short version. I decided on the short version. If I was going to be working with her for the foreseeable future, I'm sure the long story would come out eventually. "I moved out after high school graduation and have been too busy to stop by too often."

She just nodded and didn't pry any further.

Those first few weeks I stayed late into the night, planning for the upcoming weeks because I was second-guessing every choice I made. Sherri joined me on more than one occasion to help squelch any anxiety that arose. After a month of late nights at school, she eventually invited me over for dinner with her and Paul. And thus began our bi-weekly dinners.

Eventually my parents moved out of my childhood home and offered to give the house to my brother and his wife because, *"They have a family, Graham."* But my brother already had a house. He tried to encourage them to give it to me since they planned on giving it to him, and in the end he did end up talking them into selling it to me.

Once I moved back into the neighborhood, our bi-weekly dinners turned into weekly get-togethers, not just for dinner, which sealed their fate as my second parents—my preferred parents if I'm being honest. So watching Sherri get so sick with cancer, and Paul sitting by her side, looking lost, breaks my heart.

A knock at the door brings me back to the present as Paul gets up and runs to the door to keep whoever knocked from doing it again. "There's plenty of food in here if you'd like to eat with Tess and I," he says when he returns, holding a bag of takeout. "Just don't touch the garlic knots," he whispers.

I glance at the enclosed area that Tessa was working out in. "Yeah, I'd like that. Thanks," I answer, standing up to help.

Chapter 16

Tessa

I reach into the maple-colored cabinet, grabbing two plates when I hear my dad offer some food to Graham. Okay, make that three plates. I set the plates down on the kitchen island and turn around to grab a glass from the next cabinet.

As the two walk into the kitchen, I quickly turn toward the refrigerator. "Graham, would you like water, tea, or lemonade?" I ask without turning around. I wasn't prepared for how my body would react to seeing him after my moment in the bathtub.

"Lemonade would be great, thanks," he says, and I feel his eyes on my back. At least, I think it's his eyes. I grab the lemonade pitcher and suck in a deep breath before turning around.

I'm instantly assaulted with the sight of his six foot, lumberjack-built frame. Holy shit, he's attractive.

He somehow managed to move to the space right behind me without me being aware, and now my body is very aware of his presence as his musky aroma fills my nostrils in the best way. "Sorry," I say, taking a quick step to the side so I don't collide right into him.

He goes to take a step in the same direction as me which leads us to doing that awkward dance of *you first, no you first*. "Oh for fuck's sake," I say, earning a chuckle from Graham. The sound sends a warmth straight to the apex of my thighs. "You can move, I'll stay right here." I hand him the lemonade pitcher and give a smile that I hope doesn't come off as awkward.

He takes the pitcher from my hand and goes to walk away then stops and turns back to me. "Where are the glasses for this?" he asks in a way that makes my smile grow wider as I point to the counter behind him. "Right. Thank you." He smiles, turning around again.

I steal a glance at my dad and notice he's watching us, trying to hide a smile behind his water glass. I stick my tongue out at him as I grab the plates, causing him to laugh. We all sit at the island where my dad has emptied the contents of the bag of Leroy's takeout.

Leroy's sells a smorgasbord of cuisine that doesn't really fit into one specific category. The Combo 13 that I ordered is Italian—stuffed mushroom pasta and meatballs. My dad's favorite dish is their fried chicken enchilada with queso and green chili sauce. And my mom's favorite dish, or what she used to order before the cancer sucked away her appetite, is their barbecue pulled pork sandwich with a side of potato salad and banana pudding for dessert. You would think that with the wide variety of food that they sell, something would taste bad, but that's what makes Leroy's so fantastic. It surprisingly works and is incredible every single time.

We all fill our plates and I watch to see what Graham puts on his. But his plate isn't all that I watch. I find myself checking out the way his forearms flex as he grabs for something out of one of the containers. My mind flashes to an image of his arms flexing as he grabs my waist and pulls my body into him. He's wearing a long-sleeved, dark gray button-up shirt with the sleeves folded a quarter of the way up, and a pair of khaki pants that fit tightly around his ass.

My dad's cough startles me and I quickly move my eyes in his direction. He has a smirk on his face, like he knows what I'm thinking. My cheeks flush pink with the thought.

"Graham brought your mom over a huge bag of goodies for her to bring to her next treatment, so she'll have plenty to choose from between what you got her and what he got her," my dad finally says.

"I didn't realize you'd already gotten her stuff. She can just keep the stuff I got her here," Graham quickly adds, what sounds like guilt filling his voice.

I give myself a few moments before looking up to meet Graham's gaze. "No it's okay. She and I can go through everything and organize it so we optimize her options," I reassure him, feeling proud of myself for not breaking eye contact while I responded.

"How is your work going, Bug?" my dad asks between bites of his dinner.

I tilt my head side to side as I finish chewing my food before answering. "It's good. I'm working with a client

I've worked with previously. She's commissioned two new book covers—both for the same book. She wants one that's discreet with just a few details and one that has characters on the front."

"I remember your mom talking about you being an artist. Have you done anything I might have seen?" Graham asks, his full attention on me.

My cheeks heat with the intensity of his stare. "I do mostly book covers, with the occasional advertisement here and there." I pull out my phone and open my photos to show him some of my work.

He reaches for my phone and his fingers graze mine as I hand it over. I'm suddenly very self-conscious about my work and I chew on my thumbnail as he holds my phone and zooms in on the picture. "Are there more?" he asks, holding my phone up.

"Yeah, that whole folder is my work so you can scroll through and look." I pick up my fork and take a bite while trying to act like him looking at my artwork isn't giving me a bit of anxiety.

"These are really good. You do all of this by hand?" Graham places my phone back on the counter next to my plate.

I nod slowly. "I do. I will either use my sketchbook and a pencil, or my tablet and a stylus. I typically carry both around with me in my bag at all times."

"That's really cool. I can barely draw stick figures," he says, making us all laugh.

"We don't know where she got her talents, but Sherri and I both try to take the credit," my dad chimes in.

Once dinner ends, I start to pack leftovers up. "Would you like to take any of this home with you?" I ask Graham, holding the takeout containers in my hand.

He looks at me for a beat before smiling. "Yeah, I'd love to if you're sure you and your dad don't mind." He's motioning towards my parents' bedroom where my dad disappeared to get changed for work. My dad took the day off, but someone called and asked if he could pick up their shift tonight. He didn't want to take it because we aren't sure how Mom will be through the night since today was her first treatment, but I insisted that I'd be here if she needed anything.

"No, we don't mind. We have plenty of food in the fridge with Mom's appetite being what it is," I respond, moving a little bit of everything into a container for him, including two garlic knots.

Graham walks out with my dad and I stand at the living room entryway watching my mom sleep, trying to decide if I should wake her up so she can move to her bed. I can't help but notice how peaceful she looks right now. You wouldn't be able to tell she was suffering through so much. After watching her for a few moments, I decide that if she's still sleeping when I'm done cleaning the kitchen and taking a shower, I'll wake her up.

Forty minutes later, after I wake her up, she asks me to sit in the bathroom while she takes a quick shower in case she suddenly gets dizzy. As I sit facing the door, I hear her softly sing "Amazing Grace." She finishes her shower without an incident so I step out of the bathroom after the shower turns off to give her privacy.

I check and double check that she fell back asleep before walking to my room. I close the door and curl up on my bed with my stuffed rooster, Mr. Rio, in my arms. Once I'm in bed and utterly alone, I sob.

I cry for my mom, and the fact that she has cancer running rampant in her body, slowly killing her. I cry for my dad, and the knowledge that he's going to outlive his soulmate—my parents always joked that he'd be the first to go. Hell, I even cry for Graham, and the fact that he's losing his mentor, someone he has clearly grown fond of the last nine years.

But most selfishly, I cry for myself. I cry because I can't stop thinking about how my mom won't get to meet my future husband. She won't get to see me on my wedding day. She won't be around when that little plus sign shows up on a pregnancy test. I won't get to go to her for advice when I'm nine months pregnant and terrified I'm going to fail my child. I won't get to call her at three a.m. when I'm up with a crying baby to ask her how to get the crying to stop. I cry because she won't be around to watch her grandchildren grow up. We had all these plans that she won't be around for, and I cry because when she's gone I will never be truly happy again. My mom is too young to die, so I lie in bed crying because this is just so damn unfair.

Chapter 17

Graham

It's Saturday and Sherri is having a relatively good day so she texted and asked if I wanted to come over and play board games with her and Tessa. When I arrive at Sherri's house, Tessa opens the door before I get a chance to knock.

"Good, you're here. We can't decide what to play and Dad had to work, so you're the tie-breaker. Clue or Monopoly?" she asks with a pressing look on her face.

"Don't let her pretty face sway your decision! You come in here before you answer. I need to know she's not trying to bribe you to pick her choice." Sherri's voice comes in from the other room, causing me to laugh.

I follow Tessa into the living room where there are board games spread all over the floor. Sherri is sitting on the floor leaning against the recliner with a plate of saltine crackers and bottle of Pedialyte next to her. Next to her, on the floor, is a couch pillow with a blanket tossed aside, where I'm guessing Tessa was sitting before she answered the door, and she's got a fluffy blanket over her legs.

My eyes shift from Tessa, to Sherri, to the mess of games in front of me, and I laugh. "And are those the only options? Clue and Monopoly?" I inquire with an eyebrow raised.

Tessa and her mom exchange looks before Tessa responds, "I guess we can be persuaded to a different game. Make your case." She gestures to the lot of games lying around.

I take a moment to assess the games at our disposal before settling my sights on a deck of UNO cards. A small smile plays on my lips. "Care for a game of UNO?" I ask as I reach down and grab the deck.

They look at each other again and nod. "Good choice," Sherri says, doing a little shimmy. A full smile tugs on my lips this time seeing Sherri seem like her usual self.

I take a seat on the floor across from Tessa, on Sherri's other side, so we're sitting in a small triangle. "I'll shuffle and deal, sound good?" I wiggle the cards in my hands.

"While you do that, I'm going to grab a drink. Do you want something?" Tessa says standing back up, giving me a full view of her thick thighs covered in lime green leggings.

I swallow, my mouth suddenly feeling very dry. "Yeah, um. Water, please."

An hour later, Tessa and I are still playing the first hand of UNO. Sherri gave up about fifteen minutes ago and announced that she was feeling tired so she was going to nap.

We're staring at each other, me with five cards in my hand, her with eleven. I'm trying not to get cocky because

I know how quick a game of UNO can shift out of your favor. "Care to make a wager?" She looks at me through her lashes.

I look at my cards then back up at her. "What do you have in mind?" I ask, knowing this could be dangerous territory.

She sits up a little straighter and looks down at her cards. "Loser has to run through the neighborhood singing 'Feliz Navidad' at the top of their lungs."

"It's March," I say through a laugh. "Why would we sing that?"

"Okay, fine. No bet," Tessa says. Before her turn, she glances down at the yellow five card, then back at the cards in her hand. The tiniest hint of a smirk plays at the side of her mouth as she lays down a red five, changing the color.

"Damnit," I mutter under my breath. I only have yellow cards in my hand so I was hoping she'd keep it yellow. I draw, and draw, and draw again. Finally, ten cards later, I pick up a green five and lay it down.

"Oh, you didn't have any reds?" Tessa asks after I discard. I roll my eyes and nod at her to go.

She lays down a red draw two and chuckles. I pick up my two cards and watch as she puts another draw two down—this time a yellow. I draw two more cards. Her eleven cards quickly turns to eight, as my five turns to eighteen.

"You can give up now. Nobody is around to see you forfeit," she says and then looks around the room as if looking to make sure there really isn't anyone around.

"Oh, not in your wildest dreams. Take your turn." Her eyes flash and her nostrils flare as I say the word dreams. She puts down a yellow reverse and then a blue reverse, leaving her with six cards.

I watch as she quickly lays down her remaining cards, one after another, all reverse cards. When she gets to her final card she yells "UNO!" so loud I look behind me toward the bedrooms to make sure Sherri isn't going to come out and get on her for being too loud. She lays her final card down and it's a draw four. I shake my head and toss my cards down.

"Good thing you didn't make that bet." She wiggles her eyebrows and does the same shimmy her mom did an hour ago.

I stay and talk with Tessa for another hour before I head out. On my walk home I look toward the sky and think that maybe I don't have to be alone the rest of my life like I thought. Maybe Tessa being home is a good thing.

Chapter 18

Tessa

"She had her first treatment a week ago. The doctor said she should start to feel less nauseous now, but it doesn't seem to be letting up any," I say into the phone, answering Nell's question on how my mom is doing. This is the first time since moving that we've had the chance to talk, besides texting.

There's movement on her side of the phone and a soft purring lets me know Lizzo has decided to join the conversation. "Is there anything that can help? I know there are different medications that can help prevent nausea."

I know Nell is trying to be helpful, but I can't stop myself from rolling my eyes. We've already asked the doctor for all the remedies. "She's tried everything the doctors have offered, even some home remedies we've found online. Nothing is helping." I kick a rock I see on the sidewalk as I continue down the path. I decided to take a walk and make this phone call because I didn't want to just talk about my mom. And I don't need either of my parents hearing the other topic I want to discuss.

Nell sighs into the phone. "I'm sorry, Tess. I really wish there was something I could do or say to help." And I know she's being genuine. There's never been a time, since I've known her, that she hasn't done everything in her power to help me when I've been going through something.

Taking in the sights on my walk, I see flowers are slowly starting to bloom, giving me the hope of an early spring, and I notice that some people already have election signs out for the state senate, even though the election isn't until the end of the year. On quite a few signs I see the familiar name, Franklin Feldd.

The Feldd family is widely known in these parts because the patriarch, Daniel Feldd, has held a seat on the senate for many years and they happen to be from here. Franklin was a few years older than me in school, his sister Tabitha was a year older than me, and if I remember correctly, the youngest sister, Sarah, was a few years younger than me. I had received an email from Franklin Feldds's assistant recently inquiring about designs for their election advertisements. I asked them if I could get back with them, and they gave me until the end of the week. I don't usually do designs like that, but looking at the signs makes me think I should take the job—the signs are boring with just his name and the words "for Senate" underneath.

Swallowing, I come back to my conversation with Nell. "So, you know how I told you about my childhood friend. The one who is close with my mom?" I absentmindedly bring my thumb to my mouth and start chewing on the nail.

"Yeah, you said he worked with her or something? Why?" Nell asks, intrigue dripping from her voice.

I take a minute before diving into this conversation. I've been wanting to talk to her about it since the first day he came over. I need advice on whether the feelings I'm having are weird or if it's okay to feel, I don't know, interested in him. "So, he's kind of hot now." I pause for a minute, hoping she jumps in, but her silence tells me she's waiting for me to continue. "And I may or may not keep fantasizing about what it would be like to climb him every single time he comes over to visit. Which happens to be every day. Every. Single. Day." I make sure to emphasize how often I'm having to see him.

A full-on belly laugh comes from Nell's side of the phone. "Girl, it has been too long since you've had any. I'm sure that's all it is. This man can't be that good looking to the point that you're soaking your panties daily." Once she's finished I hear a deeper laugh in the background. Felix. Fuck. Of course he would be there listening.

I scrunch my nose up at her even though she can't see me "Bitch, you better not have me on speaker." I half admonish before continuing. "I never said my panties were wet, but they are pretty damn near close. I was recently, 'flicking the bean,' as I've heard Felix refer to it a few times in conversations my innocent ears had no right in hearing, might I add. I came so fucking fast just imagining Graham touching my thigh. My thigh! He's *that* hot."

Again with her belly laugh. "I'm going to need you to give me this man's socials so I can get an idea of what you're going on about." She doesn't even comment on being on speaker, even though I hear Felix snickering in the background.

I sigh in response. "No can do. He's not on social media. I don't know the story behind why, but it's an unfortunate fact."

Nell grunts and then makes a sound that I take as she's had an idea. "Take a picture of him. But be sneaky about it," she says, like it's such an easy thing.

"Yeah, don't be obvious about it, it might freak him out," Felix adds.

I rub my hand down my face and try to fight a smile. Gosh I miss them. "I'll do my best." I pause. "Hey, Nell, can you take me off speaker for a minute?" I instantly hear a click and the sound of a door closing.

"What is it, Tessa?" Her tone tells me she caught on to the seriousness in my voice.

"As much as I'm enjoying the eye candy, and the fact that the orgasm helped with some stress I've been feeling, I can't help but feel guilty that I've been having any type of feelings outside of being focused on mom." I arrive at my house and sit down at the end of the driveway.

Nell makes a noise I can't decipher. "I can't tell you what's healthy or what's not healthy when it comes to all of that, but I will say that it's not good for anyone to just focus on the bad. There's nothing wrong with getting your rocks off to help relieve the stress you're feeling due to all of the seriousness going on at home. And I'm sure your mom doesn't want you to be mopey all the time either."

I shake my head. "I'm not being mopey."

"Girl, don't lie to me. I will drive the three hours to slap that nonsense right out of your mouth." She laughs.

"Okay, maybe I'm mopey. Nell, I moved home to help out, but I've ended up hiding out in my room most of the time. It's harder to be here watching her decline than I predicted." I let out a huff and run my hand through my hair. "But I'm home now. I'll think about what you said. Tell Felix I said bye. I'll talk to you later. Love you, Nell."

"Love you too, Tessa," Nell says before we end the call.

She said to sneak a picture of him. Maybe I will. It'll give me something to actually look at if I decide to take more time for some self-care.

Chapter 19

Graham

For the entire week after our game of UNO, Tessa has been distant. When I come over for dinner she stays in her room, and the off chance she joins us she barely speaks. And by the looks of the dark circles under her eyes, I'd say she's not getting much sleep.

Tonight, she's sitting at the table with us, and I'm trying to include her in the conversation. "How was your day?" I point the question at Tessa since Paul and Sherri have both already discussed theirs.

"Fine," she says, playing with the food on her plate. Her elbow is on the table with her cheek resting in her hand.

"Have you been working on that cover you were telling me about?" I glance at Paul and Sherri as I continue to talk to Tessa, confusion written on my features. They both slowly shake their heads at me.

She lifts her head enough that her eyes meet mine. "No." She sets her fork down on her plate and stands up from the table. "I'm going to bed." She looks at her parents and grabs her plate before walking to the kitchen.

Once Tessa is out of the room, Sherri releases a deep breath. "She's been hiding in her room all day every day. She'll come out and sit with me for a few hours but the second Paul is home she goes back in there." I watch as Sherri looks down the hall with sorrowful eyes. "I hate that she moved home to help because it has only killed her spirit," she admits as shakes her head.

We sit at the table talking quietly about the not-so-subtle changes they've noticed in Tessa when Paul changes the subject. "Graham, I hate that I'm asking this last minute, but do you mind taking Sherri to chemo tomorrow?"

My eyes dart between the two of them. "Of course I don't mind. I'll email Dr. Kingsley in the morning letting her know I won't be in. Can I ask why you need me to take you, Sherri?"

She nods her head and looks to Paul to answer. "Tessa has agreed to meet with a potential client; the only time he could see her is during the chemo appointment. The moment I got home from Sherri's diagnosis appointment, I called to make one for myself, for preventative measures." He takes a breath before continuing. "The only day that was available for a full workup was for tomorrow. I scheduled the appointment before we knew when Sherri's treatments would be." He looks at Sherri with guilt in his eyes.

"He wanted to call and cancel, but I told him it's more important that he does this screening than come and sit with me while I get my treatment." Sherri reaches for Paul's hand and gives it a squeeze.

"Of course I can help. What time do you need me over here?" I take out my phone to set an alarm.

Somehow, it's already Sherri's second round of chemo and I'm the one taking her. After pulling my car into Sherri's driveway, I piled her large bag of goodies that she and Tessa sorted through into my backseat, along with a blanket and pillow. Sherri tried to help, but I insisted that I take care of it. I help her into the front seat and double check that she has everything she needs before pulling out in the direction of the treatment center.

After driving in silence for ten minutes, Sherri finally speaks. "Thank you so much for bringing me today. I probably could have driven myself there, but I don't think I would have been able to drive home after." She gives me a warm smile.

"Sherri, how many times have I told you, I'm here for you. Whatever you, Paul, and even Tessa need. As long as it's something I can provide, I'll do it." Stopping at a red light, I glance over at her as I pat her hand. "Now, would you like to talk, listen to music, or just sit in silence? You can take my phone and control the music. I have that playlist I made for you."

Smiling even bigger, she grabs my phone from the cupholder and holds it out for me to unlock. We sit in comfortable silence as she scrolls through the playlist. I mostly added songs that she has talked about in passing, but I also asked Paul what songs were her favorite when they were younger and he happily sent over a long list. She just so happens to hit play on the song that made the top of that list. "I Won't Back Down" by Tom Petty plays through the speaker and Sherri sings along at the top of her lungs.

When we arrive at the center and get her checked in, I look around at the others in the waiting room. The friends and families look like they are trying to stay positive with forced smiles on their faces, while the cancer patients look sullen. I glance at Sherri and can't help but smile as she holds her head up high with what looks like a genuine smile on her face.

Once she's attached to the machine and the curtain is pulled back, I pull my chair in closer to her. "So, Mrs. G, what would you like to do first? Color, knit, read, play a card game?" I ask as I rummage through the bag, missing the look on her face until I pick my head up in search of an answer.

"Can we just talk for a little bit?" she asks, tears forming in her eyes which instantly put me on alert.

I sit up straight and drop the bag. "Is something wrong? Are you in any pain? Do I need to get a nurse?" I ask in a mild panic, searching her face.

She shakes her head and I let out a relieved breath. But I still watch her in anticipation. "It's Tessa." She sighs. "I know we talked about this a little last night, but the poor girl is withdrawing and isn't doing what she used to love. Pauly and I had to force her to take this meeting with Franklin. She hasn't been doing her exercises that she used to love, she hasn't been drawing, and I think she's even giving *me* a run for my money in the loss of appetite department," she finally says, staring at me.

I nod, even though I'm utterly confused as to what she wants me to do. "I've noticed that since I came over for that game day she's been a little different. Do you think being home is more taxing than she anticipated?" I lean closer to her.

She takes a deep breath and looks like she's contemplating whether she wants to say what's on her mind. I don't want to rush her to answer, so I sit, waiting as I give her the time she needs. "I think that's most likely the case. I'm just worried that with everything going on we didn't consider what being in her childhood home and watching me go through this would do to her mentally." Her body chooses that exact moment to force her into a coughing fit. "I think her watching me decline is making her depressed." She grabs her water bottle and takes a generous gulp before putting it down and looking at me.

"What if she comes to stay with me for a bit? So she has a place she can go when she feels like it's getting to be too much." I meet Sherri's eyes. "I know she might not like the idea, but even if we just mention it to her . . . I'm two minutes down the street; she'll still be within walking distance if you need anything." The more I think about it the more this makes sense. If we can get Tessa to agree to come stay at my house so she isn't surrounded by the reminder of her mom's diagnosis twenty-four seven, it might help her.

Sherri releases another sigh and with it comes another cough attack. "We can't ask that of you." She pauses to cough again. "Plus, I don't even know if she'd agree to that."

I don't hesitate. "You're not asking me, I'm offering. If she agrees then I'll be more than happy to have her stay with me." I don't mention that, selfishly, this is a dream come true. Especially because, while this seems like a drastic move, it might be exactly what Tessa needs. "I can have one of the spare rooms set up by the end of the day. That way it's ready whenever she is." I grab her hand and give it a squeeze.

Chapter 20

Tessa

The picture I sent was one I snuck the night Nell joked about me taking it. Graham was wearing a pair of dark denim jeans that hugged his ass so well they made me jealous. He was leaning against the kitchen counter with his arms crossed over his chest, wearing a light blue sweater the color of a Robin's egg. He looked so at ease standing there talking to my dad. Before I could think better of it, I pulled my phone out and took a picture. Two days after that text I had a package full of brand new panties and a note that said: **You know why.**

Nelly-Belly Peters:

I'm thinking about you.

Nelly-Belly Peters:

Hey, Tess. I miss you. I love you.

Bennett Thatcher:

Just wanting to check in again. I haven't heard from you in a while and Nell said you haven't been returning any of her texts or calls either. We're worried about you.

I took the meeting this morning with Mr. Feldd with the intent of just getting out of the house to appease my parents. I accepted the job because, even though political marketing isn't typically my thing, it'll at least get my creative brain working again.

I walk into the living room after my meeting and notice my mom is back from her appointment. She's sitting on her recliner while Graham sits on the sofa next to her; they're watching something on TV I've never seen.

"Hey, Mama, how was your treatment today?" I lean down and give her a kiss on her head.

She smiles up at me. "Oh it was okay. I made it through without needing the nurse, so I call it a win."

I give a small smile at her response. I know she's trying to keep the mood light, but it's hard to smile when thinking about her hooked up to that machine again. "Graham, thanks for taking her for us," I say, giving him the same smile I gave my mom.

"Oh, don't mention it. I'm glad I was able to help." He looks at me with a smile reaching his eyes, causing the corners to crease.

"Come sit down and join us," my mom says, motioning to the couch next to Graham. My eyes shift between the two of them before I shrug my shoulders.

I set my bag down and sit at the edge of the couch, chewing on my nail as I pretend to focus on the TV. Graham and my mom are talking, trying to bring me into the conversation. But I'm not in a talkative mood, so I keep my eyes glued to the TV.

I wonder how chemo really went. I want to steal a glance to see if she looks any better. It's supposed to be helping extend her life, but honestly it just seems to be sucking her energy and making her sicker, and being home to help with everything is harder than I thought it was going to be. It's like watching the light slowly drain out of the sun. I can feel my world growing dimmer each time I hear her cough, or see her reach for the trash can to throw up.

An hour passes and my dad walks in. "Hey! What are we watching?" he asks as he leans in and kisses Mom.

"It's something about the Egyptians on the History channel. Tessa is really engrossed; she hasn't taken her eyes off it since sitting down." I can hear teasing in my mom's voice as she talks to my dad.

"Oh, you know how much she loves the Egyptians and their cats," my dad jokes, causing a chuckle to leave my mouth, surprising me.

"Hey, you can't fault me for thinking they were on to something with the esteem in which they held cats," I say with my palms up in the air. Out of the corner of my eye I see Graham purse his lips and nod his approval.

"Tess, you want to walk me out?" Graham asks as he stands up. I blink a few times at the abruptness at which he decided to leave, but I nod and stand. As I reach the door I turn around in time to see Graham hugging my mom, whispering something to her.

When we get outside, he sits down on one of the rocking chairs. "Join me for a bit?" I arch an eyebrow at him before taking a seat.

"If you aren't ready to head home, why did we leave the living room?" I ask pointedly.

"Oh, you mean so you could keep watching that riveting documentary?" His eyebrow bounces up in accusation.

I let out another surprising laugh and take a seat. "Okay, so I wasn't watching the documentary. You caught me."

He doesn't say anything for a few minutes, just silently studies me. I shift in my chair, uncomfortable with the attention he's giving me, but also curious about what he's thinking. I'm about to say something to break the silence when he finally speaks.

"Why don't you come stay at my house?" He must see the mixture of confusion and frustration written on my face because he hastily adds, "It doesn't have to be permanent. I know you came home to be here for your mom and dad, but Tessa, come on. This isn't necessarily healthy for you. Being in this house day in and day out, only leaving when your mom has an appointment—"

I cut him off. "How do you know I don't go anywhere during the day?"

He just stares at me, eyebrows raised in disbelief.

"Okay. Fine. I don't leave the house. But I came home to be with my mom. So I'm here. I can't stay at your house when I'm supposed to be *here*." I huff.

"I'm not saying you move from your house to mine to just sit at my house all day—Lord knows that's not healthy either. But having my place as a landing pad, for when you're starting to feel too much could be a good thing." His face is full of concern. I know he's not saying any of this out of malice, it's all coming from a good place.

I shake my head and look down at my hands. "You don't think they would think less of me?" I half whisper. "If this has become too much and I need a little space." My voice catches as I fight back the emotions.

Graham reaches for my hand. "Tessa, your parents love you so much. They know this is a lot. I'm positive that if you decide you need a break, even if it's just a place to go at night to sleep, or for a few hours during the day, they would support that decision. They want you to be happy, and I'm going to risk sounding a bit harsh here, Tessa, but you don't seem happy."

"How long do I have to think about it?" I ask while picking at the hem of my shirt.

I hear him inhale. "I'm going to fix up my spare room as soon as I get home. You can make the choice whenever you're ready. It'll be there for you." I look up. First I catch sight of his hand landing on top of mine, and then I see the sincerity in his face. He really doesn't mind if I use his house as a safety net—a landing pad, he called it.

I continue to sit on the porch long after Graham left to go feed his cat and prepare his house for the possibility of me coming to stay. I ponder what it would be like living at his house, away from the middle of the night cough attacks that lead to barfing. Away from the lingering smell of vomit that no amount of cleaning products can remove. I moved home to be here for her and I feel guilty for even considering taking Graham up on his offer.

Lost in my thoughts, I literally jump when my dad places a hand on my shoulder. "Holy—" I stop myself. "You scared me." I let out a chuckle.

"Sorry, Bug, I was just worried about you. You've been out here for a while. Your mom's already turned in for the night." He leans his head towards the door. "What's going on in that pretty head of yours?" He takes a seat in the empty chair.

I exhale while trying to find the words. "Graham offered to let me stay with him. He said it's obvious I'm not happy here and I need a break."

"He said that?" my dad asks, his gaze drifting to Graham's house across the street.

"Maybe not exactly that. But close to it." I lift my shoulder. "Am I a horrible daughter for considering it? Daddy, this is more than I expected, and I want to be here and be strong for Mom, but . . . I don't know if I can." I let out a sob.

He's up in a heartbeat, pulling me into a hug. "Listen here, Tessa Elaine. If you think that going to stay down the street will help you in any way, you do it. This is your home and the door is always open for you, but if this is getting to be too much to handle all at once, you do what you need to do." He leans in kissing my temple. "Your mom and I won't think any less of you."

As he holds me in his arms, I can't help but wonder if putting a little bit of distance between me and all of this for a day or two might be best for my mental health.

Chapter 21

Graham

"So, let me get this straight. You just offered to let the woman you've been pining over for years move in?" Grant asks over a fork full of spaghetti. He was in the kitchen making dinner when I made it back from the Gunter's house.

I spin noodles around on my fork before answering him. I've told him the whole story twice now, but somehow this is the part he's stuck on. "I have not been *pining* over her for years," I deny. "But yes, I did offer to let her move in if she's comfortable with it. I have three rooms being unused, except when you and Lisa need me to keep the kids. Why not let her stay?"

He holds his fork out toward me with an expression on his face I can't interpret. "You have, and denying it is only going to get you in trouble if she moves in."

I hold his stare before responding to give myself time to come up with a response that doesn't sound stupid. "I'm doing this as a favor. Her mom is dying. I think I'll be able to keep my dick under control while she's here." He gives me a smirk that says he doesn't believe me. "Oh, I guess I can say congratulations now," I say, changing the subject.

"Congratulations on what?" He looks away, trying to play dumb. I know good and well he's the mastermind behind Corinne telling me the baby news. I also know he wanted to talk about it at the park but I wouldn't rat out my niece. Desperate times call for desperate measures, and I'm desperate to get him to stop making a big deal of the possibility of Tessa moving in. I level him with a stare saying as much.

"Oh, on what? Hmmm, let's see. Maybe the fact that after ten years you're going to have another baby!" I let the excitement show through my voice. "I know you've been wanting another kid, but I also know it's nobody's business to ask how it's going. So, truly, I'm happy for you, bro." We both smile at each other.

His grin lights up his whole face. "All right, all right. On the way to the park I kept talking about how much her Mom didn't want anyone knowing about the baby, so we have to remember it's our family secret for a while. I knew Cori wouldn't be able to resist." He scratches his beard and laughs. "I'm actually surprised it took you so long to say anything. I was beginning to think I don't know my daughter as well as I thought."

His last sentence brings a laugh out of me. "Poor Corinne walked right into that one, but I also wasn't going to let you know that I knew." I think about how she made sure I promised not to say anything. "If it helps, she didn't tell me right away."

"Thanks, we're really excited. It's still early so we don't want to go telling a bunch of people yet," Grant says, taking a swig of his beer.

I nod in acknowledgement and take a drink of my lemonade. "Well, would you like to help me get one of the spare rooms ready, or did you just come here to eat my food?" I stand, taking my empty plate to the dishwasher.

"Yeah, yeah. I'll help. Which room are you letting her have? Or should we get them all ready so she can choose?" My big brother, ever the thoughtful one, thinking ahead about letting her pick which room she wants.

"That's not a bad idea. How about you get Ethan and Cori's rooms situated in case she wants one of those. And I'll get the one closest to my room and the bathroom ready." I grab his plate off the table and add it to the dishwasher with mine.

Grant turns on music through the speakers and we get to work. "You Belong With Me" by Taylor Swift starts playing, making me laugh. I don't know when or if she's going to take me up on my offer, but I want to make sure I'm prepared in case she does.

I'm cleaning the toilet when Grant pops his head in to let me know his rooms are complete and that he's going to head out. "Thanks for the help, man. And congrats again on the soon-to-be little one. I really am happy for you both," I say as he walks out of the room.

Two hours later, Jay Catsby and I are lying on the bed watching reruns of *Battlestar Galactica* when my phone vibrates on the nightstand.

Paul Gunter:

> *Tessa has agreed to come stay with you. She seems a little reluctant, but also a little excited. Will tomorrow after work be too soon for her to start moving her stuff?*

Me:

> *Of course not! I have three spare rooms; she can have whichever one she wants. I can drop my key off with her in the morning before school and she can even move stuff during the day if she wants. She'll just have to be mindful of Jay Catsby. He might try to sneak out if she leaves the door open too long.*

Paul Gunter:

> *Thank you again so much. This means so much to me and Sherri—you opening up your home for Tessa. I think it'll be good for her.*

Me:

> *Don't mention it. You're family to me, I'll do anything for you guys. I love you both.*

Paul Gunter:

> *We love you too.*

I set my phone down and lean my head back. I can't believe I'm really going to have Tessa Gunter living in my house. What I said to Grant stands, I won't make any moves on her—she's going through a lot right now. I'm giving her a place to stay so she isn't around Sherri's illness twenty-four seven. But damn if my dick isn't getting excited just thinking about seeing her in my house, sitting at my kitchen table, on my couch, knowing she'll be naked under my roof. I close my eyes and let myself dream about the possibilities that could come with having Tessa live here.

Chapter 22

Tessa

Am I really doing this? Am I really moving in with a guy I've known for years but have only recently reconnected with? Sure we grew up being friends and he's close with my parents, but the small conversations we've had here and there the past few weeks don't mean we know each other. Not as adults, at least. What if I can't control the urge to climb him? I won't have my parents there as a buffer. What if I walk in on him naked? Not that I think I'll need to go in his room for anything.

The only time I don't feel completely numb and distant is when he's at the house visiting. I don't even understand what that means. But he's doing me this huge favor by letting me have a safe haven to escape to, so I'd be crazy not to accept his help.

Standing in my room looking at the boxes I feel like I just emptied, I try to decide how much I want to take with me. How long will I be staying there? I just need to escape for a little while, but how do I determine how long that is?

I finally decide that I don't need to pack too much. After all, if I need more stuff I'll only be a few houses away. Putting the boxes aside, I opt for my duffel bag. I pack a few pairs of jeans, some leggings, sweaters, a few T-shirts, socks, a few bras, my untouched box of panties from Nell and Felix, and a few pairs of pajamas. I also add my bathroom supplies: my razor, shampoo, conditioner, body wash, toothpaste, toothbrush, and my tampons. In my backpack, I put my electronics and all their various charging devices, a sketchpad, and some colored pencils. I look around the room one last time and turn out the lights.

I walk sullenly into the living room where my parents are sitting watching *Who Wants to be a Millionaire.* "Well, I guess I'm going to head on over to Graham's and get settled," I say, shrugging my shoulders. I feel a little uncomfortable thinking that my parents might think less of me for needing this break even though I moved here to be *here.*

"That's all you're bringing?" my mom asks, looking me over. "Or do you have more things in the other room?" She looks behind me toward the dark hallway.

I glance down at my duffel- "Nope. This is it. I figure if I need more things I can grab them one of the many times I'm over here visiting." I try my best to smile at my response.

My dad stands up and walks to me with his arms stretched out. "Tessa-bug, we're going to be right here whenever you are ready to come back—we're not going anywhere. We love you and understand the need to have a neutral zone." As my dad is talking, my mom starts gagging and reaches for the trash can.

I put my duffel down and go to the kitchen to get a damp washcloth. "And what about you, Dad? You're also around this twenty-four seven. Do you feel like you need a neutral zone?" I ask, bending down to help my mom clean up.

He looks at me and sighs. "No, Bug, I don't feel like I need a neutral zone. Not only do I leave for work each day, but thirty-five years ago I vowed 'in sickness and in health.' I meant it then and I mean it now." He takes the can once she's done getting sick so he can clean it out. "I would sit by her side all day every day if I didn't have to work."

The reality of it hits me all over again. I stand up and give my parents each a quick hug and leave before the tears can escape my eyes.

My mom is dying.

My dad is losing his best friend and partner.

And I can't be strong enough to stay by her side every-day. What kind of daughter am I?

As I walk to Graham's house I let the tears flow freely. I don't trust myself to drive my car, even if it is just a few houses away. My eyes are so blurry I barely trust myself to walk.

Graham dropped an extra key off at the house before he left for work so I let myself in. I catch a glimpse of a tail from a cat as it darts under the couch and remember Graham has a cat. I shut the door behind me and lock it as I take in my new space.

I find myself standing just inside the door of Graham's house, which also happens to be the living room. There's a sectional facing a large flat screen TV that's mounted on the wall. In front of the sectional is a glass coffee table with various novels laid upon it. Under the mounted TV is an entertainment center that has more books and video games on the shelves. I walk further into the house and come into the kitchen and dining area. The kitchen has ash wood cabinets and white marble counters. There is a small island in the middle of the kitchen with two stools, and off to the side is a dining table that can sit six. On the island is a piece of paper. Walking closer I see it's a note addressed to me.

TESSA,

WELCOME HOME I GUESS? I KNOW THIS PROBABLY ISN'T EXACTLY WHERE YOU THOUGHT YOU'D BE WHEN YOU DECIDED TO MOVE BACK HOME TO HELP WITH YOUR MOM, BUT I'M HAPPY TO HAVE YOU STAY HERE AS LONG AS YOU NEED. THERE ARE THREE ROOMS FOR YOU TO CHOOSE BETWEEN. I LEFT ALL THE DOORS OPEN SO YOU CAN PERUSE THEM AT YOUR LEISURE. I DO APOLOGIZE IF JAY CATSBY IS HIDING WITHIN WHICHEVER ROOM YOU CHOOSE. HE'S USED TO BEING ABLE TO ROAM FREELY, BUT FEEL FREE TO KICK HIM OUT IF HE'S A BOTHER. TREAT THE HOUSE LIKE IT'S YOUR OWN—EAT WHATEVER LOOKS APPETIZING, WATCH WHATEVER YOU WANT ON TV. I'LL BE HOME AROUND FIVE AND THEN WE CAN GO TO YOUR PARENTS FOR DINNER.

I'LL SEE YOU THEN,

GRAHAM

At the bottom of the note, as if added as a last minute thought, is his phone number telling me to call if I need anything. I pick up my phone and add it into my contacts.

I take in a breath and look around again. I continue walking deeper into the house and check out the rooms as he suggested. I decide on the one directly across from the bathroom. It's located next to the only closed door in the house besides the one that leads to the garage. The room I'm assuming is Graham's. I set my stuff on the bed and lie back on the pale green comforter. Once I'm comfortable, a black and white tuxedo cat jumps up on my belly.

"Oh hello there, big guy. You must be Jay Catsby. I'm Tessa." I introduce myself by stroking his soft fur on the back of his head. "If you don't mind, I think I'd prefer to call you by your last name." His only response is a quiet purring sound. Having Catsby snuggled up on my stomach oddly puts me at ease. Probably because he reminds me of Lizzo, Nell's calico cat. Thinking of Nell, I grab my phone and finally text her back.

Me:

I'm sorry I've been the world's worst best friend. I hope you can find it in your heart to forgive me.

Nelly-Belly Peters:

Shut up, you're not even close to the world's worst best friend. There's nothing to forgive. You've got a lot on your plate.

Me:

kissy face emoji

Me:

So, you'll never guess where I am right now.

Nelly-Belly Peters:

Please tell me you're lying in bed after being fully satisfied by a man whose name rhymes with ham.

I audibly laugh at her response. Because only her mind would go there.

Me:

Oddly enough you're not too far off. I am lying in a bed, and Graham is involved.

Me:

Sort of.

Nelly-Belly Peters:

OMG!

My phone immediately starts to chime, indicating I have an incoming video chat. Nell's face is on the screen, her eyes wide. I roll mine, giggle, and then answer, "What if he was in bed too? I did say he was involved."

"Because if that hunk of a man was with you, you wouldn't have been texting me. Now, where are you? I don't recognize that bedding," she responds, as if she knows all the bedding I own. Which, okay, she does.

I let out a long sigh before rehashing the details that led to me living in one of Graham's spare rooms. As I tell the story, Catsby moseys his way up to my face and plops down in the crevice of my neck. This elicits a gasp out of Nell. "You're cheating on Lizzo with another cat! How could you?"

I hold up one of my hands in a *hey now* gesture. "He's not my cat. This handsome fella is Mr. Jay Catsby—Catsby for short. He's Graham's baby, and I think he thinks that me being here means he's going to get fed early. But there were no rules about giving him anything." As if he understands I'm talking about him, he starts nuzzling my chin and purring louder which makes me laugh.

"Well, I guess Lizzo will forgive you. But that just means when you come back home you owe her lots of love." Nell's comment about me coming home hits a nerve and my eyes well up. "Oh, honey! Lizzo forgives you whether you bring her treats or not!" She misunderstands why I'm crying.

I let out an ugly sob. "Nell, I don't think there will be a coming home. I don't think I'll have the strength to leave my dad once my mom is no longer with us." I take a few shuddering breaths and continue. "He's going to be losing the person he's loved for over half his life. I don't think I can just move back to Richmond and leave him."

"Of course not! Tess, sweetie, please don't cry. I can't do anything to comfort you while you cry right now," Nell says in a soothing voice. "Do you want me to sing to you? Will that help?" When I don't answer, Nell busts out singing "Big Bottom" by Spinal Tap—the only song she ever sings to make me laugh. Which works because I stop crying tears of sorrow and start crying because I'm laughing so hard.

Chapter 23

Graham

I arrive home from work on Tessa's first day at my house to find her sitting on the floor at the glass coffee table. She has her long brown curls in one of those buns that somehow manages to look put together, a pair of green fleece St. Patrick's Day pajama bottoms paired with a black T-shirt that says: *"Two fonts walk into a bar, and the bartender says 'sorry lads, we don't serve your type."* Jay Catsby is lying on her lap while she absentmindedly rubs his back, and her sketchpad sits on the table in front of her. The sketchpad is open to a blank page and she's just sitting there, staring at it.

"Hey, did you get settled in okay?" I ask, causing her to gasp and grab her chest.

"Shit! You scared me," she responds, patting her chest. "I didn't hear you come in. Yeah, I'm as settled as I can be for now." She switches the position she's sitting in, and picks Jay Catsby, up and snuggles him into her neck.

"I'm going to put some food in Jay Catsby's bowl, and then we can head to your parents for dinner," I say, walking toward the kitchen.

She gets up and follows me, setting my cat down. "I'm not going to my parents tonight," she says, not looking me in the eyes. "I realized while sitting here today that I really do need to take some time for myself—even if it's just for a few days. I'll just find something here to eat if you don't mind and do some work on that design for Franklin Feldd."

I take a minute to let what she says sink in. "You sure? Your parents still want to see you. They still want you to come for dinner." She shakes her head but doesn't say anything. "Okay, I'm sure they'll understand. And you're welcome to have anything here. If there's anything you'd like that I don't have, I have a grocery list hanging on the fridge, just add it on there." After another moment of silence and her still not meeting my eyes I ask, "Is there anything you want me to tell them? If they ask why you aren't there?"

She looks at me and I see tears brimming her eyes. "Just tell them I'm trying." After she says it, she turns around and walks to her room, leaving me with only the sound of Jay Catsby chewing his food.

It's been a couple of days since Tessa moved in and she still hasn't gone to her parents' house. She originally agreed to go twice a day. Once in the morning to sit with Sherri for an hour or so after Paul left for work, and then again for dinner. Every day she just gives me a shake of the head when I ask if she's coming. Her parents weren't lying when they said she's pulling into herself. She barely says five sentences to me a day. Not that I'm expecting it; it's not like she owes me anything. I was just hoping getting her into a fresh environment would help her come back to her bubbly personality.

Sherri gives me a sad look when I walk in for dinner tonight. "Still no Tessa?" She glances behind me, probably hoping that Tessa was just a little behind.

I shake my head. "Not tonight. I'm sorry, Sherri, I tried to talk to her. She's still not really talking to me either." I pull her into a hug and give her a little squeeze. "She'll come around. She just needs to determine when she's had enough time."

Paul reaches for his wife's hand. "It's only been four days, Sher. If she hasn't come over by Tuesday, I'll go talk to her." Then he plants a kiss on her head.

We eat dinner in the living room like we've spent the last few meals. Sherri hasn't been in the mood to sit at the table with so much food directly in front of her—it makes her feel nauseous. So Paul and I sit on the couch with dinner trays in front of us while she sits in her recliner, snacking on whatever her body is tolerating that day. Today it happens to be apple slices.

"So, what are the plans for this week at school?" Sherri asks, trying to keep the conversation light.

I set my fork down before taking a sip of my tea. "We're writing essays. I told them it had to be an essay about who they admire. So, on Friday, they started brainstorming ideas on who they wanted to write about. I wrote an example essay and talked about you." I watch her face as I continue. "I wrote about how I admire you because of your generosity when it came to helping me when I was new to teaching. How I admire your integrity and how you stand up for what you believe in. Most importantly, I wrote about how I admire your bravery. You have gone through so much adversity in the past few weeks and you've been so damn resilient through it all."

By the time I finished talking, Sherri is smiling at me, but she has tears running down her face. "Oh, Graham," is all she says before she's overcome with a coughing fit. I didn't mean to make her cry, but I had to tell her how much she means to me.

When I get back home that evening, I notice all the lights are out except the light in front of the freezer. I try to move around quietly—I'm still not exactly used to having an additional person in my house. As I walk past Tessa's room to get to mine, I'm stricken by the sound of her sobbing. It takes everything in me not to knock on her door and check on her.

Chapter 24
Tessa

Bennett Thatcher:

Haven't heard from you in a while, I hope you're doing okay.

Me:

Yeah, I'm sorry about that. I've been going through it. I think I might be on the other side of it soon. Thanks for checking though.

The first time I leave Graham's house is Monday morning. I sit at the window and watch my dad leave my parents house. As soon as he's gone I jog over, get in my car, and drive to a meeting with Franklin Feldd. I turned in a design idea and he wanted to meet in person to give feedback. He's been around politics his whole life, with his dad being a former senator, so I was honestly confused as to why his signs looked plain and why he wanted to hire me to "spruce" them up. But it's a job, and I couldn't turn down the money, especially when it's to draw something.

For the design. I kept it simple. Not as simple as his original design, but simple. I drew a red outline of the state of Virginia and put blue stars around the border with "Franklin Feldd for Senate" in the middle. I'm not really too concerned about whether they approve it or want to fire me. Since my mom's gotten sicker I honestly haven't had the energy or desire to really care about work. Besides this job, I haven't picked up my sketchbook since her first chemotherapy treatment.

For this meeting, I'm wearing my nicest pair of black skinny jeans, a soft yellow sweater with a puffy scarf-like neckline and a black and white coat over top. It doesn't exactly scream professional, but I left all my professional attire at my parents house and I'm not ready to go back there yet. I walk into the building, pulling my coat tighter around me.

"Good morning, I'm Tessa Gunter. I have a meeting with Mr. Feldd," I say in greeting to the receptionist. She has long blonde hair in a fishtail braid resting over her shoulder, and she's wearing a well-pressed tailored navy blue jacket with a brilliant coral blouse underneath.

She greets me with a smile and holds her finger up. "One moment please." She picks up her phone and dials a number. A second later she says into the speaker, "Yes, Ms. Gunter is here for her meeting." A brief pause. "Very well." Then, back to me, she says, "Mr. Feldd will be right with you. Please, have a seat." And she motions to a couch by the door.

Sitting down, I don't bother to pull out my tablet to look at my sketch—I know what it looks like. Instead, I opt to chew on that damn thumbnail again, glancing around the office space. I was here a week or so ago for the first meeting to discuss the design job, but I didn't really look around. There are tables spread out in an open space behind the receptionist's desk. At the tables are what look like very young employees, possibly interns stuffing envelopes and stapling papers. There's a kitchenette toward the back of the office, and to the right of the kitchenette is Franklin's office, and he picks that moment to walk out.

When I see him walking toward me, I stand up and wipe my hands on my pants. "Good morning, Ms. Gunter. I'm so glad you were able to come in this morning," he says in greeting. "Monica, please hold any calls for me," he says to the receptionist as he guides me back to his office.

I give him a small smile. "Good morning," is the only thing I say in response. What else was I supposed to say? *"Of course I came in, what else would I do this morning?" "You're the one paying me, the least I can do is come to you."*? No, neither of those sound appropriate.

When we're in his office, he closes the door and I notice his assistant, Tracy something, is her name, I think. She's wearing a similar outfit as Monica, the receptionist. Except, where I couldn't tell the type of bottoms she wore, I can see that Tracy is wearing a pair of pressed slacks that match her navy jacket, and in place of the coral blouse, she's wearing a salmon color. "You remember my assistant, Ms. Voight?" he says, gesturing toward Tracy.

I nod my head. "Good morning." And then I take a seat across from the desk without waiting for him to give any directions.

Tracy—I mean, Ms. Voight—taps a few times on her tablet before looking my way. "Good to see you again,

Ms. Gunter," she says, looking up at me with a smile that shows off a perfect set of white teeth.

Ms. Voight hands Franklin her tablet and then sits in a chair off to the side, behind his desk. "We love your design, it's simple, yet gives enough to our signs that it doesn't look over crowded. My father liked his advertisements basic and to the point, which is where my original design inspiration came from." He takes a minute and taps on the tablet. "This is what my father used." He holds the tablet out to me so I can see. "And he held a position in the Senate for two terms, so I thought *why not follow the old man's lead*. But then my sister told me it was boring and I shouldn't do what Dad did. She thought I should pave my own path. So we looked for local designers, and found you."

I have to fight the urge to roll my eyes at the redundancy. He said almost the exact thing during our initial meeting. Instead, I just look at the images on the tablet and offer a small smile and a brief nod. "I'm glad you liked the design."

"We wanted to have you come in today to give you your paycheck, and let you know to expect to be hearing from us again. We have more projects coming up that we could use your help with," he says, extending an envelope out to me, then offering his hand to shake as I take the envelope and extend my thanks. After, Tracy leads me back out to the front of the building.

Getting back into my car, I sit in the driver's seat for a moment and take in a few breaths. I open the envelope to look at the check and realize it's double the amount we originally agreed on and has me second guessing whether I should go back inside and say something, or just accept it. Looking between the check and the building, I realize I shouldn't look a gift horse in the mouth and open my bank app to scan the check into my account.

My playlist is on shuffle as I drive back to Graham's house. Martina Mcbride's voice comes through the speakers, causing my eyes to well up, leading me to pull off the road. Half tempted to change the song, I hover my hand over the knob as I listen to her lyrics, the song hitting close to home, about a man loving his wife and helping her cope with her cancer diagnosis. The words echo through my car as I sit on the side of the road, tears coating my cheeks as I finish the song.

I wake up to a knock at the front door. Forgetting Graham is at work, I ignore it for a bit, thinking he will get it—it's his house after all. But then I remember it's Wednesday morning and he has work. *Duh.* So, I get out of bed and pad my way to the front door. Not bothering to check the peephole, I open it to a disheveled version of my dad.

"Tessa!" My dad walks in and envelops me in a hug. "God, we miss you." He breathes into my hair, stroking his hands up and down my back.

"Hey, Dad. What are you doing here?" I hug him back, but not as tightly as he's hugging me. He releases me and walks into the living room. "Yeah, come on in," I say, trying to sound light when I really want to cry.

He sits down on the couch, looks at me, and then stands back up and starts to pace. "Why haven't you been by the house? What's wrong?" he asks. Not giving me any time to respond, he continues on. "Your mother misses you—*I* miss you. And while Graham doesn't know everything that goes on while he's at work, he doesn't think you've been leaving the house. I thought we talked about this? I thought coming to stay over here would be to give yourself a breather from being around the house day in and day out, not to disappear."

The dam that is my tear ducts breaks and I sit down on the couch and sob. "I'm sorry, Daddy. But once I got over here, I realized just how much space I needed. Being at home, hearing Mom cough and get sick, was taking a toll on me, one I didn't fully understand until I wasn't there anymore. I know I moved home to be with her, but I don't know how to be there right now."

My dad sits next to me and wraps his arms around me and the tears fall harder.

"Bug." He sighs. "We don't expect you to be at your mom's side all day every day. But since you've moved here, you've shut us out completely. This is the longest we've gone without talking to you and it's sad. But we understand you need time." He moves my hair out of my face and wipes at the falling tears.

"I just feel . . . I feel so guilty. I can't look at her right now. It breaks my heart seeing her like that. And I know—I *know* it's going to get worse. And I'm not prepared for that," I choke out. My dad just holds me as I cry in his embrace.

I don't know how long we sit there before he speaks. "Here's what we're going to do. You're going to go take a shower or bath, and then take a nap. This evening, you're going to come over and have dinner when Graham comes over, and you're just going to visit with your mom. Just sit with her—you don't even have to talk. And then you can come back here and take another break from it all," he says.

I reluctantly agree, and he kisses me on the forehead and leaves. Once I'm alone again, I curl up on the couch and cry some more.

Chapter 25

Tessa

By the time Graham gets home, I've already fed Catsby, and am dressed and ready to go to dinner with my parents. I sit on the couch, chewing my thumbnail and bouncing my knee while he gets ready. I can feel the nervous energy radiating off of me. I only hope it dissipates before we get to their house.

"You ready?" I startle at the sound of Graham's deep voice. I'm so deep in my own head that I didn't hear him walk into the living room. I nod my head once and stand up from the couch.

Graham is wearing a pair of dark gray slacks that seem to fit just as snuggly as his jeans, a burgundy sweater, and a pair of black loafers. His chocolate brown hair is disheveled, like he's run his hands through it multiple times throughout the day, and his beard is starting to thicken really nicely. While Graham's dressed in his nice work clothes, I'm wearing an outfit far less dressy—workout attire. A pair of forest green leggings and a white T-shirt under a gray hoodie, despite not having worked out today.

We walk the five minute distance in silence. When we arrive at my parents house, Graham knocks once before opening the door. The ease at which he feels entering the house shoots an odd feeling through me.

"Good evening!" he calls out. "I brought a surprise!"

Walking into the living room, I stop at the sight that I'm not prepared for. My mom is sitting in her usual brown leather recliner, and she's covered in what looks to be possibly three blankets. Her typically beautiful olive skin is now sallow, her bright brown eyes dull in comparison to how they once shined. The bits of her once thick, curly brown hair that I can see have become thin, and the rest of her head is hidden beneath a brown handmade beanie. But the thing that startles me the most is the sagginess of her skin, the tell-tale sign of her weight loss. It's only been a week since I've last seen her, how has she deteriorated so quickly?

She turns to me and gives what looks like a pained smile as she reaches her arms up. "My Tessa." The sound is barely above a whisper. I walk to her, lean over, and hold her in a hug.

Terrified that my face will show every feeling and emotion running through my mind, I keep holding her. I try to command myself to pull it together. "Hey, Mama, I'm sorry I haven't been here sooner," I whisper in her ear, thankful my voice doesn't crack.

My dad comes over and taps my shoulder, pulling me out of the embrace with my mom and welcoming me into one of his own. "Thank you," is all he whispers into my ear before kissing my cheek and letting me go.

We sit in the living room while we eat dinner and watch an episode of *The Masked Singer,* which, according to Graham, has become my mom's favorite show. "We had to start from season one, and she makes us watch an episode a night," he says through a laugh.

My parents try to make guesses as each new performer appears and gives clues. Graham watches with amusement on his face and occasionally adds his two cents. Meanwhile, I sit there, watching the three of them, feeling like an outsider. I can't look at my mom without tears threatening to fall. Not just from how different she looks in such a short amount of time, but because of the guilt and shame I feel about not wanting to be here.

I didn't want to leave when Graham suggested I come stay at his house for a bit, but now that I'm not there, I'm relieved. Granted, I'm not in a better headspace in my new accommodations, but at least I'm not here. The feeling of relief makes me feel like a bad daughter, I moved home for this. I should want to be here and help. I should want to keep her company during the day, or try to get her out of the house, even if it's just a walk around the neighborhood. But I don't want to do any of that. What I want to do is to go back to Graham's house, put on my pajamas, and crawl back into bed and cry.

On the way back home—I guess that's what Graham's place is now, home—I look up at the sky. We walk in silence all the way to the front door before I finally speak. "Why didn't you tell me?" I ask softly, letting the tears finally fall.

Graham stops and stares at me. "Tell you what?" He genuinely sounds confused.

"How bad she looks. You or my dad could have prepared me." I'm sobbing and not even trying to hold back the tears that are running down my face. "One of you could have said *'Hey, just so you know, she's lost weight and her hair is starting to fall out. And it's starting to show on her skin that her organs are officially failing her!'* OR ANY-FUCKING-THING!" At this point I'm full-blown yelling.

I don't wait for a response. I open the door and run to my room, slamming the door behind me before I slide to the floor and cry. Why didn't they tell me?

Chapter 26

Graham

I definitely deserved to be yelled at. Neither Paul nor I told Tessa what to expect when seeing Sherri. At first, we weren't sure what to do. It started out as a gradual decline, but then her hair started falling out in chunks and the decline sped up tremendously. In the end, Sherri's the one who told us not to say anything. She was afraid that if Tessa knew how bad it's gotten she would either insist on moving back, or refuse to come see her all together. I still don't know if we made the right decision forcing her to get that shock. Because that's what it was. When you see someone who once was so healthy, happy, and full of life all of a sudden be none of those things, it's a shock to your senses.

Me:

She was not very happy we let her walk into dinner unprepared.

Sherri Gunter:

I know, but thank you for not telling her. And I know she probably won't come back for a few more days, so please just be there for her. She's lost right now. Losing me isn't going to be easy on her.

Me:

You know I'm trying. She doesn't talk to me when I'm home. When we're both in the same room, it's just my voice being met with silence.

Sherri Gunter:

I know, but don't give up on her. She'll want to talk eventually, and she'll more than likely be willing to talk to you over Pauly or myself.

Sherri Gunter:

Well, I'm going to bed. I'll see you tomorrow, Graham. Goodnight.

Me:

Goodnight, Sherri. Sleep well.

I'm lying in bed after taking a shower to wash the day off of me. It's been a tough couple of days—work is getting to be a lot. But I'm thankful it's almost spring break and I'll get a week off to just relax. And knowing that Sherri is getting worse quicker than expected is gutting me. Tessa didn't ask her mom how she was feeling. In fact, she barely said anything at dinner tonight. I'm guessing, though, with her comment tonight about how Sherri's looking, she knows. That thought gives me an idea that has me scrambling out of bed.

I knock on Tessa's door and wait a few moments. I don't expect her to open the door. Hell, I don't even know if I fully expect her to even respond.

I hear the sound of repressed sobs and I knock again. "Tessa, I know you probably don't want to see me right now, but please, at least listen." I slide down the wall outside of her room and lean against it, getting comfortable.

"Okay. I don't know if you're listening or not, but I'm going to talk anyway," I say, angling my head toward the door. "I know you're upset with your dad and me—rightfully so, in my opinion. We didn't prepare you for how bad your mom's health has gotten—how quickly the cancer is ravaging her body. And I'm sorry for my part. I know you're scared. You're scared of losing her. You're scared of her missing out on all that life still has to offer."

I take a breath. I can feel the words getting caught in my throat, but I need to say this. "I'm going to tell you something. I'm scared, too. For the past nine years, your parents have been the only constant in my life. Your mom took me under her wing when I first started at the school. She asked me once about my relationship with my own parents and she sensed by my response—or really, lack thereof—it wasn't something I wanted to talk about. So she didn't ask again."

I sit there leaning my head back against the wall for a moment. I swear I think I hear her move closer to the door, but I don't want to risk spooking her, so I continue. "My parents never treated me like they wanted me around. My brother, you know Grant, he was planned, and he was the perfect son. He had perfect grades, played all the sports, had all the friends, and all the girls wanted to date him. For as long as I can remember, my parents made me live in his shadow. Or at least, that's how it feels. *He* never treated me that way, but they did. Nothing I did was ever good enough. I'm sure you remember me trying to make excuses for why I didn't want to be home. But the moment I graduated high school, I moved out. I got a scholarship to college and I worked my ass off. I invited them to my college graduation and they didn't come."

Taking another breath, I can feel the tears building, the pressure in my eyes as I try to contain them. "The only reason I'm able to live in this house—my childhood house—is because my brother talked them into offering it to me once he turned it down. They paid it off years ago and offered to give it to Grant and Lisa. But they made *me* buy it from them. And even though I don't have a million fond memories in this house from my childhood, I have enough that made me agree to buy it. I paid for a house they were going to *gift* to my brother . . . Anyway, when I started at the school, your mom treated me how I feel a mom *should* treat her child. She was so happy that I became a teacher and was pursuing my dreams. She told me countless times that she's proud of me. My own mom has never once said that to me."

I swallow back tears as I continue. "So watching your mom wither away, while it's hard to witness, I do it because it gives me more memories of her that I can cherish. Because she's more of a mom to me than my own mom, and once she's gone, I'll be losing someone special to me too. I know she's not my actual mother, but that doesn't mean I don't love her like she is. So while you might not want to talk right now, just know that I'm here for you. Whenever you're ready." I say the last bit as I stand up. "Goodnight, Tessa."

Chapter 27

Tessa

I stay awake, leaning with my back against the door and my knees pulled up to my chest long after Graham tells me goodnight. I can't stop thinking about his story. I knew he didn't love being at home growing up, but I didn't realize just how much he didn't get along with his parents. How could someone treat their child that way? Especially a child with such a big heart like his. It makes my heart hurt in a different way for him.

Finally, I find my way back into bed. I toss and turn until my mind finally shuts off long enough for me to fall asleep. Once I wake up, I check my phone and see a message from my mom, sent last night not too long after I fell asleep.

Mom:

Thank you for coming to dinner tonight. I know it was difficult for you. I love you so much, Tessa.

Blinking back tears, I set my phone back down. I need to go over there and see her—talk to her. I need to share my fears with her, but at the same time, I don't know if I can voice my fears out loud. She needs to have positive thoughts and energy around her right now, and I'm not quite sure I'm able to do that. I grab my phone and send a short *"I love you too"* back so I don't leave her on read, before lying back down and pulling the covers over my head.

Maybe I need to talk to someone.

I move the covers off my face and grab my phone.

Me:

Hey, do you have a few minutes?

The response comes in almost immediately.

Bennett Thatcher:

Of course. What's up?

Me:

Do you mind if I call you?

My phone instantly starts ringing. "I guess that answers my question." I laugh into the phone.

"I'm just sitting at my desk staring at this blank sketchbook—I could use a break. What do you need to talk about, T?" Bennett's voice comes out soft and worried.

"I just think I need to talk to someone who isn't here and won't judge me or try to placate my feelings." I sigh. "Can you be that person?" I close my eyes, anticipating him saying no, he can't.

I hear a soft exhale come from his side of the phone. "I can be whatever you need me to be. I'll just listen and not give any advice unless you ask."

I open my eyes and stare at the closet door, collecting my thoughts before I begin. "I saw my mom for the first time in a week last night. Please don't say anything about it being that long, I'm already punishing myself. She's doing worse. Much worse." I swallow back a lump forming in my throat. "Sitting on the couch feeling like a stranger in my own home made me realize why I haven't wanted to go over there."

I hear Bennett shift in his seat. "And why haven't you wanted to go over there?" he asks in the silence I left.

"I think I've been trying to prepare myself for what it'll be like when she's gone." The rush of emotions that creep up my body at admitting that out loud is overwhelming and I start to cry. "She's the one I want to share all my happy news with. Once she's dead what will be the point in being happy again? I won't have my person here to share it with."

Bennett doesn't say anything for a few minutes and neither do I. I lie here, letting the silent tears fall down the side of my face into my hair.

"T, I know I said I won't offer advice, so I'll try to say this without sounding preachy, but don't let this horrible situation keep you from being happy. Go see her and share happy memories with her. Talk about the good times you once had. Just enjoy her company while you still can."

I shake my head knowing that what he's saying is true. But knowing it's true and actually believing it are two different things. "I'm going to let you get back to staring at your sketchbook. Thanks for letting me talk."

I can almost feel his reluctance to hang up when he says, "For you, anything. If you need me to come see you, just let me know. I can take a few days off."

"I'll let you know. Thanks again, Bennett." I hang up before he can say anything else.

I spend most of the day lying in bed, switching between scrolling mindlessly on my phone and sleeping. Even though I've been resting so much, I still feel like I haven't slept enough. I leave the bed long enough to go pee and grab a snack, and then I slink back under the covers. I lie in bed until I hear the front door close, letting me know that Graham is home from work. His usual routine of getting home, feeding his cat, and doing whatever he does in his room before going to my parents typically takes thirty minutes.

Sitting in bed, I listen to the sounds of his routine, watching the clock, waiting to hear the front door close again before I get out of bed to shower. However, the sound of him leaving the house never comes. I wait ten more minutes, thinking maybe he decided to change, which is unusual, but not necessarily unheard of.

Getting out of bed, I tug at my pajama shorts, adjusting them after having been lying down so long. I quietly open the door and peek toward his room and see the door closed, like always, and I turn my head to look down the hall. I walk down the hall as stealthey as I can manage—that's when I hear the sound of the TV and abruptly stop. Seeing the back of Graham's shoulders and head on the couch makes me double check the time on my phone. He didn't come home early, and it's dinner time. Why isn't he going to my parents?

"Hey, I ordered some pizza. I got one meat lovers and one vegetarian. I don't know what you like on them," Graham says over his shoulder as if he knew I was standing in the hallway.

I hesitantly walk to the couch and stop at the edge. "Why aren't you going to dinner at my parents tonight?" My voice sounds timid and frail in my ears.

He turns around and takes me in, his throat bobbing up and down with a swallow. "Um. Your dad called when I was on my way home and said your mom isn't in the mood for company tonight." He says this while looking at my thighs that are on full display. With my mind confused about why he hadn't left yet, it didn't register that I'm not wearing my typical long pajama pants. The March weather in Northern Virginia is still not quite shorts weather, but Graham keeps the house toasty enough I felt like wearing shorts today.

I'm just now realizing that because of that, he hasn't seen me in shorts in a very long time. I don't shy away from his gaze though, instead it makes my stomach flutter. "Did he say why? Is everything okay?" I ask, worry lacing my words.

"Oh no," he says standing up, immediately understanding why his words could evoke concern. "No. I mean, yes. Everything is okay. He said she's just tired today. He did say he might stop by this evening though." He takes a few steps, as if about to round the couch.

We stand there, looking at each other for a few seconds before I finally speak. "Okay, that's good. And meat lovers pizza sounds good to me. I like meat." I grimace as I realize what I said and how it could be interpreted. At the same time, Graham perks up one eyebrow in a way that I've always been envious of people being able to do, and he lets out a soft chuckle.

Graham sits back down and motions to the rest of the couch. "Feel free to join me. I was planning on watching the rest of this episode and then finding a movie to watch. Pizza should be here"—he looks at his phone for the time—"in about ten minutes." He watches me expectantly.

"Yeah, I think I will." I smile and walk around the coffee table to the opposite side of the couch.

We sit comfortably with only the TV to break the silence. He has on an episode of *Battlestar Galactica*—a show I've never seen before—so I'm utterly confused but don't ask him what's going on. As we sit watching the TV, I steal more than a few glances at him. He's not in his work clothes anymore, and even though I've lived here for a week, he's wearing clothes I've yet to see him in—a red T-shirt, a pair of gray joggers, and a pair of black socks. When he stands up to get the door after the doorbell rings, I see every inch of the appeal that is the gray sweatpants. I swallow audibly.

Before digging into the pizza we look through movies and decide on an oldie but a goodie: *Space Jam*. Once the movie starts, we sit in our self-designated positions on the couch and eat our pizza. After watching about forty-five minutes of the movie, I break the unspoken *no talking* rule. "Do you remember the basketball hoop you used to have out front?" I ask, thinking about our childhood.

Graham looks at me and nods. "Yeah, my parents bought it because Grant wanted to play basketball. They got rid of it once he moved out—didn't care that I still liked to shoot hoops on it." He takes a swig of the Dr. Pepper he ordered with the pizza. "What about it?"

"I remember coming over and playing HORSE with you and Grant," I say with a smile. "I really sucked and y'all both took full advantage when playing against me."

Laughing, he agrees. "You really did suck. No matter how low we put the hoop you could not get it in to save your life." He looks at me again and this time his eyes roam over my body, causing heat to pool in places it shouldn't.

I shift my legs under me as his gaze lingers. "You both tried to give me as many pointers as you could. I was hopeless though," I say laughing at the memory. "Those Looney Tunes wouldn't stand a chance against the aliens if they tried to enlist my help."

"They probably wouldn't stand a chance with my help either. Maybe Grant though. Him and Ethan like to play basketball together. He used to coach one of the little league teams until Ethan grew out of it. Ethan plans on going out for the team next year." This is the first time Graham has spoken about his family besides last night—what he said through the door.

Since he mentioned his brother, I assume it's a safe topic. "How is Grant?" I set down my glass of Dr. Pepper and bring a blanket over my legs.

He looks at the ceiling as if to find answers there. "He's good. I was sworn to secrecy about this news, but I trust you." He gives me a crooked grin before continuing. "He and Lisa found out recently she's pregnant again. So they're pretty excited about that."

I gasp at the news. "That's exciting for them! Congratulations, or, wait, no. I guess since I'm not supposed to know I can't really say congratulations." I start to get flustered and I have no idea why. "Did they want this? I believe she was pregnant after I graduated college, right before I officially moved, right? That's a big age gap."

"Yeah, they had been trying for a while unsuccessfully, but then they got lucky, so they're really excited. And the kids seem to be thrilled to be getting a new little brother or sister. At least Corinne is, Ethan will get used to the idea." Another smile tugs at the corners of his mouth.

"What about you? Do you see kids in your future?" I immediately regret the question as soon as it's out. It's none of my business if he wants kids.

He looks at me contemplating his answer, "I don't know. I never really saw a family of my own in my future. But now I'm not so sure."

An unexpected blush creeps up my chest. Changing the subject I ask, "Do you remember riding bikes around the neighborhood? You taught me how to ride without holding on to the handlebars."

This time he gives a full smile, one that allows me to see the slight imperfections in his teeth even from this distance. "You were terrified, if I remember correctly—rightfully so. You fucking broke your arm trying to copy me." He shakes his head and rubs his hand through his beard. "Your mom and dad were so pissed at me for showing you how to do that. But that broken arm didn't deter you. The moment you got that cast off, you were back up there trying again."

"I would've been back up with the cast if my mom wouldn't have freaked out. I couldn't let you show me up all the time," I say, my own smile breaking through at how right this feels. Comfortable, even.

Chapter 28

Graham

Sitting on the couch reminiscing and laughing with Tessa feels like the most natural thing in the world. And God, seeing her smile again . . . it's like medicine for the soul. I'm about to remind her about the time she insisted on riding on the back pegs of my bike when there's a knock at the door. I get up to answer it without looking through the peephole, knowing it's more than likely Paul.

"Hey, Paul!" I say, giving the older man a hug. "Come on in—help yourself to some pizza. Tessa and I were just watching *Space Jam*." I motion to the couch and step aside so he can come inside.

"Graham, Tessa." He steps past me and greets his daughter who stands up to give him a hug. "How're you doing, honey?" I hear him ask while giving her a squeeze.

"I'm okay. Graham got us pizza for dinner, so I can't complain too much." The cheer that was just in her voice moments ago falters.

I walk into the kitchen to grab Paul a water—his choice of drink every time he comes over—and watch as he sits on the couch in the space between Tessa and me.

"So, Paul, what brings you over tonight? Not that I'm not happy to see you," I add as I hand him the glass of water.

He nods, taking the water and immediately takes a sip. "Well, I told you that Sherri wasn't in the mood for company tonight and she fell asleep early. We had a pretty eventful day, so it zapped her energy real quick." He looks at me as he says it, but then he looks at Tessa for the next part, "I had my follow-up appointment today to go over the tests they ran."

My heart starts racing as I hear the words Paul is saying. It takes everything in my power to not walk over to Tessa and hold her hand as he delivers whatever news he's about to tell us.

"And . . . What did they say?" Tessa asks, her voice shaking. I can see that she's trying to keep her composure, unsure of where this is going.

"The doctors say I'm as healthy as a horse. There wasn't anything abnormal in any of my blood work and nothing was found on any of the scans," he says and I hear Tessa's breath of relief leave her body. "They said it's smart that I came in to get everything looked at and it would be smart for me to continue to do so yearly just to be proactive." He grabs Tessa's hand and gives it a squeeze. At the contact, Tessa starts crying.

"Oh, Bug!" Paul scoots closer to her on the couch and pulls her into a hug. "This is good news, sweetie."

She hugs him back and I can tell she puts all her strength into the hug. "I know. I'm just so relieved that it was positive."

I stand up and walk out of the room to give them some privacy. Instead of walking to the kitchen or my room, I go into the garage. All the talk about our childhood gives me an idea, which leads me to remembering that my parents left their bikes behind when they moved. Once out in the garage, I head to the bikes that are on a rack hanging from the ceiling. I pull each one down to check the tire pressure.

Chapter 29

Tessa

I'm not sure how I found myself riding Graham's mom's old bike down the road, but if I'm being honest, it's actually helping my mind from wandering. I woke up this morning and walked into the kitchen to see Graham smiling, saying he had a surprise for me. He told me to go get changed into comfortable clothes and tennis shoes, then we walked into the garage where he presented his surprise—two bicycles. I wasn't sold on it at first, but then he reminded me about our conversation the night before and how much fun we had riding bikes growing up, and now, here we are.

We've been riding for almost an hour in companionable silence, one of us occasionally breaking the silence to point out something we see. Finally, I speak up, "You were right the other night." I quickly glance over at him before I continue. "When you said I was scared. But it's not just that I'm scared. I'm also angry. I'm angry that God allowed this to happen. I know I might not be the best Christian, but my mom is. She goes to church every Sunday—or at least used to before she got too sick. She reads the Bible. She was part of a Bible study group. He's taking away a wonderful, Godly woman, and it makes me angry."

He doesn't say anything in response, just watches me as we ride. I know he's allowing me to feel my feelings and think of what else I want to say. Which is something I appreciate more than he knows.

"I'm angry because there's so much she's going to miss out on. I always thought she'd be around to see my kids, ya know? I was never in a hurry to get married or have kids—she's young; I thought I'd have time for all that and she'd still be here." My voice shakes with emotion. "Do you remember how my family used to go on family vacations every summer with my dad's side of the family? I always assumed we would carry on that tradition when I had kids—my parents, and the family I create."

Neither one of us says anything else for what feels like another hour, but in reality it's only minutes. Then Graham asks, "Why don't you tell me about one of your vacations? I know you always told me stories when you got back from the trip, but why don't you share a memory anyway." He glances over at me before turning forward while we take a turn.

I think for another minute, trying to decide what story to share. We did so many things with my dad's parents, his sister, and her family. "Well, you know we'd go every summer starting as far back as I can remember, until I left for college. We tried to go someplace new, and if I had fun at any location, we would go back—just the three of us—at another time so we could experience more of what that place had to offer."

I take a steadying breath and glance up at the trees as we pass, the leaves slowly growing back after a long winter, and listen to the birds sing to one another. "This one summer we went camping out at the James River State Park. I was maybe five or six—I think it was before we met. I remember we all rented canoes to travel down the river—" I stop and start to laugh at the memory before I even get it out.

Instead of interrupting and telling me to continue, Graham just chuckles along and waits for me to resume my story. "Well, I wanted to sit in the canoe with my grandparents—which they were fine with—and my cousins were in the canoe with my Aunt Val and Uncle Dave. So, that left my parents in their own canoe. My mom packed way too much stuff for a trip down the river and my dad didn't try to stop her." Again, I start laughing before I can finish the story, this time I have to stop pedaling my bike and take a moment to catch my breath.

"They didn't even make it out of the shallow end before the canoe sank. She basically packed everything but the damn kitchen sink in that canoe. She and my dad were both sitting inside of it and it just started sinking. My aunt and uncle paddled back to the shore to help them get the canoe situated again, while my grandparents and I stayed out in the middle of the river just laughing at the sight unfolding in front of us." The sound of Graham's hearty laugh is music to my ears. I wish I could record that sound and make it my ringtone without it being weird. "We finally made it down the river without any more incidents, but it was enough trauma on my poor mom that she refused to go in a canoe on any more of our camping trips." I finish the story wiping tears from my eyes. I haven't laughed this hard in what seems like years.

"I can only imagine the sight. Were there any other families around to witness it, or only your group?" Graham asks, residual humor still in his voice.

I nod. "Oh yes, there were probably three or four other groups that got to witness it. I'm sure it made for a very entertaining story for them to share when they got home."

Once I've fully recovered from laughing and taken a good enough break we get back onto the bikes and head back toward the house. "Your mom might not be around for any future vacations, but at least you have a memory bank full of great adventures y'all went on in the past. You can always share those stories with your kids." Graham has such a gentleness in his voice as he speaks. "The way you just told that story—it made me feel like I was there. As long as you share your memories with your kids, they'll know your mom through you."

I choke on the lump of emotion forming in my throat. He's absolutely right, but it doesn't make me feel any less angry.

I'm sitting at the table, staring at my tablet, trying to come up with an idea for this drawing when Graham sits down with Guess Who?. "Care to play?" he asks with a smile.

I look up at him and then glance back down at my tablet. "I'd love to. I wasn't getting anywhere with work right now anyway." I slide my tablet away from me and reach toward the box.

"How about we make this interesting? We didn't bet when we played UNO, which ended up being a smart choice because I would've lost. But why don't we make a bet now?" Graham asks as he grabs the blue board.

"And what do I get when I win?" I ask with a cocky smile on my face.

He returns the smile with one of his own. "Oh, and who says you're winning?"

I reach into the box and grab a card without breaking eye contact with him. "How about something easy? Loser has to change Catsby's litter box for the foreseeable future," I say, throwing out a lame punishment.

He quirks his eyebrow. "But I already change his litter box. If you're so confident you're going to win, that's not a suitable prize on your part."

I bite my lip in thought. "How about the loser has to participate in an activity of the winner's choosing. For example, when you lose, you can sit next to me and draw an outline for the cover I'm working on."

"Okay, I can get behind that. So when *you* lose, we can go to the park and play a game of HORSE." He gives me a devious smile that causes the butterflies in my stomach to go crazy.

"You're on!" I say, extending my hand across the table, waiting for him to shake.

His eyes flick from my hand to my face before reaching over to seal the agreement. When he pulls away, he grabs a card from the box and raises his eyebrows. "Ladies first."

Chapter 30

Graham

Sunday morning Tessa and I are at the park. She's wearing baby blue workout leggings, an oversized hoodie, and a baseball hat with her curly hair pulled through the hole in the back. She's holding my basketball under her arms and looking at me like I took the last bite of her favorite dessert. "You remember the rules of the game?" I ask, reaching for the basketball she's holding. "I stand wherever on the court and throw it in the hoop. If I make it, you have to stand in the exact spot and throw it. If you miss, you get a letter. If you get the shot then you get to move positions and take a shot. Then I'll move to where you were standing and take a shot." I watch her as she rolls her eyes.

"I remember how to play—you and Grant always kicked my ass," Tessa grumbles as she looks from me to the basketball hoop. "I can't believe I agreed to this." She crosses her arms as I dribble the ball a few times.

I stand about two feet away from the hoop, giving her an easy shot to start out with, and sink the ball in the net effortlessly. I jog to grab the ball before it bounces away and I hand it to her.

She walks to where I was standing and tosses the ball and it goes into the net. I catch it once it bounces after hitting the court. Her eyes light up and she squeals as she jumps for joy. "I made it!" she yells. "I don't have a letter yet! *And* I get to shoot first now." She sticks her tongue out at me as she grabs the ball out of my arms.

We each take a few more turns standing close to the hoop. She makes every shot she takes. As I walk to half court so I can take my next turn, I look at her and see her smiling. She looks carefree at the moment and it has my pulse quickening.

"So, if you could travel anywhere in the world, where would you go?" I ask the first question that comes to my mind.

She looks at me with confusion on her face. "Um. Greece. I'd love to go to Santorini." She answers my random question. "What about you?"

"Well, I've been to most states, so I'd probably say Europe. I'd like to backpack across Europe and stay in hostels—get the whole experience," I say, glad I'm prepared with an answer to give.

"That could be fun. What made you want to become a teacher? I don't remember that being your dream growing up," she says, reaching for the ball after I score.

I wait to answer until after she shoots the ball so I don't distract her. I blink my eyes and watch as she bends down to throw the ball, granny style. Laughing, I collapse to the ground. I haven't seen anyone shoot granny style in years.

"What? You didn't say I couldn't do that. And I made it in." Her face is shining as she stares at me while lying on the ground, still laughing.

I shake my head once my laughter is under control. "You're right. I didn't. Good shot, by the way. Half court, nice." I stand up and walk to get the ball. "To answer your question, it's not some noble reason. I didn't pick my major until I finished my pre-reqs. My roommate was an education major and the way he talked about everything he looked forward to about being a teacher made me interested."

Tessa shakes her head. "It's okay. It's a good reason, though. Better than doing it because that's the major all the chicks were doing." She laughs as she lunges at me, trying to steal the ball from my grasp. Instinctively, I pull it closer into my chest, causing her to stumble into me. We lock eyes for a few seconds before mine steals a glance at her lips. She gently bites at her bottom lip, pulling me out of the trance I had fallen under. I release the ball into her hold and step away, coughing to clear my throat.

She takes a step back with the ball in her arms and sucks in a deep breath. I catch her eyes looking at my mouth before she turns around, running and dribbling the ball down the court. She jumps, as if she's going to try to dunk it once she reaches the hoop, and completely misses, making herself laugh.

Lying in bed, I replay the weekend in my mind. The almost-kiss has been on a steady loop in my mind since the moment it happened. I feel like Tessa and I had a breakthrough of sorts. While she still hasn't been back to see her mom, she has opened up to me about some of her fears and things that make her angry about her mom's prognosis.

Baby steps.

It makes me feel confident that she'll be ready to go see her mom again soon.

Chapter 31

Tessa

Hey daddy, sorry I didn't answer your call, my phone was dead and I had it turned off to charge faster. What's up? How was mom's treatment today?

That's what we wanted to talk to you about. Do you think you'd be willing to come over? You can wait for dinnertime when Graham comes over, or you can come now. Whichever you prefer.

I should probably wait for Graham. I know y'all probably want to tell him the news too and there's no point in having you repeat it.

That's totally fine. I look forward to seeing you, Bug. I love you.

I love you too, daddy.

I've been an anxious mess since receiving the text from my dad asking to come over. There was another round of treatment today, and while I originally planned on going, I couldn't bring myself to walk across the street before they left. Instead, I've paced the length of my room and the living room multiple times.

I lied when I told him I didn't want to make them repeat their news, kind of. I don't want them to have to say it twice, especially if it's as bad as my mind is making it out to be, but Graham has become a great sense of comfort for me since this past weekend. I think having him next to me when my parents give me this news will help keep me from breaking down right there.

My parents haven't pushed me to come visit since my shocking visit last week, which I've been very grateful for. But Graham has still gone over every night, even if it's just to bring my dad some dinner. After he goes over there, he comes home, sits with me, shares how my mom is doing and lets me vent my feelings. He allows me to share as much or as little as I want and never prods for more.

As soon as I hear the door open, I run to the living room and throw my arms around Graham, startling us both with this act of affection. "My dad texted. They got some news today that they don't want to share over text. Graham . . . I'm really scared." I start to cry into his shoulder.

He hesitantly wraps his arms around my back and guides me out of the doorway so he can shut the door with his foot. "Whatever it is, I'm here for you." He rubs my back with one hand and brings the other up to stroke my hair. "I'm always going to be here for you," he whispers into my ear then places a gentle kiss on my temple.

We stand in the foyer, hugging for what feels like an eternity, but in reality was actually five minutes. I pull away from him when Catsby starts weaving himself between our legs, letting us know he wants attention and dinner. "I'll get you some food, Mr. Catsby, no need to get all needy." I wipe the tears off my cheeks and pick the tuxedo cat up and stroke his chin. "You can go get ready and we can head over when you're done," I say over my shoulder to Graham.

Walking over to my parents house, I can't stop feeling like this news is going to shake my world more than her diagnosis did. When we reach their house I stand there, staring at the red door that I've walked through without a thought my entire life. Now, I have to try to muster all my courage before even reaching for the handle. Graham, sensing my hesitation, reaches for my hand and gives it a squeeze, I look at him with a forced smile and squeeze back. I'm really thankful he isn't rushing us to get inside. I inhale and hold for a count of five, exhale and hold for a count of five. When I release his hand, I open the door.

I walk through the hallway and into the living room where my mom is bent over a trash can, while my dad is slightly rubbing her back. I close my eyes and turn my head. Graham is there, with his hand on my back, reassuring me that he's here, like he promised. Again, he doesn't force me to move any faster than what I'm ready to, he just patiently waits for me to move into the living room.

Our entrance makes my dad look up, his gaze landing on Graham's hand still on my back. His lips perk up a little and I'm not sure if it's at the contact or at the fact that I actually showed up and didn't bail. Again.

Mom sits up straighter, sets the trash can to the side, and gives me a weak smile. Holding her frail arms up toward me, she says, "Tessa, thank you for coming to see me today."

I lean into her and fight back the tears as I wrap my arms around her thinning frame. "Of course, Mom," I say when she releases me. "I'm sorry I wasn't here sooner." I walk backward to the couch and take a seat. I glance around the living room and see my dad sitting in a chair next to the recliner. On the couch, sitting so close my thigh is touching his when I sit, is Graham.

"Do either of you want something to drink?" my dad asks as if the thought just occurred to him.

"No, thank you," Graham and I both respond at the same time. My dad looks at my mom who has a slight gleam in her eye as she observes us.

"All right." My dad nods his head. "So, as you both know, Sherri was supposed to have her third treatment today," my dad says with his hand resting on my mom's arm. We both nod but don't say anything so he will continue. "Yesterday, she went in for her bi-weekly labs to make sure her levels are stable enough for chemo. Well, yesterday's labs came back with some unsettling news." I instinctively grab Graham's hand that is resting atop his leg.

My mom takes a shuddering breath and says, in a tone just barely above a whisper, "My labs show that the chemo isn't doing its job." She takes a break to cough into a tissue she's holding. "My levels are climbing at an unfortunately high rate. They aren't comfortable continuing any treatment because it'll do more harm than good at this point." She looks between Graham and myself, then looks over at my dad and nods her head.

Graham rubs my fingers in a gesture that feels reassuring. Letting me know he's with me.

"The doctor suggested we start looking into hospice care." My dad gulps, eyes brimming with tears.

I run my hand over my face. "Does that mean the prognosis has changed?" I ask, trying to keep the tears back.

She silently nods her head. "They're now saying it's only a matter of weeks." As she watches me I take a moment to observe her through the tears swelling in my eyes. Her frailness, her sallow skin, the dark circles under her eyes. The brightness that is typically in her brown eyes, so much like my own, is gone. The woman I grew up watching and admiring is sitting here deteriorating, the weight of this illness sitting heavily in the room.

Swallowing through the lump in my throat I manage to ask, "Are you thinking about home hospice, or are you going to want to be admitted into a hospice facility?"

My dad looks at her with a look of question on his face.

She responds in a murmur, "I'd very much like to be in the comfort of my own home when the good Lord calls me home." She takes a moment to reach for and get a sip of her water before continuing. "I know it might be hard on you and your dad to continue being in this house if this is where I have my final moments though. So if you aren't comfortable with me doing home hospice, I will consider going into a facility," she says the last sentence with a steely resolve.

I move over and grab my mom's free hand. "If you want to do home hospice then that's what you'll do. And I want to be here with you—please don't say I can't be." I let my tears fall freely as I beg her. "I stayed away from you out of fear that my sorrow was too much of a burden on you, and it stole precious time I could've had with you."

My mom lifts her hand to my cheek and gives me a sad smile. "Oh, honey, if you want to come back home for this, I won't stop you. But I want you to know, you were never a burden. Even though my body is weakening, I am strong enough to be around your sadness." She rubs her finger across my cheek, catching a loose tear.

Graham clears his throat behind me. "Is there anything you need me to do?" he asks, looking between my parents. This man, who has become such a steady figure in my life, is here, making sure my parents have as much help as he can give. It makes my shattering heart feel not so broken at the moment.

"Not that I can think of at the moment. We will be making a phone call tomorrow to the woman at the hospice center," my dad answers. "I might need you to help me move the furniture around though. We're going to set the living room up as her room so she isn't locked away in the back room. It'll also be easier for people to come and visit with her," he says as he takes stock of the living room, probably making mental notes of what needs to be done.

By the time Graham and I get up to head back to the house I'm emotionally spent from crying. "Would you like a piggy-back ride?" Graham asks, looking at me. I can't help but to laugh.

I must be delusional. Did he really just offer to give me a piggyback ride?

"Is that a no?" He turns around so he's walking backward, facing me. "Honestly, I don't mind, and no offense, but you look exhausted—like you might not make it all the way back." He throws his thumb up and points towards the house.

I sigh. "Honestly, that would be great." I stop walking and he gets in front of me, turning so his back is facing me, and kneels down. "I can't believe we're doing this." I laugh as I climb onto his back.

He links his arms under my thighs, making my body shiver and my mind race. I'm suddenly overwhelmed with the heavy emotions from the news and this current feeling of desire for Graham. He stands up and starts walking like this is just an everyday thing for him. When we're at the bottom of the driveway I start laughing which makes him stop and turn his head around to look at me over his shoulder.

"I can't believe you actually carried me all the way here."

Chapter 32

Graham

Having Tessa's legs around my waist and soft curves pushed against my back as I carried her down the street had my dick straining against my pants. I offered to give her a piggyback ride because she looked exhausted and I honestly didn't think she'd successfully make it back to the house without tripping a few times. I didn't, however, expect her to say yes. So when she did, my heart rate picked up.

Actually, my heart has been working overdrive a lot today. It started when she ran into my arms when I got home from work, and while I'm not a fan of why she ran into my arms, I could definitely get used to that being how I'm greeted when I come home.

When she starts laughing it stops me in my tracks. The fact that she's still able to laugh even with the news that we found out tonight makes me want to put her down, turn around, and kiss her.

"I just can't believe you actually carried me all the way here." She takes a big breath through her laughter.

"Did you think I was going to let you walk here when you looked like you'd make it three steps before you passed out?" I question glancing at her over my shoulder. "Do you want me to carry you all the way to the door, or do you think you can manage the rest of the way?" I ask, giving her thighs a squeeze with my arms, which elicits another giggle from her.

She wiggles on my back before replying, "I think I'd prefer you to finish the piggyback ride all the way inside, please," causing another fit of laughter to spill out of her. Her wiggling causes her tits to brush against my back which has my growing dick very uncomfortable.

I pop her up on my back to readjust her then continue walking. "Aye, aye captain," I say through a laugh of my own.

When we get inside, I bend down to let her climb off my back, and my body immediately misses the feel of her. "Are you going to head to bed, or are you going to be up for a while?" I ask while looking at the clock. It's only eight, so it's still early, but it's been a long afternoon.

"I was actually thinking about making some hot chocolate and watching a movie if you want to join me," she says with a hint of a smile.

I smile back. "Yeah, I'd like that. I think I'm going to put on some comfortable clothes and then I'll be out."

Walking into my room, I grab a pair of black basketball shorts and toy with the idea of walking out shirtless. Taking my pants off allows my boner to stand up behind my briefs. I fist my dick in my palm and let out a groan. As much as I want to fix this, the desire to go back out and be in Tessa's presence is even stronger. I force myself to think unappealing thoughts, hoping it kills the mood. Getting dressed, I decide on wearing a red t-shirt because I don't want to risk Tessa feeling uncomfortable if I went shirtless.

I walk into the kitchen and notice Tessa also changed while I was getting comfortable. She's got on a pair of lime green shorts that show off her voluptuous thighs and a gray tank top that's tight enough I can see the outline of her bra—her very thin bra—which allows me to see the hardness of her nipples. I have to swallow the saliva accumulating in my mouth before I start to drool at the beautiful sight in front of me.

"I didn't know if you joining me for a movie meant you also wanted hot chocolate, so I made you one just in case," she says, handing me a mug of hot chocolate with little marshmallows on top.

I grab the mug and smile at her. "Thanks." I turn around and head into the living room. "What movie are you thinking about watching?" I ask, grabbing the remote and offering it to her once she's sitting right next to me. I suck in a breath at the closeness and inhale the smell of her coconut lotion. Typically, when we're both on the couch, she sits as far away as possible, so I'm a little surprised at her decision to sit so close. Not that I'm going to complain.

A sly smile appears on her face. "*The Princess Bride.* Does that change your mind about wanting to watch with me? It's one of my favorites—my mom and I used to watch it all the time."

I shake my head and respond in one out of the two ways I know will garner a smile. "As you wish." And I'm rewarded by exactly that. A wide grin spreads across her face as she pulls a blanket on her lap and snuggles into the couch, slightly leaning toward me.

Chapter 33

Tessa

I turn on the movie and snuggle in close to Graham. I haven't quite begun to unpack why he feels like such a comfort to me lately, but I've decided not to question it. He feels like home and I'm going to lean into it. As the movie plays, I find myself watching Graham more than the movie, which is inconceivable, because this is *The Princess Bride* after all. There's never been a time when I didn't pay one hundred percent attention to it.

A few times I've caught him mouthing along to the movie, which leads me to ask, "Exactly how many times have you watched this movie?"

A smile teases at the edge of his mouth as he turns his head to look at me. "That question is rather hard to answer," he says as he looks down at his fingers like he's trying to do the math. "I would say over fifty, but maybe not quite one hundred. I've watched it with your mom a few times, and to say I've never watched it alone since she introduced it to me would be a lie." He looks at me smiling with a twinkle in his hazel eyes.

I study him for a few more moments without breaking eye contact and then I hear the beginning of one of my favorite scenes, making me avert my gaze. If I would have paused the movie before I asked him that question, I don't know that I would have stopped from trying to lean in to kiss him.

Once the movie ends, Graham and I go our separate ways—him to his room and me to the bathroom so I can take a shower. Now that I'm alone, I get to thinking about my growing attraction towards him. Obviously he's good looking—anyone with eyeballs can see that. He's got broad shoulders and muscular arms, and the fact that he doesn't have a flat stomach with sculpted abs just adds to my attraction to his appearance. The brown hair atop his head that I'd love to run my fingers through, the hazel -green eyes that I've caught watching me on numerous occasions, and his beard that I imagine scratching against sensitive parts of my body all add to the allure. But even more than his looks, the way he opened his house for me without even a second thought—his generosity is an endearing quality. The relationship he has with my parents, watching him interact with my mom and how animated he gets when talking with my dad, it's easy to tell that they care for him too. I can't help but think how effortlessly he would fit in if our friendship became more.

Spending time with him tonight, watching a movie, helped me not wallow in the news about the new prognosis. Now that I'm alone in my room, I start to think about what they told us tonight. How could we have gone from predicted months with her to just weeks? I knew she was sick, but I guess I was foolish enough to believe that the chemo would buy us more time.

The more I think about it, the angrier I become. I can't believe I've spent the past week and a half over here sulking. My mom didn't even seem upset with me for not being there, which makes me even more bitter. She should have yelled at me, or at least scolded me in her new whisper-voice. Instead, she said she understood why I haven't been around.

I'm not mad at her, I'm angry at the fact that she has cancer. And I'm angry at myself for not being strong enough to put my own selfish feelings aside to be there for her. I'm thankful that neither she nor my dad tried to argue with me when I said I wanted to be there everyday once they get her settled into in-home hospice.

I will make up for not being there for her—I have to.

Or I'll never be able to forgive myself.

Chapter 34

Graham

Last night, Sherri told us that her in-home hospice care was going to start today.

I have to admit, Tessa's decision to move back hit me hard. I understand why she's going back, but if I'm being honest, I'm not looking forward to her not being here after work every day.

I felt something shift between us Wednesday after we got news about her mom and watched *The Princess Bride* together. I'm not sure what, but a few times during the movie it felt like she was watching me. When she asked me how many times I've seen it, I swear I could've kissed her after the way she eyed me so intensely. I probably would have if she didn't break eye contact. Another missed opportunity.

The early April evenings still have a bit of a chill in the air, and I want to be warm while I walk between houses, so after work I put on a pair of joggers, a T-shirt, and a hoodie. After I change, I feed Catsby, which is what I've taken to calling him after Tessa informed me she dropped the "Jay" when she talks to him, because *"Gatsby didn't always use Jay when being talked to or about,"* and I admit, she has a point.

"Come on in," Paul says, opening the door before I get a chance to knock. "Tessa and Sherri are in the bedroom doing who knows what so they don't get in the way of the 'living room shuffle,' as Sherri called it." He's already got a light sheen of sweat on his brow and on his bald head. Once I glance around the living room, I see he's made some progress in moving around the furniture.

I take my hoodie off and place it on the counter in the kitchen before I walk back to the living room. "Let's do this." I rub my hands together looking around the room. "What do you want help with currently? I see you've started some moving. What's your plan?"

"Well I figured we could put the bed here." He moves to stand in an area almost in the center of the wall. "Then we could put the couch over there, and the recliner over there—leave the TV where it is because that'll give Sher the best view of it." He points to every location as he says it and I nod along, seeing his vision in my mind.

We work in comfortable silence, moving the furniture around to make space for the bed. Once the couch is pushed aside, we put the bed frame together to get it set up and plugged into the wall so Sherri will be able to use the buttons to adjust the mattress. With the living room how Paul envisioned it, he walks into the back room to get Sherri and Tessa. While he does that I go into the kitchen to get a drink.

"Oh, Dad, it looks great!" I hear Tessa exclaim as they enter the living room. I also hear a very soft response from Sherri, but her voice has become so low I'm unable to make out what she says.

"Well it wasn't just me. Graham helped. He's in the kitchen getting a drink or something." Paul's voice booms loudly as I walk back into the living room with everyone. My eyes immediately find Tessa. Fuck, she's gorgeous. She's wearing a pink oversized sweatshirt and a pair of black leggings, her brown hair in a braid laying over her shoulder, reminding me of Princess Elsa. I may have seen *Frozen* a time or two with Corinne.

When she looks at me a smile spreads across her face, causing my breath to catch. "You did good, Graham," she says, walking over to me and squeezing my arm. "Now Mom can have all the visitors while she's comfortable in bed." With that comment, I look down at Sherri sitting in her wheelchair. She's looking at me with a small smile on her face.

"Well, don't just stand there," Sherri murmurs. "Someone help me into the damn bed." As she starts to stand up, Tessa and I reach out to help before the struggle can fully show on her face. The cancer has zapped her energy to the point where it's a feat for her to make too much movement.

We eventually settle into our nightly routine of dinner and *The Masked Singer*. But tonight, instead of sitting a foot or more away, Tessa takes a seat right next to me, our legs touching. I steal a glance at her and see that she's watching the TV. I look over at Paul and Sherri, my gaze settling on Sherri who is eyeing Tessa and I with a knowing smile on her face. She catches me looking at her and nods her head then wiggles her finger between Tessa and I. I just shrug my shoulders and give a small smile in return.

Chapter 35

Tessa

It's been four days of being back home with my parents and even though Graham still comes over, I miss being at his house with him. He's on spring break this week so he's been here visiting at all hours, but at the end of the day he goes back to his house.

My room here is available, but I've taken to sleeping on the couch in case my mom needs anything in the middle of the night. A few times she's woken up from a coughing fit and has asked for water. Another few times she's woken up unable to find a comfortable position and has asked me to rub her back in the hope of helping her relax.

My dad unfortunately still has to work. So, to keep her company during the day, we watch movies and *The Masked Singer* when she's not resting or chatting with visitors. She's had the church's deacons come pray over her and some of her friends have come by to keep her company. When she has visitors I like to stay close but try not to hover in case they want privacy. Today's one of those days that she's got company—a friend she's had since childhood. Graham is here when Angie arrives so we go out to the enclosed patio to give them time to visit.

"How was she last night?" he asks, taking a seat across from the couch I'm sitting on.

I unconsciously play with one of the coasters sitting on the table. "She slept most of the night, maybe woke up once or twice. My dad keeps telling me to sleep in my room, but I can't bring myself to leave her side through the night." I look up at him and meet his stare with my own. "The nurse who was here this morning said she's still having urine output, so that's a positive sign right now."

"Well that's good news. We want all the positive news we can get, right?" He gives me a weak smile that doesn't reach his eyes.

I inhale and nod. I don't want to talk about her right now, but my mind is blanking on what to say. As if reading my thoughts Graham says, "I think Catsby misses you." He looks up through his thick eyelashes. "He paws at your door until I open it, he prefers to sleep in there at night instead of my room."

The mention of his tuxedo cat makes me smile. "Oh, it's Catsby that misses me?" I tease, even though I don't know if what I sense between us is something he feels too. "You know, you could bring him by tomorrow. My mom loves cats and it might cheer her up," I say before taking a sip of my tea.

He sits, shaking his foot as it hangs off the edge of his knee. "You know, that's not a bad idea. He will get to see his new favorite human"—he points at me—"and it could make your mom smile to have a cat to love on for a few hours. I read that cats are good therapy animals for cancer patients."

While I doubt I am Catsby's favorite human, I just nod along in agreement. I take our momentary silence as an opportunity to think of a topic change. "Are you happy to be on spring break?" I ask as I subconsciously bring my thumb to my mouth. The moment I start to chew on my nail I realize I haven't partaken in this particularly nasty habit in a while and that thought makes me drop my hand.

He chuckles. "More than you can imagine. I love those kids, but it's been a year. And this being the last break before summer, it always goes by too quickly." I watch him as he fiddles with his pant leg. "You know, it's not just Catsby that misses you being around the house." He doesn't look up from his hand as he messes with the cuff of his pants. "I miss you being there, too."

I feel my body flush with his admission. Maybe he does feel the connection too. All of a sudden my mouth and lips are too dry. I swallow a large gulp of my tea and then lick my lips as I try to think of what to say in response. Do I admit that I miss being there? Do I say thank you? No, that's awkward. But before I get a chance to respond, Angie pops her head out of the door. "Hey, Tessa, honey, I'm headed out. Your mom's fallen asleep and I have a few errands to run. When she wakes up let her know I'll try to stop by again tomorrow."

I stand up and walk over to give her a hug. "Thanks for coming by; I know it means a lot to her. Everyone stopping in to visit means a lot, even for a short while." I glance back at Graham and motion toward the other room. "I'm going to walk her out." He looks at me with a shy smile and nods.

A few hours later, Graham's gone home and my dad and I are sitting in the living room with the TV turned down low while my mom sleeps. "So, you and Graham have been getting along really well lately," my dad says, eyeing me conspiratorially.

I give him a sideways glance and shove a bite of cake in my mouth. "Sorry, my mouth is full, I can't answer," I say, causing him to shake his head and laugh.

He leans back in the recliner and sighs. "You know, it's not a bad thing for you to be happy—for Graham to make you happy. Your mom and I love that boy. He's been a big part of our lives for a long time." He looks at my mom and then adds, "There are definitely worse guys you could fall for than Graham Link."

I smile down at my chocolate cake and mumble, "I don't know when it happened. I just all of a sudden started to feel like my day isn't complete if I don't see him. When I was staying at his place, at first I kept to my room, and then the next thing I know . . ." I take a breath and look over at my dad, who is now watching me intently. "Next thing I know I wanted to be in the living room to greet him when he got home from work. Even when I was being a stubborn ass and not coming over here, I was waiting for him to get back because he would sit with me at the table and talk while I ate, even though he ate over here. He would let me know how everything was with y'all, helping me feel like I was still part of everything I was refusing to be part of."

My dad just nods as if he knows what I'm talking about. "Tessa-bug, that boy has loved you since you were children. I remember him coming over just to sit in the front yard with you to talk about whatever it was that *you* wanted to talk about. I don't know if you know this, but he had a pretty serious girlfriend a few years back, about the same time you were dating that Darren fella." He swallows before continuing his thought, his gaze shifting back to my mom, asleep in her bed. "He would bring her over for dinners occasionally, I could see his fondness for her when he'd look at her. But honey, when he looks at you his whole face lights up. He never had that look when he would look at her."

I don't know what to do with that information. I didn't know Graham had been in a serious relationship, especially one that was serious enough he'd bring around my parents. For some reason that knowledge makes me jealous. Did Catsby like *her*? Did he miss *her* now that she's gone? I don't even know why I'm thinking about that—my dad said it was a few years ago. I was dating Darren then. That feels like a lifetime ago.

My mom's soft voice startles me out of my mini spiral. "If you hear music, you might be pregnant." My dad and I look at each other in confusion.

"Mom? What are you talking about?" I stand up, walk to the side of her bed, and grab her hand.

She looks over at me, in her dazed and sleepy state she repeats, "If you hear music, you might be pregnant." Besides looking tired, she looks like she believes she's giving the wisest advice known to man.

I rub my hand over her frail one and nod. "Well, Mom, I'm not sure if this information will be welcomed news to you or not, but I won't be hearing music any time soon." I let out a wet laugh, tears brimming my eyes, not at what I'm about to say, but at the thought of her not being here for when I do hear music. "I haven't had sex in an unbelievably long time."

My dad coughs, choking on a laugh. "Fuck, Tess, that's not something a father wants to know." He shakes his head and runs his hand down his face, muttering something under his breath.

"What?" I ask with a shrug. "She's the one telling me to listen for music. I just gotta remember to take my birth control pills," I add, laughing at the fact that I'm making my dad blush. He looks like he's seconds away from sticking his fingers in his ear and singing *"lalala"* to drown me out.

I look back to my mom and notice she's fallen back asleep. Then I look at my dad and point to the bathroom. I'm going to use this time to wash up, get ready for bed, and let my dad sit with my mom for a bit.

I curl up on the couch and take out my phone. I look over at my mom, watching as her chest rises and falls as she sleeps.

I think it's time to text Bennett and let him know I don't have any intention of moving back to Richmond.

Me:

Hey, you busy?

Bennett Thatcher:

For you? Never. What's up, T?

I let out a breath as I read his text a few times. Oh boy. This is not going to be easy.

Me:

I wanted to let you know that I don't think I'll be returning to Richmond besides short visits after my mom passes.

The three dots appear and disappear multiple times before his text finally comes through.

Bennett Thatcher:

It's that guy isn't it? The one Felix told me about. It's okay, Tessa, I get it. You told me we needed to pump the breaks while you went home. And I haven't heard from you much since you've been gone. I'm not going to lie and say it doesn't suck a little, but I just want you to be happy.

Happy. That's the thing though—I look up from my phone again and watch my mom through watery eyes—once she's no longer around, I don't know that I'll ever be happy again. Even if it is with Graham.

Me:

I'm not sure what Felix said—nosey ass needs to keep his thoughts to himself—but no, it's not about another guy. I just think I need to stay close to my dad. It's going to be difficult losing her, for both of us. I think being here will be best for the two of us.

Me:

*I really do like you. It's just that I don't think a long distance relationship is what I want. And you deserve someone who's there and able to give you 100%. I'm sorry, Bennett. Blair might be interested *winky face emoji**

Bennett Thatcher:

No need to apologize. And no offense to Blair, she's great, but she's not my type. Can we still be friends? Hang out when you're in town?

Me:

Of course! I wouldn't want it any other way. Goodnight, Bennett.

Bennett Thatcher:

Goodnight, T.

I put my phone on the charger and lay my head on the pillow. As soon as I close my eyes, I'm jolted awake by my mom coughing.

Chapter 36

Graham

This morning I woke up with a text from Tessa asking if I'd mind coming over to sit with Sherri for an hour or so later this morning. Sherri's parents are flying in and they refuse to take any type of car service and Paul has to work. She ended the text saying that Catsby is very welcome to come along with a winky face emoji. I sit staring at my phone longer than I should, trying to decipher if the winky face was her way of flirting or if it was a typo and meant to just be a smiley face.

Once I put Catsby in the carrier, I grab the travel litter box and the carrier then head over to the Gunter's house. Tessa opens the door and I fight to get air in my lungs. The weather is finally warm enough to bring out the warm weather clothes, and Tessa is wearing a light pink sundress with various types of flowers on it. The material hugs her breasts in a way that leaves no room for my imagination, and it flows out right after her waist.

Her eyes are bright and her smile is wide as she takes in my furry friend in the carrier. "Why hello there, Mr. Catsby. My mom is very excited to see you this morning."

She talks to him as she opens the carrier and reaches in to grab him. "Good morning, Graham. Thanks again for coming to keep her company. My stubborn grandparents don't believe in any form of ride share services and don't want to pay for a rental. They think they will get kidnapped and sold on the underground market." She chuckles, rolls her eyes at her statement, and gives me a one-armed hug.

I lean into the hug and get a whiff of her coconut lotion. "Oh, it's not a problem. I planned on coming over today anyway and your mom is great company." I walk into the house and lift the litter box. "Where should I put this? I want to keep it out of the way, but in a place where Catsby can easily find it."

"Oh! Smart for bringing that! I wouldn't have even thought of what he would use if he needed to go to the bathroom while here." She grabs the box from me with her spare arm and walks through the house. "We can keep the back door open, I'll put it on the patio."

Once the litter box is down we walk into the living room. Sherri is sitting up in bed, a smile on her face and a skein of yarn on her lap. She's knitting. It makes me smile to see her acting like her old self, but I've done my research and I know what this means: terminal lucidity. It means she's got hours, maybe a day or two left. "Hey Sherri, it looks like you're having a good day," I say in a light voice.

Sherri looks at me and then at Tessa. "Hey, Graham. Tessa, honey, you need to get going if you want to be there to pick Granna and Pop up on time." This causes Tessa to look at the clock and jump a little.

"Fuck, you're right!" she says, bending over the side of the bed giving her mom a kiss on the cheek. She walks around the bed, gives me a hug and kisses me on the cheek, causing my face to flush and my body to forget how to breathe. "Really, thanks again. If anything happens or anything changes please call me and tell me to get home right away. I won't ever forgive my grandparents if something happens to my mom and I'm not here because I had to go get them."

I stand there, still holding my breath, as she walks out of the room. "You know you can sit down, it'll be easier to catch your breath that way." Sherri laughs.

I look over at her as I walk to the couch to sit, and she's smiling at me, "I don't know what you're talking about," I lie.

"You and Tessa are both terrible liars. That's good in a relationship though. It means you won't ever be able to hide things from each other," she says, causing me to choke on the spit that was accumulating in my mouth.

I take a few moments to compose myself before asking. "And what relationship might you be talking about?" I eye her suspiciously.

She just rolls her eyes and sighs. "I may be dying, but I'm not blind. The attraction between you two is magnetic and I wish y'all both would just acknowledge it. I'll say the same thing to you that Pauly said to Tessa the other night. The way the two of you look at each other when the other isn't looking—it honestly reminds me of how Pauly has looked at me for most of my life." She pauses to catch her breath. "I understand not wanting to rush anything or try to force something if you're not ready. But a mama knows what a mama knows."

I sit up a little straighter trying to comprehend what Sherri just said. I'm an educated man, I don't *need* her to clarify, but I still ask, "What do you mean? Exactly?"

She points to a jewelry box sitting on the table next to her bed. "Can you hand me that box, please?" Standing up, I grab the box and place it in her outstretched hand. I watch as she pulls out what looks like a wedding ring set. "This is the engagement ring and wedding band that Paul got me when we first got together. The one I wear now is the one he bought me for our fifteenth anniversary." She holds her hand out, palm up. I hesitantly reach mine out to her. "Tessa always wanted this to be the engagement ring and band she wore," she says, placing the rings in my hand.

I know the confusion on my face is obvious, but Sherri just stares at me and folds my fingers over the rings.

"If Tessa wants these, then why don't you have Paul keep them to give to the man she's going to marry one day?" I ask, as if that's the most logical question.

She smiles and shakes her head. "Honey, I told you, a mama knows what a mama knows. You may not be together now, and you may not even get together in the next couple of months. But the way the two of you have been interacting—the stolen glances you give each other—it's only a matter of time. I will roll over in my grave if she marries someone that isn't you." I blink at her, emotion thick in my throat. "And I don't plan on being buried in a grave, so that makes that statement all the more interesting." She gives a laugh at her own joke.

I squeeze my hand around the rings and watch Sherri shift around on her bed. "Do you need any help? You look uncomfortable." I move a little closer to her side.

She nods her head. "Can you take the jewelry box back and then move this yarn? I'm starting to get tired again. Oh, and there's a small satin bag on the table—it was under the jewelry box. You can put the rings in there for safe keeping, turn on the TV, and get comfortable. I'm just going to take a nap." She presses the button to lower the bed to a more comfortable position. Then she lies back on her pillow and falls fast asleep.

I grab the bag she mentioned, but before I put the rings in there I sit down and really look at them. The engagement ring is simple but very elegant. It's a gold band with a single round diamond—it can't be more than half a carat. The gold wedding band has small diamonds embedded within the band itself. It's truly a beautiful set of rings, but not at all what I pictured Tessa would want. I wouldn't describe her as high maintenance at all, but I would've thought she would want something bigger, a bit more flashy. More like the ring her mom wears now.

I put the ring set in the bag and put it in my pocket. Then I glance at Sherri's left hand, and the ring set atop her ring finger. That diamond's a cushion shape—at least two carats—with two smaller diamonds next to it. The band is one where the engagement ring sits in between two separate bands making it three rings in total.

I let my mind wander as I sit on the couch while Sherri rests. Catsby climbs up on the bed and curls himself up into the crook of her shoulder. They look so peaceful, I can't help but snap a picture and send it to both Paul and Tessa.

Chapter 37

Tessa

Don't get me wrong, I'm very grateful that my Granna and Pop were able to fly in and see their daughter before it's too late, but if she ends up passing away while I'm having to go pick them up, I'll never be able to forgive them. They could call a ride share or rent a car. There are plenty of other ways to get from the airport to our house.

I step out of the car and plaster on a smile as I see them walking out of the airport doors. "Granna! Pop! It's so good to see you." I take turns hugging them. "I wish this visit were under better circumstances, but we'll have to make the most of it." I grab their suitcase from Pop and put it in the trunk, then I open the passenger door followed by the door to the backseat to let them get in.

"You look like you've lost weight. Are you eating enough?" Granna says, getting comfortable in the back-seat.

I take a deep breath in and release it before answering. "Honestly, probably not. With all this stuff going on with Mom, eating hasn't been my number one priority." I look in the mirror to make sure it's safe before I pull out of my parking spot.

Pop just sits stoically in the front seat. I can't imagine the emotions the two of them are feeling. My mom is an only child, like me. But unlike me, she's never had a great relationship with either of her parents. They used to make comments about her weight, and when I came along they started making comments about mine. Finally, she had had enough and snapped at them, and now we only see them once or twice a year.

When my mom got her diagnosis back in February she called to tell them the news and they've made a point to call and talk to her at least twice a week. Once her prognosis changed, they decided they would come and stay indefinitely to be with her and help out in any way they could after. Luckily for us, they're staying in a hotel. Unluckily for me, they don't have their own vehicle while they're here. But my dad said he would do most of the driving for them if I just pick them up today.

Granna breaks the silence we're sitting in. "So, how was she doing when you left?" She leans forward far more than I feel comfortable with while I'm driving.

I glance back at her through the rearview mirror. "She was actually in good spirits this morning. She had some energy she hasn't had in a few days and was working on a scarf when I left." I switch lanes and turn my attention fully on the road, trying to give her the hint that I don't feel like talking.

"Well, that's positive isn't it? Her having this burst of energy. Maybe those doctors don't know what they're talking about after all," she says, tapping my shoulder.

I have to take another breath and give myself a mental lecture. She's just being hopeful because she doesn't like the idea of her only child dying. I get it—I don't like the idea of losing my mom. But even I know enough to know that this random burst of energy isn't some miracle. It happens to most—if not all—people within their last few days of life. Instead of trying to explain that to her, I just say, "Maybe."

I think Pop can sense my disinterest in wanting to talk because he chimes in, "Jeanie, why don't you play that game of yours on your phone and let Tessa concentrate on the road."

He gives me a look and I mouth, "Thank you."

We finally arrive back at the house after getting them checked into their hotel and their bags put in their room. Granna and Pop kept quiet for the remainder of the ride with music playing low so we weren't riding in complete silence.

When we walk in the first thing my Granna notices is Graham sitting on the couch. "And who is this fine specimen of a man? Tessa, is this your boyfriend?" She turns to glance at me before returning her attention back to Graham. She visibly checks him out while Pop stands next to her.

Graham stands up from his spot on the couch and reaches his hand out in introduction. When he goes to shake my Granna's hand she pushes it away and grabs him in for a hug. "I'm Graham," he says, not answering the comment about being my boyfriend. "Nice to meet you both." He returns Granna's hug half-heartedly.

"Tessy-dear didn't tell us we would have eye-candy while we were visiting," Granna says, pulling out of the hug and holding Graham by the shoulders, inspecting him. "If I would've known I would've insisted to Sherri and Paul we stay here." She looks at me and wiggles her eyebrows.

"Granna!"

"Jean!" Pop and I both scold at the same moment.

"This young man doesn't want to be ogled by an old bitty when he's got Tessa," Pop says, pulling Granna away from Graham. "I'm so sorry, young man. Forgive her for acting like she's never seen a man before."

I don't correct my grandparents when they talk about Graham and I, and I notice he doesn't either. "How long has she been sleeping?" I ask as my grandparents settle themselves on the couch.

He looks at the clock and tilts his head from side to side. "She fell asleep about thirty minutes after you left, so an hour and a half. We were talking about—" He cuts himself off and a faint red creeps across his face making him look a little embarrassed. "Um." He coughs. "We were talking about—" He looks around. The look he's giving me is like I caught him with his hand in the cookie jar before dinner.

"Were you talking about me?" I ask after allowing him to flounder for a few seconds, a small impish grin playing on my lips.

A sheepish smile spreads on his face. "Yeah. I wasn't sure how you'd feel if I told you that, but I also didn't want to lie. So, I was trying to think of something safe to say," he says through a small laugh.

I put my hand on his arm. "It's okay. We've talked about you too." At this his face perks up and he eyes me with curiosity. "Oh no. I'm not telling you what we talked about if you don't tell me what the two of you talked about. I very much believe in tit-for-tat," I say through a wry grin.

"Tit-for-tat, huh?" he asks thoughtfully. "Okay. I think I can get behind that." He winks at me then turns to walk back over to the couch where he starts talking to my grandparents. He left me standing there turning five shades of red wondering about all the things he could be thinking about to cause him to wink at me.

My mom wakes up about ten minutes after we get back and my Granna starts crying and runs over to the bed. "Oh, Sher-bear! I didn't know if we'd make it in time, but then Tessa said you had some energy this morning! Are you feeling better?"

Graham looks over at me looking a little uncomfortable. If he's thinking about what my Granna just said, I feel the same way. "Hi, Mom," my mom says in a raspy sleepy voice. She looks around and spots Pop still sitting on the couch. "Hi, Pop." She smiles at the old man.

At her acknowledgment, Pop stands up and walks to the other side of her bed. "Sherri. I'm sorry we haven't been here." He grabs her hand, his eyes glimmering with unshed tears.

I grab Graham's hand and lead him out of the living room to give my mom some privacy with her parents. We walk into the back room after stopping in the kitchen to grab a snack.

"So . . . You talk about me with your mom?" he asks with a knowing smirk on his face. I immediately lift my cup to hide the blush creeping across my face. Unfortunately, I can't do anything about the blush that appears along my exposed chest.

"We may have said a thing or two about you. But if I'm being honest, it was mostly my dad and I talking about you. Mom was in and out of sleep." My eyes dance over his face watching for his reaction.

He leans back in his chair and nods his head. "And, you don't feel like sharing what y'all discussed?" He brings his cup to his mouth but doesn't take a sip, eyes studying me.

I bite my lower lip and shake my head. "I think I'll keep it a secret." I look down at my lap then look up at him through my eyelashes. "For now."

As we sit and cautiously flirt, I can't help but think about when the awkwardness between us turned to solace. Living at his house, having him there to let me vent, all the small moments where our friendship slowly started to return, it all led to this moment. When a comfortable silence appears we both just look out the screen and watch the birds. Just being in his presence makes me feel calm. I don't feel like I'm seconds away from a panic attack thinking about her dying. It's comforting.

Chapter 38

Graham

Thursday morning Grant calls and invites me over for breakfast with him and the kids since it's spring break. I check the time and decide it's still early enough that I have time before going to visit with Sherri and Tessa. Pulling into his driveway, I take a minute before getting out. I love Ethan and Corinne to death, but I always need to prepare myself for the hormones these pre-teens are going through.

"Uncle Graham!" Corinne yells as she comes racing out of the house. "I'm so happy you were able to come over! Daddy said you might not be able to because you have a girlfriend now, so I'm not the most important girl in your life anymore." I shoot a *what the fuck* look at my brother who is standing in the doorway. He just laughs in return.

I pick her up in a hug. "Cori, you're always going to be my favorite little girl. Even though you're not so little anymore." I walk inside the house holding my niece in one arm and giving my brother a stink eye. "How is it that you're taller than you were when I saw you just last month?" I ask as I put her down.

"Well I eat my vegetables. Those help you grow. Right, Daddy?" she says, matter-of-factly.

I nod. "Yep, that'll do it. Where's that brother of yours?" I inquire, ruffling her hair and making her squirm under my hand.

She grabs my hand from the top of her head and flings it down. "He's in the living room playing video games." She sits at the kitchen table and picks up the book she must have been reading.

I walk through the house and see my nephew sitting in a bean bag chair playing some football game. "What? You're too good to come greet your uncle?" I joke, tapping his foot with my own.

He pauses his game and looks at me. "Is breakfast ready yet?" No *"Hey, Uncle Graham," "Good to see you, Uncle Graham."* Not even a smile. Yep, these hormones are a blast.

Rolling my eyes I answer. "It's good to see you too. And I wouldn't know, I just got here." The amount of fucks given by him is absolutely zero. Was I that way when I was eleven? No, probably not. I was obsessed with Tessa and tried to spend as much free time with her as I could.

"Hey, Dad!" he yells across the house. "Is breakfast ready?" He waits a beat before setting his controller down and getting up with a "hmph" and walking into the kitchen where I hear him ask again, "Is breakfast ready? I'm starving and you said we would eat when Uncle Graham got here."

I sigh, roll my shoulders, and walk back into the kitchen. Ethan is setting the table, grumbling under his breath. I can only assume Grant had some choice words with him. Corinne is sitting at the table drinking some milk and reading a book. The sight of her makes me smile. Grant and Lisa always joke and ask if I'm sure she's not my kid with her love of reading.

I grab the plate of pancakes and the pitcher of orange juice before walking to the table. Sitting down next to a preoccupied Cori and a disgruntled Ethan, I look up at my brother and smile. "So, how's Lisa?" I take my fork, grab a few pancakes and place them on my plate.

Grant walks to the empty seat at the table holding a plate of eggs and one of bacon. "She's good. Annoyed that her boss wouldn't give her the week off to spend with the kids during their spring break. But he said she'll be taking enough time off for appointments and then maternity leave."

"Sounds like a dick to me," I say, covering my mouth so the food I'm chewing doesn't ruin anyone's appetite. "Also, that sounds a little illegal. Can he really get away with not letting her take leave because of upcoming days she'll need to take off?"

He nods while he chews and swallows his bite before speaking, showcasing his manners. "Well, she technically could have gotten this week off. But she wouldn't have been able to use her PTO if she wants to be able to use that for upcoming appointments."

"I guess that makes sense. How is this pregnancy treating her? I know with Cori she was really sick," I say, glancing over at my niece who is still engrossed in her book.

"Thankfully she hasn't shown any signs of hyperemesis gravidarum being an issue this pregnancy. She thinks that means we're having a boy, because it reminds her more of her pregnancy with Ethan," he says as he picks up his glass of orange juice. "How are Tessa and Mrs. Gunter?"

I inhale deeply and wiggle my jaw. "Well, Sherri's on her last days, unfortunately. Paul and Tessa are handling it very differently. I know you didn't ask about Paul, but he's taking it better than I would be. I mean, he's losing his wife of thirty-plus years. But Tessa . . . " I take another deep breath as I think of how to explain how Tessa is coping. "Tessa is trying to be brave. You know she wasn't taking it well for a bit—that's why she moved in with me. But now she won't leave her mom's side unless she has to pee. She reluctantly leaves her side when there are people visiting." I stop talking and look up at the ceiling.

Grant can sense I'm not finished talking so he lets me sit for a minute. He bends over and says something to Ethan that I don't hear because I'm focused on my thoughts of Tessa. I am vaguely aware of Corinne and Ethan picking up their plates and leaving the kitchen. "And how about you, little brother? How are you doing with it? I know Mrs. Gunter has been more of a mom to you than ours has."

Blinking, I bring my gaze back down to my brother. "I'm hanging in there. I've done my share of crying, and I'm sure I'll do more when the time comes. But I'm trying to be strong for Paul and Tessa. Especially Tessa." I take one last bite of my breakfast before taking my plate to the dishwasher. "Sherri point blank said she knows I love Tessa. She even gave me her wedding ring set to give to Tessa one day."

That news causes him to cough. "Wait, wait, wait. You're going to propose to her? You're not even dating." He stares at me expectantly.

I huff out a laugh and shake my head. "Sherri's under the impression that Tessa feels for me, the way I feel for her. She said, and I quote, *'A mama knows what a mama knows,'* and told me to keep the ring set." I chuckle at the memory. "I mean, I might be crazy for thinking this, but I have been feeling like there's something growing between Tessa and myself. But I don't think right now is the time to make a move."

He nods in agreement. "Yeah, hitting on her when her mom's dying isn't classy. But, what you should do—you should invite her up to our cabin when everything is said and done. Get her into the mountains and let her just have some time." He watches me for a reaction. "I'm serious. Lisa and I are planning on going for a babymoon in a few months. And as long as you keep it clean when you go I'm sure she won't mind y'all using it."

I shrug but don't give a verbal response. That doesn't sound like a half-bad idea, but I'm not going to tell him I think so. We move into the living room and sit on the couch and watch Ethan play his video game.

That's where we are when my phone rings. "Hello?" I answer without checking to see who it is.

The other side of the phone is silent for a few seconds and then Tessa speaks. "Graham." It's all she says, and it comes out as a plea.

Chapter 39

Tessa

My mom is barely awake this morning when my dad leaves for work, falling back to sleep quickly after he kisses her goodbye. I check the clock and see it's around four in the morning. I woke up when I heard him telling her he'd come home to check on her around noon. I stand and walk to the bed to check that she fell back asleep. Once I see she seems to be sleeping as peacefully as she can, I lie back down and watch the rise and fall of her chest.

My dad ended up letting my grandparents borrow my mom's car since it's not being used at the moment. It frees me up from having to pick them up from the hotel, and allows for him to not have to take any additional breaks from work. Granna said they'd be over around noon, and the hospice nurse is going to be here around nine to check and make sure everything looks good.

With time to rest before anyone gets here, I close my eyes, falling asleep to the sound of my mom's struggling breath.

"Honey," Gracie says somberly as she shakes my arm. "Honey, wake up." My eyes fight to open as they adjust to the light shining in the window. As soon as they flutter open she looks at me, sympathy etched on her slim features. Quietly she says, "Your mom went to be with the Lord—I'm not sure what time. She was gone when I got here." I jolt up and throw off my blanket, her words slowly registering on my sleep-deprived brain.

"What do you mean?" I ask as I run to my mom's bed. She looks the same as she did a few hours ago—she looks like she's sleeping. "She was just awake!" I grab her slightly too-pale hand and notice how cool it feels.

"Honey, would you like me to call your dad? We will need to get the coroner here shortly," she says with care in her voice. "Also, you might want to step out while I clean her up. Give her some dignity of you not having to witness this."

I nod my head and grab my phone from the table and call my dad. The phone only rings one time before he answers. "Tessa? Is everything okay?" His voice is tinged with worry.

The tears haven't hit yet, so when I respond, I sound sort of robotic. "Daddy, you need to come home. Mom's gone." I hold the phone to my ear and listen to the sounds of my father coming undone. He lets out loud sobs on the other end of the line. I flinch at the image of his body shaking as he weeps at work. "Do you think you'll be able to drive? Should I call someone to come pick you up?" I ask in that distant robotic voice that doesn't sound like my own.

I mentally run through the list of people I can call to pick him up so he doesn't have to drive in his current state. Before I have a chance to ask him another question, I hear a muffled sound followed by another voice talking to me. "Hey, Tess, this is Larry. I'll make sure your dad gets home as quickly as possible."

Nodding, even though he can't see me through the phone, I respond. "Thanks. I have to go make more phone calls." After I get off the call with my dad I sit at the kitchen table just staring at my phone in my hand. I mechanically call both sets of grandparents. My mom's parents say they're on their way before they hang up the phone. Once I've called my dad's parents, I call his sister and let her know the news.

My mind is running on autopilot, automatically shutting my emotions off. I'm not in the right headspace to hear Nell's voice—I'm afraid the softness in her cadence will cause the dam to break. So I send her a text message to inform her of what happened, asking her to pass it along to our friends. I set my phone down then look around the dining room in a haze. I hear my dad come running into the house. Gracie sends him to the dining room and tells him she'll let us know when my mom's presentable. He comes straight to me and pulls me out of the chair into a hug.

I numbly return it, letting him hold me as he cries into my shoulder. "Did you find her?" he asks through a hiccup.

I shake my head. "I was still sleeping when Gracie got here. She woke me up and told me." My voice comes out cold, detached.

He pulls away from me and nods his head. "It's probably for the best that it wasn't one of us who found her. Do you need coffee? I need to do something. I need to call your grandparents. And my sister." He starts to pace the kitchen.

"No, I called everyone. They're all on their way. The living room will be crowded with family members soon so everyone can say goodbye before the coroner gets here." I completely forgot he asked about coffee as I sit back down on the chair.

"Good. Good. Is Graham coming over too?" he asks, looking over at me, tears spilling freely from his eyes.

My eyes bulge for a moment. *I haven't called Graham!* I pick up my phone and walk to the back patio. The phone rings twice before he answers, "Hello?"

My emotions are thick in my throat, still not ready to be released. "Graham." My voice cracks on his name, emotion trying and failing to break through.

Immediately his tone changes. "Tessa? Is everything okay? What happened?" I can tell he moved from a relaxed position to one of high alert from the way his voice changed.

I try to swallow. "Graham, she's gone. My mom's gone." Still, tears don't fall. The numbness has taken over. I feel the emotions, but my body isn't allowing me to react to them.

He says something to someone in the background and I bite my thumbnail as I strain to listen to what he's saying and who he's talking to. "Tessa," he says into the receiver, "I'll be right there. I'm over at Grant's right now, but I'll be there as fast as I can. Is your dad home? Do I need to pick him up?"

Again, I nod as if I can be seen through the phone. After nodding for a few seconds I realize I need to verbalize my thoughts or he won't know. "Yes, I called him home."

"Good. I'll see you shortly," he says before I hang up the phone.

Gracie comes out and lets me know I can go sit with my mom if I want—she tells me my dad is sitting with her now. I nod my thanks but just sit in the chair, staring out the screened in patio.

Why did I allow myself to go back to sleep after my dad left?

Did I tell her I loved her before she went to sleep?

What was the last thing I said to her?

Did she feel any pain?

The questions are like a tsunami crashing around my mind, waiting for a barrier to stop them.

I hear the sound of voices coming from inside the house. From the sounds of it, my grandparents have arrived. Which ones, I'm not sure. But at the moment, I just sit on the chair. Unmoving. Unblinking. Possibly unbreathing.

"Tess. Tessa." I feel a warm hand on my cheek and blink a few times before I focus on Graham's mossy green eyes with a burst of golden brown around the pupils—the look of concern marked across his handsome face. "I've been saying your name for a solid minute, are you okay?"

I hold his gaze and nod. He holds his hand out and I take it to help me stand. Once I'm standing, he wraps his muscular arms around me, holding me tight. He strokes the back of my head with one hand and moves the thumb on his opposite hand over my lower back. I sink into his embrace without returning the hug. Still, the tears don't come.

"Do you want to go in there and see your mom? The coroner just got here a few moments before I did," he says with his cheek resting against the top of my head. His voice is soothing—he doesn't sound like he's trying to rush me.

I shake my head no, and then nod yes. "I don't know. I don't want to see her alone," I whisper, afraid to feel judgment for my answer.

"I'll be right by your side for however long you need." He leans his head back and tilts my head so I'm looking at him. "And if you want to come stay at my house when she's moved out of here, you can." His eyes search mine for something.

Instead of responding, I pull out of his hug and turn toward the living room. As I start to leave the patio, I hear my phone ring on the chair I left it on. Graham turns to grab it but I just shake my head. I don't want to talk to whoever's calling.

I have to walk through the kitchen to get to the living room and I see both sets of grandparents crowding around the island, my dad's sitting on a stool next to it. I don't acknowledge anyone as Graham and I walk to the living room. I go straight to the side of the bed and stand there, staring down at my mom. Gracie pulled what little hair she had left into a side ponytail that reminds me of someone from an 80s jazzercise video. That alone almost elicits a chuckle from my mouth. Almost. Besides her out-of-style hair and her too-pale skin, she looks normal. She looks like she's sleeping.

Graham's presence behind me gives me a little more courage and I reach for her hand. "I know you're not here anymore, so I'm not really talking to you, I'm talking to myself, but—" I take in a shaky breath. "I'm glad you're no longer in pain, but selfishly I wish you were still here with me. I love you." I lean down and kiss her hand. Then, I head straight out the front door and don't turn back.

Chapter 40

Graham

It's been three days.

Three days since I promised Sherri's lifeless body that I'd take care of Tessa and Paul for her.

Three days of me failing at that promise.

Tessa's back at my house, in her room. I've been bouncing back and forth between my house and visiting with Paul at his house. I've been trying to give him as much support as I can, but he keeps assuring me he's okay since his parents are there to support him.

Meanwhile, Tessa only leaves her room to go to the bathroom and to eat, which is maybe once a day. I say *maybe* because I've only actually witnessed her leave her room and go to the kitchen twice in the three days. But there's been evidence that she's been in there on other occasions. I haven't heard her cry, but that doesn't mean it hasn't hit her yet. Paul's worried about her. He's concerned with how calm she was when it happened. She was so detached that I'm sure her body just shut out all emotions.

They're going to the funeral home tomorrow and then up to the church to talk about the arrangements for her service. I offered to take the day off to help, but Paul told me he couldn't let me do that. He did tell me he'd let me know if there's anything I can do, though.

Regardless, I can't stop myself from feeling so helpless.

It's Sunday morning and Paul wants to go to church. Tessa didn't respond when I asked through the door if she wanted to go, so I decided to go with him alone. It's been a while since I've gone to church. I've come a few Sundays with Sherri and Paul in the past, but I definitely wouldn't say I was a regular church-goer.

I walk into the small church and find Paul standing with a group of people, all with their heads bowed. I don't want to interrupt what I'm sure is a prayer, so I walk along the tables set up and look at the flyers on each. I'm greeted with smiles and even a few hugs by ladies who recognize me from my previous visits. The ladies who hug me give me their condolences, which I accept with a genuine smile.

Paul catches my gaze once his group has dispersed and he heads over to me, pulling me into a hug. "Thanks for coming this morning." He looks around me and his face falls slightly. "No Tessa?"

I squeeze his shoulder. "She didn't even respond when I knocked on the door. I knocked a few different times and told her where I was going each time. I'm not sure if she was even awake." He nods his head in understanding.

Music from the sanctuary gets a little louder as the organ is played. The crowd starts shuffling in to find seats. On our way to our spots, we're stopped by multiple people who hug Paul and shake my hand, they all whisper their sympathies for our loss. We find our seats as the music comes to a stop. The pastor walks up to the podium and opens the sermon with a prayer. Within the prayer, he mentions the passing of Sherri. Paul softly shakes as he's overcome with emotion and I reach over, grabbing his hand.

We make it through the sermon and I stand to leave when we're approached by more people wanting a moment of Paul's time. "You head on home, go check on Tessa. Thanks again for coming," he says, patting me on the back before he turns to talk to the members of the church who await his attention.

Pulling into my driveway I take a moment to myself. "Sherri, I feel like I'm letting you down. Tessa isn't talking to me. She isn't answering Paul's calls or texts. Actually, from the amount of times I've heard her phone ring, I'm not sure if she's answering anyone's calls. I don't know what to do." I lean my head back on the headrest and close my tear-filled eyes.

Walking into the house I head straight to the kitchen to look for signs that Tessa might have come to get food. I see an empty cup and plate in the sink and exhale a sigh of relief that she at least had something today.

I knock on her door. "Hey, Tess, I'm home." I lean my ear against it to see if I can hear movement from within. I don't even let myself breathe as I strain to hear any subtle movements that might come from the other side. I don't hear so much as the bed creak.

Once I've changed into comfortable clothes—a pair of basketball shorts and a white shirt—I sit on the couch and turn on the TV. I put on a show I've seen Tessa watch a thousand times in the hope that the sound will entice her to emerge from her room. I sit there, watching episode after episode as the hours tick by before I realize she's not going to come out.

I stand up, head to my bathroom, and turn on the bath. I run the water until it heats to a desirable temperature. I put the stopper in and let the tub fill up. Tessa hasn't taken the opportunity to bathe or shower since before her mom died. If she's expected to leave the house tomorrow to run errands, regardless of how depressing they are, the least I can do for her is make sure she's clean and feeling a little better. Even if only physically. Once the bathtub is full, I head to her room. This time I knock but don't wait for an answer before I walk right in.

Chapter 41

Tessa

It's been three days.

Seventy-two hours.

Three days of me feeling nothing but unrelenting exhaustion, the urge to pee, and the dull ache of hunger pains.

I still haven't cried. I sleep, I go to the bathroom, I eat enough to satisfy a bit of the hunger pain, and I listen to my phone ring and vibrate. During my awake moments I lie in bed, curled up, hugging my legs, staring at the wall. My phone died sometime yesterday afternoon; it's just been sitting on the nightstand. I haven't bothered to plug it in.

I haven't talked to anyone since agreeing with my dad to go to the funeral home and the church on Monday to plan the service. My dad, Nelly, and my friends from Richmond have all tried to call or text. I haven't answered because I know what they will say *"I'm sorry for your loss." "You have my sympathy." "At least she's no longer in pain."* I just don't want to hear any of that right now. Graham has talked to me through the door, but he hasn't pushed.

I'm lying in bed, staring at the door, listening to one of my favorite guilty pleasure shows play on the TV in the living room, when there's a knock at the door, followed by a stream of light filling the doorway as Graham walks in. He walks over to me without saying anything, bends down, and picks me up. I let out a gasp but I don't protest and I don't question it, I just lean my head into his chest. The scent that releases from his nose as he exhales fills me with an odd sense of comfort.

He's got a firm grip around my back and under my legs as he walks me into his room and through to his bathroom. He moves so quickly I don't have a chance to look around as we pass. When we get to the bathroom, I notice the tub is filled almost completely.

"You need to take a bath," he says in such a way that has my body waking up from its fog. He sets me down gently, feet first. "Now, you can either bathe yourself." He swallows and catches my gaze. "Or I can do it for you. But either way, you need this."

I just stand there unblinking, watching him. I want to respond, react somehow, but I don't. I can't. He reaches for my shirt, and when his fingers graze the softness of my curves beneath the hem, he stops and waits for my permission.

I nod and lift my arms.

He slowly raises my shirt up, and I have half a second to feel self-conscious that I'm not wearing a bra before my shirt is off and placed on the counter. His gaze quickly roams over my chest and my stomach, a small smile tugging at the corner of his mouth appreciatively. His eyes look back up at me, as he gently moves his hands to my pajama shorts. I nod again, my eyes never leaving his. He inhales deeply and pulls my shorts and panties off in one quick move.

It looks as if it's taking all his willpower to keep his eyes on mine as he takes my hand and leads me to the bathtub. I break eye contact so I can watch where I'm stepping as I lift myself into the tub. Before I can sit down, Graham climbs in behind me, fully clothed, and sits down. Once he's seated, he guides me to sit with my back towards him. He reaches around me and grabs a clean washcloth that was sitting on the edge of the tub. I relax a little in the water but don't turn to see what he's doing.

The air fills with the intoxicating lemony scent I've come to associate with Graham as I hear him squeeze body wash onto the washcloth. "I'm going to wash your back now," he says in a low, husky voice. Unable to find my voice, all I can do is nod in response.

My body stiffens as he places one hand on my shoulder and uses the other hand to glide the washcloth over my body. After my mind gets adjusted to the idea of Graham's hands on me, I relax again. That is until I feel him shift behind me as he raises my arm to wash my sides. The level of intimacy that is in this simple act of kindness has a jolt of lava churning in my core. The amount of tenderness he's putting into the strokes as he washes away the past three days of sleep and sadness scratches away at the dam that has built itself around my emotions since my mom died.

Suddenly, that dam breaks open and I let out a sob that has to be the most unattractive sound I've ever heard leave my body. I lean forward and put my face in my hands as I release all the sadness and sorrow that has been safely tucked away.

My mom is gone.

She passed away.

She's with the Lord.

She's no longer in pain.

No matter how you say them, all four phrases mean the same thing.

She's dead.

She's never coming back.

It hits me like a ton of bricks and I have a hard time breathing. I'm crying so intensely.

I'm lost in the pain that has taken over my body, so I don't register Graham pulling me into him. I instinctively rotate my body so I'm in a fetal position, leaning my head against his chest. He doesn't say a word as I grip his shirt in my fist and weep in his embrace, he just gently strokes my head with one hand and rubs my arm with the other.

Once it feels like I've cried all the tears my body has, I slowly pull away from Graham. He reaches up, wipes the remaining tears from my face and says, "Now, let me get your hair."

No mention of my complete breakdown.

I nod, because I'm still unsure if my voice is able to work. I turn around again so my back is facing him. Once I'm situated, he reaches his hand up and pulls the light pink scrunchie from my hair, causing my brown locks to cascade down my back. Without warning, he leans my head back and pours a cup of water down my hair. He does this a few times before reaching for the shampoo. As soon as he's done washing my hair and rinsing it to his satisfaction, he gently pushes me forward and climbs out of the bathtub. He grabs a towel from the counter but doesn't bother drying off his drenched clothes. Instead, he opens the towel and holds it out towards me.

"Stand up," he says softly.

Without a second thought, I stand, and before I get the chance to step out of the bathtub, he wraps the towel around me. When he sees that I've secured it in place, he grabs my hand and helps me out of the tub so I don't slip. Then he turns around and grabs a second towel. This time, I think he's going to dry himself off, but I'm wrong again.

"Turn around," he insists.

Doing as he says, I turn around. I startle at the feel of him rubbing my hair with the towel. After he rubs it a few times, he wraps the towel around my hair and gives it a squeeze to help release any extra water.

He puts his hands on my shoulders and turns me back around so I'm facing him. I feel like I should feel embarrassed that he's seen me naked—that he witnessed me have a full meltdown. But instead, I feel more at ease and more safe than I've ever felt.

My mouth lifts up in a small smile. "Thank you," I say in a groggy voice as I gesture down at my body and up at my hair.

He returns my smile with one that's slightly bigger, then winks and says, "It was my pleasure."

Immediately, I feel my face heat as it changes shades of red. I lower my gaze and my smile widens. I nod at him and then I walk out of his bathroom, leaving him standing in sopping wet clothes.

Chapter 42

Tessa

The next morning I wake up feeling better than I've felt in days—less numb now that I've actually cried and felt some emotion.

Though my mood has slightly improved, I'm dreading getting out of bed and starting the day. The errands my dad and I have to do make Mom's death feel more real. It makes it permanent. Final. Even though I know it already was.

I get dressed in a pair of jean shorts and a cream colored top. I put my hair in French-braided pigtails and walk into the kitchen to find Graham's already gone for work. He left a Tupperware container full of cinnamon rolls and a note on the counter. At the sight of the cinnamon rolls my stomach growls, letting me know I'm hungry, so I grab a pastry. Taking a bite and savoring the sweetness of the icing, I read the note.

TESSA,

I KNOW TODAY'S GOING TO BE DIFFICULT FOR YOU AND YOUR DAD SO

I THOUGHT I'D MAKE YOUR MORNING A LITTLE BRIGHTER BY MAKING YOU

BREAKFAST. *I WISH I COULD BE THERE FOR YOU, BUT I AGREE WITH YOUR DAD AND THINK IT SHOULD BE JUST THE TWO OF YOU MAKING THESE ARRANGE-MENTS. IF THERE'S ANYTHING YOU NEED FROM ME, DON'T HESITATE TO TEXT OR CALL. I'LL SEE YOU WHEN I GET HOME.*

 GRAHAM

I smile as I read the note again. Inside my stomach, butterflies flutter around as I think about how intimate last night was. The way he took care of me broke me out of the spiral I had gone down. He could have easily tried to make a move, but he didn't. He didn't let his gaze linger on my body too long either. I'm choosing to believe that has more to do with him being respectful and not that he finds me unattractive.

As I finish brushing my teeth, a knock comes from the front door. Knowing it's my dad, I slip on my shoes before I answer it. He pulls me in for a hug, and instead of denying it, I hug him back.

The moment my arms are wrapped around him and I'm in the comfort of his embrace, I start to cry. "I'm sorry I've been keeping myself locked up here and haven't been there for you." I sob.

He rubs his hands over my back in a comforting motion. "It's okay, Bug. You need to cope in your own way. Granna and Pop have been staying at the house with me, so I haven't been alone."

I wince a little at that. With everything that's happened I forgot my mom's parents are still in town. "They checked out of their hotel?" I ask, pulling away from his hug.

He nods his head. "Yeah. I told them there's no point in paying for a hotel when I have the space. And—" He takes a deep breath and swallows hard. "And your mom isn't there in need of rest, so, no use in them staying at a hotel." He reaches behind me as I walk out of the house to shut the door.

Our first stop is the funeral home to go over all the details of how to handle her remains. She wanted to be cremated and have her ashes put in a columbarium—what I affectionately call a *P.O. Box*—at one of the local cemeteries. She and my dad bought a unit where they'll both end up when she was diagnosed. While we were there, we discussed the type of urn her ashes would be in, and I asked to have a small amount of it placed in a necklace.

Our second stop is the one that takes the longest. We sit with the pastor and discuss what we'll be doing for my mom's celebration of life. She insisted that we celebrate the life she led instead of mourning her loss, so we're planning a celebration open to the whole congregation, as well as her friends and family outside of the church, for the following Tuesday.

The pastor left my dad and I in the conference room to discuss other parts of the celebration. While we talk, I pull out my phone and post on social media, asking friends and family to send me any pictures they have of or with my mom so I can make a slideshow. We work together to write her obituary, and agree that we won't have just one person eulogize her. We figure whoever feels it in their heart to speak should have an opportunity to do so.

After everything is planned, we leave the church and stop at Zigglers—mom's favorite—for brunch and place a catering order for after the celebration.

On the drive back to Graham's there's a tense silence.

"I don't know when I'll be able to go back to the house," I say in a whisper. "I don't think I'm ready to be back in the place where she took her last breath. I feel selfish for thinking this, but I wish she would have chosen to do hospice in a facility so I wouldn't be so afraid of going back home." The guilt hangs above me like a rain cloud and I'm afraid to look at my dad for fear of the judgment I might find in his eyes.

He takes a slow, deep breath, inhaling and exhaling a few times before he says anything. "I don't think that's selfish. I think it's really healthy that you can identify that as part of why you haven't been to the house since she passed. I understand that feeling." I can feel him looking at me as we sit at a red light, but I don't turn my head to meet his eyes. "I haven't been able to go into the living room since . . . I spend most days on the patio listening to Jean and Nigel bicker like the old married couple they are. Honestly, it makes me jealous, watching them. I was supposed to have that. Your mom was supposed to be here longer." His voice gets thicker as it fills with emotion.

Even though I know my dad isn't saying any of this to make me feel worse, I can't help the shame I feel building inside me for not being brave enough to go back to the house.

But I don't say anything, making the cab of his truck fill with a heavy silence once more.

Chapter 43

Graham

Sherri passed away a week ago and Tessa is slowly starting to pull herself out of the sadness she's cocooned herself in. When I get home from work, she and Paul are sitting on the couch, talking about something. Catsby is curled up in a ball perfectly content in her lap.

"Hey, how was your day?" Tessa asks with a soft smile on her face. She's gently rubbing Catsby's shiny black fur.

"It was good. Tiring, but good," I respond as I take my shoes off and pick a spot on the couch.

Paul glances down at his watch, then leans over and gives Tessa a kiss on the cheek. "I gotta go get ready for work—I asked if they could put me on nights. It's been difficult sleeping in my bed at night, so I needed to change it up at the station. I love you, Bug." He nods to me and walks out the front door.

"Is his bereavement leave over already?" I look at Tessa and notice she's moved a little closer to me on the couch. Ever since the night I gave her a bath, where she cried in my arms, she's seemed to gravitate toward me a lot more frequently. It makes me feel like she might consider me a place of safety. At least, I hope that's what it means.

By the time she answers she's directly next to me, sitting with her legs tucked under her, facing me. "Yeah, today's his first day back. His chief told him he could take more time if he needed it, but he said he couldn't stand being at the house much these days. Especially with my Granna and Pop still in town."

"I can't imagine how difficult it must be for him. He's more than welcome to use one of the rooms here if he feels the need to escape the house," I say, pointing down the hall at the two bedrooms not being used right now.

Tessa gives a small chuckle. "You want my dad to move in here too? Either you're a literal saint or you have a thing for us Gunters." The smile playing on her lips makes my dick stir. It feels like it's been years since I've seen that beautiful smile.

I give a small laugh and shake my head. "Nah, he's just been through a lot. I want to be able to help as much as I can. I owe that to him."

She stares at me with a look in her eyes that I can't decipher. I watch out of my peripherals as her tongue sweeps across her lips causing me to swallow. My mind wanders to the things she could do with that tongue. And while it thinks about that, images of a naked Tessa swim through my mind.

Fuck, seeing her naked in my bathroom was the best thing I've ever seen in my life. She didn't cover herself, or look the least bit embarrassed or ashamed. I tried not to make it obvious that I was checking her out. Besides,

I didn't insist on bathing her for sexual reasons. She was in a state of depression, and I thought her taking a bath would help wash some of the fog she was buried in away. But, I am a man after all, and she's fucking gorgeous. So when she was in front of me, completely naked, I looked.

When the dam finally broke and she cried against my chest, part of my heart broke. I couldn't do anything for her besides just letting her cry on me. I wanted to kiss her forehead and tell her everything would be okay, but I couldn't tell her that—I have no way of knowing if that's true. I've never lost someone that close to me before; I still have both my parents, pleasant relationship or not. They're both alive, and in good health as far as I'm aware. So I just held her and let her cry.

There have been moments, much like the one we're having now, where I've had to keep myself from leaning in and kissing her. While Sherri was so certain that Tessa feels the same way about me that I feel about her, I don't want to ruin her safe space by making a move if it's unwanted.

In order to break myself out of the trance I've worked myself into, I clear my throat and ask, "So, what would you like for dinner?"

She blinks and shakes her head as if she too had been in a trance. "I actually took out some chicken and was planning on trying to make chicken parmesan. Does that sound okay to you?" she asks as she stands up and starts walking around the couch into the kitchen.

"Yeah, chicken parm sounds delicious. Do you need any help?" I go to stand up and add, "The word 'try' has me a little nervous."

She laughs and shakes her head. "Yeah, you can come, but only to observe. I have to concentrate if you want it to actually be edible."

I sit at the counter while she makes her way around the kitchen. I get lost watching her as she moves about, looking so much at home. I start to picture what our life could look like if Sherri was right. A pregnant Tessa sitting at the table working on a drawing as I come home from work. Me making dinner while Tessa and our little girl run around the backyard.

I'm so caught up in my thoughts I don't hear Tessa until she puts a hand on my shoulder, scaring me. "Do you want angel hair or spaghetti pasta?" She's holding up two boxes in my direction.

"Angel hair works," I respond, coming back to the moment.

When dinner's done we sit at the counter eating. "Do you plan on taking on another client anytime soon?" I ask as she cuts her chicken.

"I'm not sure I'm ready yet. But maybe after the celebration," she answers, looking at me. "How's dinner?"

I grin after taking a bite. "It's really good. I shouldn't have doubted you."

Chapter 44

Tessa

Please tell me there's something I can do to make it up to you?

There's nothing you need to do. I understand. You're a lawyer. Lawyers have to go to court. I'm not upset.

I don't think you're upset. I just feel like a shit best friend. I want to be there for you, but this case has been scheduled to go to court today for months and I can't let one of the partners take it because I've been working so closely with the kid.

Janelle! I said I understand. You've got work. But if you must make it up to me, let's do karaoke the first time I come visit, no matter what day it is.

Nelly-Belly Peters:

> *You've got yourself a deal, Tessa Elaine. I love you *kissy face emoji**

Me:

> *I love you, too.*

My mom's celebration of life service is today and I'm standing staring at the closet in my towel unsure of what to wear. She made it clear that she didn't want anyone to wear black, even if we are still mourning, so I keep looking between two dresses. The first option is a casual, deep purple that goes about mid-thigh and hugs my curves around my waist before flaring out in the skirt. The second option is a champagne color and semi-formal in style, but is a little longer, reaching just above my knees. I pull both hangers from the closet and leave the room in search of Graham. He can decide for me.

I walk through the house, looking for him, but don't see him in the kitchen or living room, so I head back down the hallway to his bedroom. I knock on the door and wait. When he opens it I suck in a breath and forget to release it. His hair is wet and mussed, like he just got out of the shower and ran his towel through it. He's got on a pair of khaki pants and that's it. No shirt. His brawny frame is on full display. Dark hair that I'd love to trail my fingers through, covers the top of his chest, with a trail of hair that leads below his pants. What I wouldn't give to see if the hair continues beneath his boxers. I unconsciously bite my lower lip as I check him out.

He clears his throat, causing me to squeak in embarrassment. "Can I do something for you?" He asks in a sultry voice.

It takes me a minute to remember why I came to his door and I blink a few times before I'm able to speak. "Um. Yes." I feel my cheeks turn pink. "Pick a dress. Purple or champagne?" I hold the two dresses out.

For a few seconds, he just stares at me. I can't help but notice as his eyes roam over my body. At first I'm confused, but then I look down only to realize I'm still in my towel. Instead of shrinking down and getting embarrassed, I stand a little taller and shake the two dresses, bringing his attention back to the reason I knocked on his door.

He clears his throat again and then says, "Right. Which dress?" He looks at the dresses, reaches forward and moves them so each one is held up to my body. "Purple. Definitely purple," he says with a nod of his head.

I look down at the two dresses, nod my head, and say, "Thank you for the help." Then I turn around, walking back into my room to continue getting dressed.

Thirty minutes later, I walk out wearing the purple dress, my curls pulled half up out of my face, and a pair of black heels on my feet. Graham looks up from his coffee mug with a smile on his face. "You look beautiful," he says, causing me to blush.

"Thank you." I stand there, taking him in. He's wearing the same khaki pants I saw earlier, a white button-up shirt and purple tie that matches my dress perfectly. I lower my head to hide the smile that's spreading across my face at the thought of him matching me on purpose. "You look good too," I add.

"Are you ready? It's about time to head out," he says, rinsing his mug out in the sink and placing it in the dishwasher.

Nodding, I reach for the purse I left sitting on the counter. "As I'll ever be."

We planned on meeting my dad and grandparents at the church a little before the service starts to make sure everything is set up. When we get there, my Granna and Pop have already claimed their seats at the front of the sanctuary. My dad, his parents, and my aunt are standing in the grand hall. Well, as grand as the hall can be in a church this size.

"Hey, Grandma; hey, Grandpa," I say, giving them both a hug. Then I turn to my aunt and hug her next. "Hey, Aunt Val. I think you've all met Graham before, but if not, this is my friend, Graham." I turn and show Graham off, Vanna White style.

My aunt looks at me with a wry grin on her face and chuckles. "It's nice to meet you, Tessa's 'friend' Graham." She makes quotation marks with her fingers when she says the word "friend." Graham shakes my grandparents' hands and says hello while my aunt and I exchange looks. Mine is trying to convey that, unfortunately, I do mean *friend*, while hers clearly says she doesn't believe me.

After concluding that everything's set, we make our way to the pews at the front of the church where we plan to sit as friends and family start to arrive.

I need to be sitting when everyone starts to get here or I will lose all my composure.

Graham moves to sit a few rows back but I grab his arm and usher him to the front with us.

"The front is for the family," he whispers so only I hear.

I squeeze his arm. "I know, but I really need you up here with me." My eyes are pleading and I add, "Please?"

He just nods his head once and sits down next to me, sandwiching me between himself and my dad.

"Amazing Grace" plays over the speakers as everyone enters the sanctuary and finds a seat. On the screen, a slideshow of pictures of my mom, throughout her life, plays. Tears fill my eyes as I watch picture after picture of her smiling and laughing fill the screen. Mom's friends and our family members really pulled through for me and sent in great pictures ranging from birth to random events that happened at work just months ago.

Graham pulls out a handkerchief from his pocket and hands it to me. "I figured you'd need this," he whispers in my ear, causing goosebumps to pimple across my skin. I look at him and offer a small smile as a thank you.

The pastor walks up to the microphone standing at the front of the room and welcomes everyone. He starts the celebration off with a prayer, and when he finishes, he opens the mic up to anyone who would like to speak—share stories about Mom, memories, or anything they feel moved to share. Person after person gets up to say the most kind things about my mom, which keeps my tears flowing, and causes my dad to get emotional as well. I squeeze my dad's hand with one hand, and as I sit there crying, Graham reaches over, taking my other hand in his, rubbing his thumb over the back of it.

"Hi! I'm Angie, Sherri has been my best friend for as long as I can remember. My story isn't going to be a sad one because she made me promise I wouldn't be a blubbering mess up here, so, here goes. I remember one time, when we were teenagers—this was before she met Pauly—we rode our bikes up to the corner store and there was this really cute guy working the cash register. She dared me to walk up to him and plant a big kiss on his lips then walk away. Of course, I did it—I couldn't turn down a dare. And then after, we hightailed it out of there, laughing like a couple of hyenas," Angie says, tears running down her cheeks from laughing at the memory. "I'm only sorry I never got to get her back from that dare. A few weeks later, she met Paul, and I knew from that moment on there'd be no kissing random cuties for her." Angie gives a smile to my dad and I as she walks past us to go sit back down.

A young woman makes her way down the aisle toward the microphone. "Hi, I'm Sarah, and Mrs. Gunter was my seventh grade English teacher. I was going through a pretty rough time at home, and honestly, just in general, but she would let me come in after school and during lunch to talk to her. I didn't get along great with my parents, so having her to talk to and get advice from helped make middle school a little better." I stare at Sarah, feeling a sense of familiarity. She has pink hair pulled up in a ponytail and is a couple months pregnant—she keeps rubbing her hand over her belly as she talks. "She didn't stop giving me advice once I was out of her class, though. We kept in touch through email when I went to high school, through college, and even when I moved away. We corresponded a lot when I met my husband, and Mrs. Gunter was definitely more motherly with advice than my mother or sister were. She's the one who encouraged me to amend my relationship with my family. She was a pretty remarkable woman. I'll forever be thankful to have known her." Sarah looks over at my dad and I and bows her head in condolences before she walks back to her seat. I follow her with my gaze and see her sit with a handsome man with dark brown hair—almost black—and piercing green eyes.

I lean over and whisper to my dad, "Do you know who that was?" as the next person walks up to the microphone.

He inclines his head and leans toward me but keeps his eyes facing forward. "That was Sarah Feldd. You did work for her brother recently." Recognition clicks and I steal another glance at her before returning my attention to the man sharing his story.

After the last person speaks, the microphone stands alone for a couple of minutes, and I look around to see if anyone looks like they might stand and walk up there.

Graham squeezes my hand, then stands up. I grip the handkerchief that has been sitting in my lap, forgotten, as I prepare myself for what Graham has to say.

Chapter 45

Graham

I walk up to the microphone and look out at the almost-full church, but my gaze finds its way back to Tessa. Taking a calming breath, I wipe my hands on my pants before starting. I didn't originally plan to speak—my thoughts and words aren't necessarily for everyone to hear—but I felt compelled to share. I owe it to Tessa and Paul to share how much Sherri meant to me.

"Good morning, I'm Graham, and I knew Sherri for the majority of my life. I grew up down the street from her, was friends with her daughter, Tessa, when we were kids, and then, as I became an adult, it wasn't my friendship with Tessa that allowed me to stay in Sherri's life, it was my friendship with Sherri, herself." I take in a breath. "I had the privilege, along with many of you here, of working with Sherri. I got to witness her be a beacon of hope to students in the classroom. I got to watch her mold and shape the lives of hundreds of children over the past nine years. Watching her have to leave the classroom was hard, but watching her in the classroom? Now that was a gift."

I swallow to give myself a moment as I think of what else I want to share. "I live in my childhood home, so not only was Sherri a co-worker, and my mentor, but she was also a neighbor. I've spent many nights over at her house with her and Paul, just talking about life and how much of a gift it is to be alive. That's one thing I admired about her—she loved life. She talked about the adventures she and her family went on, as well as those she never got to go on but she would read about in books. She would talk about her love for her husband." I look at Paul and smile. Then my gaze finds Tessa and I see the tears in her eyes. "And her love for her daughter. She was so proud of Tessa for going out and following her dreams. Of course, she missed having her home all the time, but she loved that she was out experiencing what else was out there." I take another breath and smile at Tessa as she wipes tears from her eyes.

"Sherri was a wonderful mom. And while she might not have been my mom, I definitely looked at her as one. She always made me feel welcome, whether it was at her house, or in her classroom. She never once made me feel like I didn't belong. She constantly told me she was proud of me for following my dreams of becoming a teacher. Her pride in me made me proud of myself. There's not a moment since she's been gone that I haven't missed her. I miss going to her for advice. I miss hearing her laugh. But I'm lucky. I was able to spend some time with her in her last days and she gave me some great advice I will cherish for the rest of my life. I'll share some of it with you all, but the rest I'll keep to myself." I inhale as I think about what she said, and I exhale before I speak. "She said, *'Go out and take what you want out of life, but don't do anything illegal, unless you have someone willing to bail you out of jail. Make mistakes and laugh at yourself.'* She said, *'You've only got this one life to live, so live it, but don't live it with regrets.'*"

Before I walk back to my seat, I look at Paul and Tessa, both sitting in their seats with tear-soaked eyes. Seeing that has me leaning back into the microphone, making an announcement on their behalf. "And with that, I think the caterers are ready in the grand hall for the reception. Please feel free to stick around, talk, and share more stories of Sherri. Thank you all for coming."

"Amazing Grace" starts back up as I walk back to the pew. I sit down next to Tessa and pull her toward me so her head is resting on my chest—she looks like she could use the support. The way she relaxes into my embrace confirms my thoughts and warms my heart.

"Do you want to head out to the hall yet, or do you need a moment?" I ask both Paul and Tessa.

Paul looks at me and his eyes flicker between me and Tessa, a smile breaking through the sorrow on his face. "I'm going to head out to the reception and thank people for coming. You two sit in here as long as you need to." He stands up and watches the two of us for a beat. And before he turns to walk away, he winks at me.

I take a deep breath and inhale the scent of her coconut lotion, a smell that I've started to love and find my own comfort in. Rubbing circles on her back, I risk leaning my head down to plant a kiss on top of her head before resting my chin there. She nuzzles her head into my chest as if she's trying to bury herself deeper, murmuring what sounds like "thank you" into my chest and wraps her arms around my back.

We sit there, holding onto each other for an eternity, before her crying slows, turning into hiccups, and she pulls back. "Here I go again, crying into you," she says, using my handkerchief to wipe her nose.

I reach up and wipe the tears off her cheeks, my thumb pausing there. "Tess." My voice comes out as a whisper. "It's okay. You can lean on me and cry whenever you need to."

She leans her head into my touch and nods. Taking in a deep breath, she stands up and grabs my hand. "I guess I should go face the crowd and thank them for coming."

Chapter 46

Tessa

I continue to hold Graham's hand as we walk through the main hall, thanking people for coming. I can feel the veil of numbness start to slide back into place as people go in for hugs and give their condolences. The slight pressure of the gentle reassuring squeezes from Graham's hand is the only thing connecting me to the here and now.

We walk around until we find a quiet spot in a corner to stand in so I can get my bearings.

"This is an amazing turnout. I knew your mom was loved, but this really shows it," Graham says, looking out at the sea of people eating brunch and mingling.

I take a few steadying breaths. The crowd of people here to celebrate my mom's life is overwhelming, and everyone wanting to talk to me is taking a toll on what little energy I have. I spy my dad talking to a group of my mom's old coworkers and notice he too looks overwhelmed.

"I'm going to go rescue my dad from the crowd." I nod in his direction.

Graham's eyes follow the direction I tilt my head and his eyes widen a bit. "I can come help; I'll take his place. Those ladies will talk for ages," he says, as if reading my mind. Thankfully, he speaks the idea that was playing in my mind. I smile up at him and start walking.

I'm still holding his hand when we make it to my dad and the group of teachers. "Hey, Dad, someone over there wants to talk to you." I motion my head in the direction behind us. His eyes give a look of appreciation before turning back to the group of women, saying his goodbyes, and turning to walk away.

Graham gives my hand a tight squeeze then releases it as he turns his attention to the group my dad just left. Immediately, my hand feels cold, and the numbness once again engulfs me. I look around for a few minutes before I spot Dad walking back into the sanctuary.

I follow behind him, and when I walk in I see him sitting on a pew, leaning forward, with his head resting in his hands. His shoulders shake as he sobs silently.

I walk up to him and rest my hand on his back. "Want company, or do you want to be alone?" I ask before I take a seat.

He looks up and pats the pew next to him. "Come on, Bug. I'll never turn down your company. But I can't promise I'll be very good company myself. I'm pretty talked out." He pulls me into him and I rest my head against his chest.

"It's okay. We can just sit here in silence. That sounds like what I need anyway," I say, resting my eyes as I listen to my dad's uneven breaths from crying.

As we sit there silently, both of us in our own thoughts, my mind wanders to Graham and the comfort I feel when I'm around him. The way his presence helps me feel relaxed and at ease. I don't think I've ever felt this way before. Darren and I dated for almost a year and I never felt this sense of peace with him.

My stomach twists with guilt for finding this sliver of happiness with Graham.

I steal a peek up at my dad who also has his eyes shut. "Daddy?" I whisper, not wanting to startle him, half afraid of the memories I might be pulling him away from.

Not opening his eyes he answers, "Hmm?" before pulling me in a little tighter to let me know he's listening.

"How did you know you were in love with mom?" I ask, not taking my eyes off him. A grin breaks across his face as he opens one eye and looks down at me.

"Tess, you've heard our story a million times. What's on your mind?"

I fidget with my hands and glance around the sanctuary before I respond. "Do you think it's possible to love someone because of the comfort they bring you? Like, if being in someone's presence makes you feel peace, when otherwise you feel so much unease."

He loosens his grip around my shoulder so he can turn his body to face me. "I think it's possible for the person you love to bring you peace by being near them. The peace and comfort your mom brought me throughout the years were one of the best things about her. No matter how stressed I was about work, or finances, or honestly anything, the moment I walked through the door and saw your mom, a sense of calm spread through my body." He tilts his head as he considers me. "You love Graham, don't you?"

I turn pink at the quickness in which my dad knows what I'm talking about. "I'm not sure. I thought I loved Darren way back when, but what I feel for Graham isn't the same. It's more . . . intense. And I feel like it should frighten me, because it happened so fast. I mean, he only just came back into my life two months ago." I swallow. "But seeing his love for mom . . . and his respect and care for you. It makes me feel—" I pause to consider the word I'm looking for. "Safe. Graham makes me feel safe in the same way you and mom make me feel safe. Like, I can be vulnerable around him and know he's there for me one hundred percent. Does that make sense?"

My dad nods his head. "Yeah, baby girl, it makes sense. And for what it's worth, he's a great guy. I can see how it wouldn't take much for someone to fall in love with him. Just like I can see how it wouldn't take much for someone to fall in love with *you*."

We fall into comfortable silence as I think over his words. It doesn't last long, however, as the sound of the door opening and closing comes from behind us. Neither one of us turns—I don't need to, a sense of comfort rushed through me the moment the door opened. The same feeling that washes over me when I'm in the same room as Graham.

"There you two are," Graham says, standing at the end of the pew. "People are starting to leave, are y'all wanting to stay until everyone is gone, or are y'all ready to get out of here?"

I look at my dad and tilt my head. "Yeah. I'm ready to go home."

"You two go on. I'm going to stay here a bit longer." He pulls me in for a hug and kisses my cheek. "I'll come by in a few hours."

At dinner, we're eating pizza and watching *The Masked Singer* in memory of Mom when Graham looks at me and says, "I think you might need a vacation."

My dad nods his head. "I agree. I think you need to get away. Go somewhere so you can clear your head for a few days. Maybe you could go visit Nell."

I look between the two of them. "A vacation from what? I haven't been doing anything. If anything, I need to get back to work. And I can't go visit Nell, she's in the middle of a big case. I can't just go stay with her while she's in prep mode."

"Grant has a cabin in the Blue Ridge Mountains I can take you to. Or I could get you the keys and you can go by yourself. Bring your work with you if you think you need to do it."

"Oh! That sounds perfect! If your brother doesn't mind, I think that's the perfect getaway she needs." My dad nods enthusiastically. "You could leave Friday after we put your mom's ashes in her P.O. Box."

I watch the two of them, the joy in their eyes at the thought of me, taking the time to clear my mind of everything that's happened the past few days. Finally, I shake my head in agreement. "Fine. What do I pack?"

Chapter 47

Graham

Pulling into the cabin on Friday afternoon feels unreal. I still can't believe Tessa actually agreed to let me take her, instead of taking the trip alone, like I offered. She slept most of the three-hour trip, so the only thing keeping me company was the music and my growing nerves. I know, rationally, I shouldn't be nervous. We've been living together for a few weeks—her in her room and me in mine. This won't be any different, considering Grant's cabin is a three bedroom that they had built with money that was left to Lisa when her grandparents died.

Tessa woke up when we were about twenty minutes away from the cabin, and she's been quietly singing along to the music, while enjoying the view out the window since.

When we turn down the lane toward the cabin she straightens up.

The driveway is surrounded by trees, opening into a clearing where the cabin sits in the middle. It's a rustic, two-story wooden house, with a wraparound porch. And on the front porch is a swing attached to the ceiling and two rocking chairs. I look over at Tessa as she takes in the cabin before I put the car in park.

"I can show you around, but then I'd like to run up to the store and grab some groceries. You can come or you can stay and get settled," I say as I grab our bags out of the backseat.

She slowly spins around, looking at the lush trees, taking in the scenery. "Sounds good to me. Show me the way."

With my bag on my back and her bag in my left hand, I gently hover my right hand over her lower back. When we get to the door, I move my hand and grab the keys out of my pocket. She walks over to the swing and gives it a push.

Opening the door, I look over my shoulder at her and ask, "Ready?"

She nods her head and follows me into the house. We walk directly into the living room. From this spot, you can see through to the back of the house, which is just a giant sliding glass door. In the living room are two couches facing a flat-screen TV that's mounted above an entertainment center. Off to the right is a staircase that leads upstairs to the bedrooms, and there's a half-bath built into the wall under the staircase. Off to the left, toward the back, is an eat-in kitchen, and the kitchen has all modern appliances and cherrywood cabinets with light gray marble countertops.

Tessa walks around, admiring the way Grant and Lisa have the area set up. "This is beautiful," she says, glancing up the staircase.

I set the bags on the couch closest to me. "We can see the bedrooms in a little bit. Let me show you the backyard." I walk across the house so I can open the sliding door.

She trails behind me, and when she gets a look at the view outside, her breath catches. "Oh my!" she says, putting her hand over her mouth. "This view!" She walks off the back porch and down the walkway toward an area with a built-in firepit where a few Adirondack chairs are placed around it. The view from the backyard is nothing but the rugged peaks and the vibrant greenery from the mountains beyond, showcasing that spring is finally in full swing.

She's staring at the view, but I'm staring at her. I could get used to watching her as she looks at what she considers to be beautiful. The awe on her face makes her look all the more breathtaking. I walk up next to her and take in a deep inhale of the fresh mountain air. "I'm going to go back to town so I can get some groceries. Would you like to come, or do you want to get settled?"

She mimics my deep inhale and smiles. "I think I want to get settled. If you don't mind."

I shake my head. "Not at all. Take the biggest room. I'll sleep in Ethan's room. If you have anything particular you'd like from the store, just text." I head back through the house and back out to the car.

On the way back from the store, I stop to get Chinese food since it's getting pretty late and I don't want to cook, or make Tessa do it. I walk into the house and notice both bags are off the couch. Looking through the door, I see Tessa's head poking up behind one of the Adirondack chairs.

I put the groceries away and put the takeout in bowls before placing two water bottles beneath my arm, then I head outside.

She looks around at the sound of me coming and smiles. She's got on a beige hoodie with a blanket wrapped around her legs. One look at everything I'm carrying has her standing up to grab for a bowl.

"You got Chinese!" she squeals and does a cute little bounce before she sits back down. After she takes a bite, she points her fork over to the tree line off to the side of the house. "I love that they have an actual tree house—built into a tree and everything." She blinks before turning her eyes back to me. "I love this place. Thank you for bringing me here."

I smile and start to feel myself turn red for some reason. "I'm glad you wanted to come." I take a bite of my dinner and look out at the view. It's starting to grow darker, but the stars twinkling in the sky make up for the diminishing sunlight. "It's a little chilly. Would you like me to start a fire?"

"No. I'm enjoying the cool air right now. Maybe tomorrow." She glances over at me. "I also noticed they have a hot tub." She wiggles her eyebrows at me.

"Yes, they have a hot tub. Why do you think I told you to pack a bathing suit?" I look at her with a smile on my face.

While we continue eating dinner we talk about everything under the sun: her job—which she hasn't yet felt ready to continue—my job, her friend that she lived with back in Richmond, the fact that her friend is planning a wedding, her dad, Grant and the cabin. It's relaxing and feels right being able to talk to her about all the random things on our minds. I never thought random conversation could be this easy. In the past, it's always felt so awkward to talk about the mundane. But not with Tessa.

I glance over at her as she tries to stifle a yawn. She catches me looking and her eyes widen. "Oh my goodness! I'm so sorry! You're not boring, I swear! I just all of a sudden feel tired."

An unexpected laugh bursts out of me. "I didn't think you thought I was boring. But now, I'm not sure. It's weird you felt the need to specify that." I give her a skeptical look, trying to hold back another laugh.

"Would it be horrible if I said I'm ready to go lie down?" she asks, looking a bit guilty.

I shake my head. "Not at all. You had an emotional morning with all the stuff with your mom. I think I'll head up too, actually."

We both stand up. I grab her empty bowl as she grabs the blanket she was covered in. I can't help as my eyes roam over her as she walks past. Those black leggings hugging her ass and thighs send signals to my dick, causing it to slightly harden. Before following her, I adjust my pants, then I head back into the house. I rinse the dishes off, put them in the dishwasher, and head up the stairs after her.

I stop in front of the first door at the top of the stairs. She hesitates before continuing on down the hall to the primary bedroom. "Thanks again for bringing me here. I know we haven't been here that long yet, but it's already helping me feel a little more like myself." She looks around as if she isn't sure she wants to say what else is on her mind.

Before I can stop myself, I pull her in for a hug. "You don't have to thank me, Tessa. I would do anything to help you feel happy. Just say the word." I lean my head against the top of her head and inhale. That breath allows me to get a whiff of her citrus shampoo mixed with the coconut scent of her lotion.

She pulls her head away from my chest but doesn't disengage from the hug. She looks up at me, her eyes flickering between my eyes, my mouth, and back again. I swallow, trying to hold back the desire to lean in to kiss her. Her gaze flicks down to my throat and back up to my mouth. She slowly leans in, closes her eyes, and tilts her head ever so slightly. I immediately meet her halfway, closing the gap as our lips collide. As soon as my mouth is on hers she deepens the kiss by pushing her tongue out, prodding at my mouth to open and let her in. I don't hesitate. I open my mouth and allow her tongue to explore as my tongue moves into her mouth. She lets out a small moan, the sound shooting straight to my cock.

Her hands move up to my neck where her fingers pull at the hair that brushes me there. I let my hands move from her back, where I was holding her in our hug—one to her hair, the other to her ass. She pushes me slightly until my back hits the wall.

When I can't move any further, she pulls back and stares at me. Then she reaches her hand up and her fingers brush her swollen lips. "That was . . ." She breathes. "Should I have done that? Was that okay?" She looks a little afraid of what my response is going to be.

Instead of answering her with words, I grab her neck to pull her back into a kiss. She exhales through her nose and opens her mouth to deepen the kiss again before she grabs my shirt, pulling me to follow her as she walks backwards down the hall. My dick is fully erect now, my mind homing in on what's finally happening between the two of us.

When we reach the door that leads into the master bedroom she pulls away and looks at me with eyes that are dilated with lust. She opens the door and walks in without saying anything.

As she stands in front of the bed, she bites her lip and looks me over as I stand in the doorway.

"Did you mean it when you said anything?" she asks in a raspy voice I've never heard come from her and my God, if I could record that sound I'd play it on repeat.

I nod, understanding exactly what she's asking. She gives a sultry smile and beckons me over with one finger. "I don't want to be presumptuous as to what you mean, but I want you to know, I don't have any condoms." My voice comes out more nervous than I intended it to. "I didn't want to assume anything would happen here."

She lifts her left shoulder in a shrug and looks at the nightstand behind her. "It's okay. I brought some." If I thought it was possible for my dick to get any harder, it definitely would be. "I didn't want to assume either. But I definitely hoped." She bites her bottom lip as she watches, waiting for my reaction.

Fuck. I take off my shirt in one fluid motion as I take a step toward her. As soon as I reach her, she puts her hand up and stops me, her eyes roaming over me, taking in my chest and stomach. She licks her lips, smiling at me, as I reach my hands up and grip the sides of her hoodie. I look at her questioningly before continuing. She nods and lifts her arms up.

My mind flashes back to a very similar scene—before I bathed her. I saw her naked then, but it was under completely different circumstances. I didn't let myself appreciate her body then. This time, once her hoodie is off, I expect to have to take off a shirt and possibly a bra. But to my surprise, she's just wearing a bra underneath. A black, see-thru lace bra that allows me to see the pink of her areolas and the hardness of her nipples. She reaches her hand behind her back and her bra falls down her arms. I inhale a breath as I take in her bare breasts.

I move greedily, kissing her neck. My hands move up to grab her breasts, and I run my thumbs over her nipples, causing them to pebble even more beneath my touch. She gasps at the touch and pushes her chest forward more. I add a little pressure as I massage her breasts and kiss down her neck to her left breast. When I'm there, I look up at her through my eyelashes. She bites her lip again and lowers her head in approval. I take her nipple in my mouth, sucking and giving a tender nip. She lets out another gasp and her hands find my head. While sucking on her left nipple, I use my fingers to tug and pull on her right one. After a few minutes, I switch my mouth to her right breast and my fingers to her left and repeat the motion I was doing.

When I stop, I gently lower her, making her sit on the edge of the bed, and I stand in front of her. I bite my lower lip as I place my hands at the waistband of her leggings and give a quick tug. She stands up enough for her leggings to slide down past her ass. "Fuck." I take in a deep breath. "No panties?" I ask, noticing that, once her leggings are down, there's nothing keeping me from seeing her bare.

She shakes her head, eyes watching me as I take her in. She's a beautiful sight to behold. Seeing her on this bed, naked in front of me, beats the view out the window by a million. I kneel down and put my hands on her knees, keeping my eyes locked on hers. I push her knees apart so she's spread out in front of me, then I lean forward so I'm in between her legs, still holding her gaze. I take my eyes off of her and lean my head over to place a kiss on the inside of her knee before I peek up to make sure she's still okay with me continuing. She licks her lips and dips her head.

I continue to lick and kiss my way up her thigh. As I go, I glance at her center and see that she keeps it natural but trimmed. I immediately feel more attracted to her. Most women I've been with insist on being completely shaved or they wouldn't let me anywhere near it with my face. Some men enjoy a shaved pussy, but to me, when a woman decides not to shave, it signifies she's comfortable in her own skin.

I stifle a moan as my face gets closer to her pussy and I inhale deeply through my nose, intoxicated by the scent of her arousal. When I reach her center I look up at her and ask, "Do you want this?"

In response, she gives a slight nod and a shaky, "God, yes."

I take one good long look at her sitting on the bed, legs wide. I tug slightly on her pubic hair. "This is a huge fucking turn on," I say, then place one hand on her pubic bone, using my fingers to open her lips, her arousal glistening in the light. I give her clit a kiss and then plunge my tongue deep inside her pussy, causing a moan to escape from her. I stroke my tongue along the inside of her pussy as my hand holds her open for me.

Removing my tongue, I hear a small groan of displeasure leave Tessa. But before she has the chance to voice any concerns, I put my mouth on her clit and suck. As I suck and tug on her clit with my tongue, I gently slide one finger inside her. I feel her lean back on the bed, her body arching into my touch as she starts rotating her hips, matching the rhythm of my sucking. I take this moment to slowly slide a second finger inside and she puts her hands on my head, pulling my hair. I can feel the walls of her delectable pussy contracting against my fingers. Her breathing is starting to get slightly erratic, the grip she has on my hair gets tighter. She's about to come and my dick throbs at the idea of me getting to taste it.

"I'm about to come," she says in a husky voice and I suck harder on her clit, not stopping the thrusts I'm doing with my fingers as she comes undone in my mouth.

"Fuck! You taste incredible," I say before I lick up the cum as it continues to spill out of her.

Chapter 48

Tessa

My body is shaking as I come down from my orgasm. I open my eyes and watch as Graham stands up, wiping his mouth and then licking his fingers.

Holy shit that's a hot sight.

He's staring at me, his pupils blown so wide I can barely see his irises.

He puts his hand on his belt and starts undoing it. *Has he been in his pants this whole time?* "The condoms are where?" He turns toward my bag that I left sitting on top of the dresser.

I swallow and answer in a voice that doesn't quite sound like my own. "In the nightstand." I point to the nightstand in question.

He gives me a quizzical look. "Tessa Gunter, why would you put condoms in the nightstand?" he asks teasingly as he saunters over to the nightstand in question, unbuttoning his pants at an excruciatingly slow pace.

I sit up on my elbows to watch him. "So they would be easier to get to if this moment were to arise. Like I said, I hoped it would," I answer without shame.

He stills as he reaches for the box and I immediately wonder if I said the wrong thing. I start to feel uncertain. I know I've been dreaming about this moment since I saw him standing in my parents kitchen, but what if this is just an opportunity for him to get laid. I brush that thought aside. I don't think he would have eagerly gone down on me, full wooly mammoth, if he didn't want this too. But then again, maybe he would have.

Sensing the change in my demeanor, he sits down on the bed with the box in his hand, placing his hand on my cheek. "Hey, where'd you go just then?"

My cheeks warm at the thought that can read me so easily.

I shake my head before saying, "Just in my head a bit. It's nothing." I give him a reassuring smile.

He holds my gaze for a few more seconds before looking down at the unopened box. He turns it over and looks up at me with an eyebrow arched. So I spit out, "I didn't know what size you were, and I didn't want to get the wrong size. I found a website that had sample kits with various sizes. I figured one of those should work." My skin heats more with what that admission means. I have been thinking way too hard about getting him in bed with me.

He nods his head while letting out a low chuckle as he opens the box. He grabs out a condom and tosses it onto the bed and putting the box back on the nightstand. I watch as he walks back to the foot of the bed, his eyes locking on mine as he slowly, oh so slowly, takes his pants off. He's now standing at the foot of the bed with his erection trying to break free of his boxer briefs. I sit up, scooting myself closer to him and reach up so I can put my fingers inside the waistband of his briefs.

I hold his gaze, and smirk as I slide his briefs down. "Tit-for-tat, remember?"

When they hit his ankles he does a little shuffle then kicks them to the side. I take my bottom lip in my mouth, holding it with my teeth, then lower my gaze to his cock, which has more girth than I'm used to, but it's perfect. I grab it in my hand and lean forward to take it in my mouth. I slide myself off the edge of the bed, sitting up in a kneeling position in front of him. As I take him deeper in my mouth, gagging on him as he hits the back of my throat, I look up and watch as his eyes flutter closed.

Oral is not my favorite sexual activity, but for some reason, with Graham, I want to experience everything. I want his cock as deep in my mouth as it'll go. I want him to come down my throat as I choke on him.

This is not a side of myself I've ever encountered, and I feel excited to discover it with Graham. Most of my past relationships have been vanilla in terms of spice, but I do enjoy reading, so I use what I've learned from my books. I reach up and grab his balls with one hand and give them a gentle squeeze. He bucks his hips forward, causing me to gag a little more. Tears fill my eyes, and for the first time in weeks it's not because I'm sad.

I hollow out my cheeks as I suck on him and he lets out a moan. He grips my hair in his hand and pulls me back from his cock. "As much as I'd love to fill your mouth, I'd rather fuck your pussy instead."

I nod at him and get off my knees as I bite back a giggle. None of my previous partners have ever talked dirty to me during sex, so if that's a preview of what I'm in store for I really hope I can keep my composure. I sit back on the bed, scooting back so my head rests on the pillows, and I watch as he kneels on the bed and grabs the condom. I'm oddly aroused at the sight of him rolling it down his shaft. I feel myself get wetter and I squeeze my thighs together to try to get some relief.

"Spread your thighs for me. I want to see your perfect pussy." He crawls forward and grabs my legs, opening them wider. I bite my lip to keep a giggle from escaping my mouth. He leans forward and for a second I think he's going to eat me out again but instead, he kisses and licks his way up my thighs. His beard tickles my body as his tongue maps its way over my stretch marks. "You're so fucking beautiful," he murmurs as he makes his way up the curves and rolls on my stomach.

When he reaches my mouth, he hesitates. I grip him by the back of the neck and pull him into me, opening my mouth and taking in his tongue. Tasting him and the aftertaste of my arousal on his breath turns me on in a way I never imagined. He reaches his hand down and slides a finger between my lips and pushes it into my pussy.

"You're so fucking wet for me."

I take in a deep breath to suppress another laugh that's trying to bubble free. This is so hot, I'm not sure why my body is having this reaction.

His eyes are closed as he thrusts his finger in and out and teases my clit with his thumb.

After teasing me with his fingers, he grabs his cock with one hand and aligns it with my entrance. He locks eyes with me and I nod, breathing out the word "please," giving him consent. We both hold our breaths as he gently slides himself in. He goes slowly at first, so we can both get accustomed to him being inside of me. With a single thrust up, I bring my hips to meet him so he is seated fully inside me and let out an elated moan. His cock stretches me in the most pleasurable way.

We move together, our bodies so in sync it feels as if we've done this a million times before. The feeling of his cock seated so deeply inside of me has my body spasming. He reaches his hand down between us and massages my clit with his thumb. My pussy starts to contract as I feel my orgasm building.

"Yes! God! Your pussy squeezing my cock feels so fucking good."

This time, I can't hold back. I start laughing. Not just a small giggle either. I let out an unattractive snort and my stomach starts to cramp from how hard I'm laughing. The intensity of my orgasm fades as I howl with laughter.

I immediately clamp a hand over my mouth and whisper, "I'm sorry."

Graham stops all movement, concern on his face as he observes me. "Are you okay?" His eyes rove over my body, tracking my movements. "Did I do something wrong?"

Instantly, I'm filled with guilt for laughing. Of course he would think something is wrong. I pull myself together.

"I'm so sorry," I say again on an inhale. As I let it out, I continue, "I've never been with someone who talks during sex. And while it's very arousing, I'm just not used to it. So what you said took me by surprise." His face scrunches up in thought. "Please don't be embarrassed. I didn't mean to embarrass you!" I practically yell as I put my hands on his face to get him to look at me. "I didn't mean to laugh. Honestly."

He lets out a breath. "Are you at least enjoying yourself?" He looks at me pleadingly.

"Of course I am. If you couldn't tell by—" I take a breath before I finish my sentence. "My pussy squeezing your cock." I bite back a smile.

Graham chuckles, then starts full on belly laughing. "Holy shit. Hearing you say that was more of a turn on than it should've been." He leans forward and kisses me.

"Did I ruin the mood? Is there any chance of me salvaging this?" I ask as I wiggle my hips, causing his cock to plunge a little deeper.

"Hmmm. I think we can figure something out," he says, grinding his hips down into me, causing my body to react to him.

He thrusts his hips forward then grabs my leg, lifting it up on his shoulder. This position opens me up to take him deeper than before. We continue this position, with him massaging my clit with one thumb and playing with my nipples with the other thumb until I come. Shortly after I finish, he pulls himself out of me and lets his cum fill the condom.

After my body has calmed down from my orgasm I get up to use the bathroom before returning to the bed.

Graham gets up, grabs his briefs from the floor, and walks to the en suite bathroom. When he comes back, he's no longer naked and leans over, kissing me. "Should I, uh . . . Should I head to Ethan's room?" he asks, pointing over his shoulder out the door, eyes pleading for me to say no.

I shake my head, pull the covers down, and pat the bed next to me. "I think it's okay if you stay with me. In fact, I'd prefer it."

He climbs in bed next to me and pulls me into him. I bury my head into him, inhaling his scent as I stroke my fingers through the dusting of hair he has along his chest. We lie cuddled into each other, him playing with my hair as I koala myself into him, completely sated, until I fall asleep.

Chapter 49

Tessa

Saturday morning I wake up and find the bed empty and cold beside me. I sit up, pulling the covers up with me as I survey the room for any signs of the activities from the night before being a dream. The box of condoms is on top of the nightstand, opened, and my clothes are tossed over by the dresser, but Graham and his clothes are nowhere to be found. I shake my head and lower my face into my hands.

Did I make a complete fool of myself? Did last night not mean the same for him as it did for me?

I startle at the sound of a throat clearing in the doorway. "Coffee?" Graham asks as he holds a mug out to me, walking toward the bed. He's shirtless and in a pair of gray basketball shorts, his hair mussed from sleep. When he reaches the bed he leans down, giving me a kiss, before handing me the mug.

I stare up at him with what I'm sure is a goofy grin as I bring the coffee to my mouth. "Thank you," I say after I've taken a sip. "How long have you been awake?"

He looks at his watch and tilts his head from side to side as he thinks. "Maybe an hour and a half. I woke up needing to pee and wasn't able to get back to sleep. Instead of tossing and turning and risking the chance of waking you up—not knowing if you're a light sleeper or not—I went downstairs, made coffee, and watched the sunrise."

I gasp, "You watched the sunrise without me!" then swat at him as he sits down on the bed next to me.

His shoulders shake as he laughs. "Hey, I've lived with you long enough to know you are not a morning person. I'm not going to be the one to wake you up from sleep." He pulls me into his chest and it feels so natural, like we've been doing this our whole lives.

I move to reach over him to put the mug of unfinished coffee on the nightstand, but he grabs it from me, setting it down. When it's safely on the nightstand he turns around, and in one quick movement, pins me on the bed, his mouth claiming mine. Kissing him leaves me feeling like no kiss has ever felt before. Dizzy and aching. Like this is how I'm supposed to be kissed the rest of my life.

I never got dressed after we had sex last night, so the only thing between him and my bare body is the sheets, his shorts, and possibly a pair of briefs. He moves his kisses down my neck and pulls the sheets down as he goes. My nipples are hardening not just from arousal anymore, but from the coolness in the air. He takes one nipple into his mouth, twisting and tugging at the other one with his fingers. My pussy is wet with desire and need. I buck my hips off the bed and into his growing erection causing a growl to escape his throat.

"Someone is needy this morning," he says before taking my nipple in his mouth and gently biting it. Instead of giggling at his comment this time, I grind my hips in a circular motion.

My hand points desperately towards the box of condoms on the nightstand. He just shakes his head as he continues peppering kisses down my stomach before he tugs on my pubic hair slightly, like he did last night. "I know I said this last night, but this"—he takes in a breath—"is a huge fucking turn on."

I feel a blush spread from my face down my chest. I flex my toes, expecting the feel of his tongue at my entrance and let out a small squeak when I feel a gentle kiss on the inside of my thigh instead. As he kisses, licks, and starts to suck on the soft, sensitive skin, he slides a finger across my entrance.

"Fuck, Tessa, you're so wet." The feel of his hot breath over the wetness his mouth is making on my thighs causes more of my arousal to gather between my legs.

He pushes two fingers inside me as he continues sucking on my thigh. The friction of his beard is an oddly satisfying feeling that I know will leave me with beard burn later, but for now, I close my eyes and enjoy. Then, I slowly start to move my hips in sync with the thrusts of his fingers.

When he's finished sucking on my thigh he keeps his fingers inside me and uses the opposite hand to open the lips of my pussy as he runs his tongue from where my ass meets the bed to my clit, shifting his fingers as he goes. Once he's there he latches on, sucking and softly nipping on it. As he sucks on the sensitive nub I feel the tension build as my stomach starts to coil. My vision starts to darken, and I tingle from my clit to my toes back to my head.

As I feel the orgasm build I reach one hand down, pulling at his hair. Using the other hand, I massage my breast and tug at my nipple. "Graham." My voice comes out ragged. "Graham, I'm about to come." The word *come* leaves my mouth as a moan as my orgasm crashes through me. My whole body tenses; I can feel my pussy clench around his fingers and my legs start to shake. He takes one more lick, from bottom to top, before kissing his way back up my body.

This time he doesn't hesitate when he reaches my mouth. Instead, he grips the back of my neck and takes my mouth with the possessiveness of someone afraid to lose their most treasured possession. Our kiss turns greedy as he grabs my hair, curling his fingers into it.

When the kiss slows, Graham releases my hair and moves his hand to my face. He pulls away from my mouth and holds my cheek in his hand. "I feel like I should thank you."

He must see the confusion on my face because he adds, "I might scare you with this admission, but after last night, and just now, I feel like I owe you the truth. And part of my truth is that I owe you a thank you." He keeps eye contact as he continues. "I've had a crush on you for as long as I can remember, Tessa. You moved away and I never got a chance to do anything about it. When you came back and took me up on my offer of staying in one of my guest rooms, my feelings returned tenfold but I was too scared to make a move, or ask you on a date—you had a lot going on and it didn't feel like the right time. But last night, you were brave enough to kiss me. Braver than I was. So thank you, for making the move I've been desperately wanting to make since you came back into my life."

My eyes sting as tears rush to the corners. I reach my hand up and cup his face. "Thank you for not trying to pressure me at a time when everything was so dark." I swallow over the lump of emotion forming in my throat. "I've also had feelings grow stronger for you in the past few weeks. But honestly, I can't say that I would've reacted well if you had made a move while I was still so focused on everything going on. So, thank you for being patient." I lean up, kissing him softly before pulling back.

We stay in that position for a few moments, just absorbing the truths we both shared. Then, I scoot back and sit up, breaking the silence first. "So, breakfast?" I ask, smiling at him.

Chapter 50

Graham

As soon as I say I'll make eggs, bacon, and toast, Tessa kicks her legs and does a little shimmy. I stand up and hold my hand out to help her out of bed. She grabs it, and as soon as she's out of bed my eyes trail down her body, taking all of her in. The way her body dips at her curves makes my dick twitch in anticipation.

Her eyes squint as she eyes me watching her. "I'm going to take a shower," she says, dropping my hand and walking to the bathroom.

My eyes follow her until she's behind the wall and I can't see her anymore. "I'll start breakfast," I call out as I leave the room. I would join her but I'm afraid I'd keep her in there so long that we'd miss out on the breakfast I promised her, only to emerge at lunchtime.

I'm at the stove making an omelet when Tessa wraps her arms around me from behind. A smile immediately breaks out across my face as I turn my head to look at her over my shoulder.

"It smells amazing," she says as she inhales deeply.

"I'm making an omelet for myself. Would you like one too, or do you prefer your eggs a different way?" I ask as I return my attention to the eggs in the pan.

Her hands caress my chest, her fingers dancing around my chest hair. Honestly, I was a little worried she'd be turned off by how hairy I am—it's a turnoff to many women—but she seems to enjoy it as much as I enjoy how natural she is.

"I'll have one too, please," she responds in a low voice as her hands continue to roam around my chest, inching further down south. I have to stop what I'm doing as my eyes flutter closed when she grazes my cock through my shorts. Then, after teasing me, she moves her hands back up, planting a kiss on my back as she pulls away from me.

I shake my head as I collect myself, grabbing a plate off the counter and putting my eggs on it. Then I add the eggs for her breakfast into the pan. As I cook, she walks to the glass door and stares out at the mountain view. "It really is so beautiful here."

Finishing up with breakfast, I pour two glasses of orange juice. "Do you mind grabbing the cups or the plates?" I ask, pulling her attention away from the window.

"Oh yes! Of course! Are we eating outside?" She scurries over to grab the plates, leaving me to grab the glasses.

I lift my chin to gesture out the door. "I figured we'd eat where we had dinner," I say as I use my elbow to open the door.

As we eat, I take in the view of the mountains, the greenery surrounding us, and Tessa. I listen as the birds sing to each other and the insects play their own music, while she keeps her stare out on the mountainscape.

"Is there anything in particular you'd like to do today? It's the only full day we have here. We can go hiking—Grant has a few mountain bikes and there are trails that we could take if you want to ride bikes—or we could stay here and just enjoy the view." I look around the yard. "We could get in the hot tub," I say with a smirk on my face, my mind picturing her sitting on top of me, riding my cock, but then I shake the idea out of my head. Sex in water is not as sexy as it's made out to be.

She tips her head to the side and purses her lips in a quizzical way. "Hmm. I didn't bring shoes for a bike ride or a hike. So maybe we can just stay here and relax—enjoy each other's company." She looks at me and smiles. "And maybe make use of the hot tub." Her eyes twinkle as she says that last part.

We stand up with our respective breakfast dishes and walk back into the cabin. Once I put my dishes in the dishwasher I turn to the counter so I can start cleaning up but notice that Tessa has already begun. I walk over and hug her from behind like she did to me only an hour ago.

I rest my head on her shoulder and kiss her cheek. She pauses what she's doing and relaxes her body into me.

"You don't have to clean up. I can do it. You go sit outside and relax," I murmur into her neck.

She squirms her shoulders—I'm assuming to try to block the tickling my beard is causing. "No, you cooked. The least I can do is clean." She turns her head to face me and leans in for a kiss, which I accept with fervor.

She groans into my mouth and turns her body around so she's fully facing me.

"I think the cleaning can wait," I say into her neck as I pick her up and she wraps her legs around my waist. Carrying her, I walk over to the couch where I sit down with her straddling my lap and deepen the kiss.

Tessa starts moving her hips in circles on top of my growing erection before leaning down to my neck, kissing and licking her way down my chest. She slowly picks her hips up off my lap, causing me to instantly miss her body against mine. Looking up at me through her eyelashes, she bites my nipple, causing me to let out a gasp. As her mouth moves down my body, she moves to the floor, kneeling in front of me. My breath catches in my throat at the realization of what's about to happen.

She puts her hands on the waist of my shorts and pulls, but with how I'm sitting, they don't move very far. I scoot my ass off the couch to help her remove my shorts and briefs—my body now angled awkwardly off the couch. Her eyes widen as she takes in my pulsing erection.

Tessa takes my cock in her hand and uses her thumb to spread the bead of pre-cum that was accumulating at the head. She lowers her head down, making me think this is it, but she just sucks the liquid off her thumb. Slowly, she starts stroking me up and down while watching my face. I can't take my eyes off of her; she's so fucking beautiful.

After rubbing her hand over my growing cock she sits up on her knees, leans over my lap, and licks my cock from base to head. It pulses in response to the sensitivity.

Once back to the tip, she licks around the head and then gently blows on it before taking it into her mouth. Still using her hand to stroke my shaft, she uses her mouth to lick and suck at the head and underside. She reaches her other hand under my cock and lightly grabs my balls, gently massaging and giving them a slight tug before taking my cock into her mouth, causing me to hit the back of her throat. Fuck, she takes my cock like a dirty girl. I reach my hand up and bite my palm to keep from saying my thoughts out loud. She didn't seem to be into that last night.

"Fuck," I moan out, managing to keep the rest of my thoughts inside. This is so erotic I want to lean my head back and enjoy it, but at the same time, my eyes are glued to her. Her eyes are starting to water and I see saliva start to drip out the side of her mouth. Once she starts to gag she pulls back but continues with the hand strokes. She pulls back to swallow then moves her mouth down to my balls. I can't fully see what she's doing, but my body tightens as I feel her lick the center of my sack.

I let out a moan as she takes one ball into her mouth and gently sucks on it, then releases it and does the same to the other. Pulling her mouth away from my balls, her hand starts back up, cupping and massaging them as she takes my length back into her mouth, taking me back as far as I can go. That motion makes me feel pressure build in my body and I pull her hair slightly, moaning out, "Tessa, I'm about to come."

Instead of pulling back, she continues the rhythm, simply humming in response, adding a new sensation on my shaft, causing me to explode into her mouth. She doesn't pull back or stop the movement once I've come. Instead, I feel her swallow with my dick still inside her mouth. Before she pulls back she sucks the tip and gives it a lick. When she's done she sits back on her feet, licks her lips, and takes her hand to wipe the spit from her mouth.

I adjust myself back on the couch and lean forward to help her up, pulling her back onto my lap, guiding her in for a kiss. This woman is remarkable. "You're so incredible. That was so hot," I say as she pulls back from the kiss to lean her head against my chest.

"Yeah. I am pretty amazing, aren't I?" She chuckles and the feel of her body vibrating with laughter sends another jolt to my cock.

Chapter 51

Tessa

I cleaned the kitchen while Graham took a shower to clean himself up. After he gets out we head back outside and I wander over to the treehouse I spotted the night before and sit on one of the swings hanging from a tree branch. Graham sits on the swing next to me and we just sway in silence for a while.

Graham glances at me with a look of hesitation before speaking. "So, I've been thinking, and I've been thinking this for a while now—about how you said before that you're sad your future children won't know your mom." He pauses as he takes in my reaction. I nod, agreeing with the statement, curious as to where his thought process is going. "The way you described that canoe trip, I felt like I was there with you. I think you should write down your memories. Make them into a book for your children. You draw—I mean, that's what you do for a living—so you wouldn't have to hire an illustrator."

I sit there taking in his suggestion.

When I don't say anything he lets out an exhale. "I did some research and it doesn't seem like too much work to create a book. You don't have to publish it for the world, so it wouldn't cost as much as if you were trying to become a full-blown published author. It would just be for you and your family."

His eyes gleam with excitement as he continues to share his ideas. I look out at the view in front of us before I say anything. I'm not sure why I feel like being so dramatic in dragging out my response, but the urge is strong so I lean into it. "That idea . . . it's not a bad one," I say as I peek over at him. "I can make a small little series of books for my kids, starting with my earliest memories of those family vacations. It doesn't even just have to be family vacations, it could be holidays like Christmas or Halloween."

I get more excited as I think of all the possibilities this idea Graham had unlocks. "Actually, that's a great idea, Graham!" I turn so my body is angled toward him. His smile becomes brighter, causing his eyes to crinkle at the sides.

We sway on the swings for a little while longer, discussing semantics of what Graham had researched. The more he shares the more eager I feel to get started on this project. Unfortunately, I didn't bring any of my art supplies so it's going to have to wait until we get back home, but it doesn't stop my mind from planning.

"You know, if it'll help, whenever you start to work on this, I could type up or write down your memories as you tell them, while you draw the pictures to go along with it," Graham says with so much earnestness in his voice.

I look at him—really look at him. "You would do that?" I ask in astonishment.

The look he gives me tells me his answer before he responds. "Of course I would do that. I wouldn't have offered it if I didn't mean it."

The heart of this man makes me swoon. But all of a sudden I get nervous, wondering what's wrong with him that could explain why he isn't in a relationship. He's perfect. He cares about people other than himself. The relationship he has with my parents is beyond anything I've ever seen. And the sex . . . I won't even mention the sex because thinking about him with anyone else like that makes me want to punch an imaginary woman.

"Where'd you go?" he asks, regarding me with concern.

"Hmm? What?" I ask while trying to think of an answer to give.

I decided to be honest. "Honestly? I was wondering what's wrong with you." The look on his face makes me giggle.

Graham blinks a few times and furrows his eyebrows. "Well . . ." He stumbles over his thoughts. "You really think something is wrong with me?"

I reach over, placing my hand on his leg. "It's just that you're so perfect. I don't understand how you're single. There has to be some hidden secret that has scared all the other women away." I give his leg a squeeze beneath my hand.

He chuckles at my answer. "Why does it have to be that something is wrong with me? What if I've wanted to be single so I haven't been looking?" he asks, arching a brow. "You know, I could say the same thing about you," he adds pointedly.

"Touché," I say, giggling. "But, for all you know, I could be a walking red flag." I shrug as I pull my hand back.

Before Graham gets to respond his phone starts to ring. He pulls it out of his pocket and looks at the screen. "I have to get this," he says before he looks at me, stands up from the swing, and walks away.

I take this moment to pull out my phone and text Nelly.

Me:

Nelly-Belly Peters:

Okay, 1. I'm glad you're alive. You've been grieving so I've been giving you space, and 2. You can't just text me all those exclamation marks and not say anything else! Is everything okay? Nothing bad?

Me:

I'm at a cabin in the Blue Ridge Mountains. With Graham. For the weekend.

Nelly-Belly Peters:

And . . . you fucked him didn't you?

Nelly-Belly Peters:

Yes, girl! Get you some good Brawny paper towel man dick! Was it good?

Me:

1. You're jumping to conclusions, and 2. SO GOOD. He gives the best head I've ever had in my whole life. That man could eat me for breakfast, lunch, and dinner and I'd still be craving his mouth on me.

Nelly-Belly Peters:

FUCK YEAH GIRL! Say more!

Me:

*Well, I laughed during sex. *Cringe face emoji**

Nelly-Belly Peters:

. . . go on . . .

Me:

He talks dirty, and I've never been with someone who does that, so it took me by surprise. And . . . I laughed.

Nelly-Belly Peters:

Shut up! I've seen the filthy books you read. You gobble that shit up. Why'd you laugh?

Me:

It's one thing to read it, but a complete other thing to experience it in real life.

I look up from my phone and find myself observing Graham walk around the fire pit, talking to whomever called. I just sit there staring as my phone vibrates with unanswered texts.

Nelly-Belly Peters:

> *Here's what you need to do. You're going to take matters into your own hands. You're going to initiate sex. And YOU are going to talk dirty.*

Nelly-Belly Peters:

> *I'm talking full on dirty! Compliment his dick. Tell him you want to ride his face. When he's in you scream, "Oh yes, daddy, fuck me like the dirty girl I am!"*

Nelly-Belly Peters:

> *I'm going to need you to acknowledge that you are with me.*

Nelly-Belly Peters:

> *Tessa.*

Nelly-Belly Peters:

> *Tessa Elaine, the only acceptable reason for you to not be answering me is if you are currently getting some dick!*

Me:

> *Holy shit, calm down! I made the move the first time. I kissed him. And . . . I'm the one who brought the condoms.*

Nelly-Belly Peters:

> *YOU KISSED HIM? AND YOU BROUGHT THE CONDOMS! You go girl! But now, you need to show him you can be good with the dirty talk. I'm sure he feels super embarrassed, ESPECIALLY because you LAUGHED at him.*

I shake my head at Nelly's texts, but I start thinking maybe she's right. Maybe I should try to talk dirty. What's the worst thing that could happen? I'm bad at it and we laugh? That already happened.

I stand up and head toward the cabin. Graham stops walking as he catches sight of me and I point to the hot tub then back to the house, silently letting him know I'm going to change into my swimsuit.

I come back down after getting dressed and don't see Graham anywhere. But as I walk to the hot tub I see that it's already turned on. I set my towel down and climb in. After a few moments alone, relaxing with my head back and my eyes closed, I hear the sound of the glass door sliding closed.

"I brought us out some lunch," Graham says, holding a plate with two sandwiches along with two bottles of water.

I sit up a little straighter, making my chest come above the water. The cool air causes my nipples to pebble with the temperature change. Graham's gaze dips to my breasts for a moment before he sets the plate and bottles down on the side of the hot tub. He offers me his towel to dry my hands before putting it down next to mine.

Then he climbs in the hot tub and sits next to me before picking up a napkin I didn't see on the plate and one of the sandwiches. "I like your bathing suit." He lifts his chin, pointing it at me.

I'm wearing a forest green, full-coverage halter top, and a pair of high-waisted black bottoms that he can't see beneath the water. "Thanks, I like yours too." He's wearing a pair of bright orange swim trunks that stop slightly above his knees.

We sit in silence while we eat our lunch, and once again find ourselves staring out at the view of the mountains. I can't get over how green the trees are and the bright colors of the flowers waking up from their winter slumber.

Graham is the first one to break the silence. "That was Grant who called. He wanted to make sure everything was good here. He pays someone to come out weekly to make sure things are in order and that the cabin hasn't taken on any squatters. So he wanted to make sure the last report he got from them was accurate." He starts rambling. "Plus, he asked if I grew balls and finally kissed you." He says the last part with his face down, his eyes looking up at me through his lashes.

I howl with laughter. "And what did you tell him?" I inquire.

He shifts in his spot and looks at me. "I told him no, I did not grow balls and make a move. However, and I hope you don't mind, I did tell him that you had the courage for the both of us and kissed me." I laugh even harder at that. "But, I didn't say anything about the other activities we participated in. He did ask though, so he might suspect."

I shrug my shoulders. "It's okay if you do. I told Nell. And honestly, my dad probably assumes we're having sex this weekend too." I say it so nonchalantly but it causes Graham to choke on his water and he starts to cough.

"Fuck!" he says when he finally catches his breath. "I didn't even think about what your dad would think with us going out of town together." He shakes his head and then adds, "But we live together. For all he knows we've been having sex since you first moved in."

This time I shake my head. "No. He knows we haven't had sex before. I told my mom it's been a very long time since I've seen any action." His eyes bug out with my openness about my sex life with my parents. "I may have mentioned something about cobwebs," I say, waving a hand in a "no big deal" gesture. Graham just looks at me with astonishment and sits back against the wall.

We stay in the hot tub, pruning, way past the recommended soak time. I get out first and quickly grab my towel to wrap around myself. The April air is a lot cooler here in the mountains.

"I'm going to go in and change. Then can we make a fire?" I ask Graham as I grab the plates and start walking toward the door.

"Yeah, that sounds great." He gets out of the hot tub and rubs the towel over himself but hangs it up after. He's made of thicker skin than I am if he's able to walk around like that after sitting in the hot tub for so long.

As I walk inside he turns to the path that leads to the fire pit. I put the plates away and go upstairs, changing into a pair of pajama shorts with my beige hoodie. I walk over to the nightstand and grab a condom, slipping it into my pocket before grabbing a blanket off the bed and heading back outside.

Chapter 52

Graham

When Tessa comes back outside I'm sitting on one of the chairs and she's sitting opposite the chair I'm in. My eyes travel up and down her body before she takes a seat, covering her voluptuous thighs with that cursed blanket. Part of me wishes she would have sat on my lap, but I guess I can't be too upset. Plus, I'm in my swim trunks, which are still damp.

"So, tell me another story you have about your mom. Something we can add to the book for your children," I say, leaning my head back against the chair, my gaze still locked on her.

She leans her head back and closes her eyes. "Hmm. Let's see." She takes in a few deep breaths, concentrating. "Do you want family vacation memories or just memories of my mom in general?" she asks, shifting her head side to side.

"Whichever memory you're in the mood to share. I want to hear them all!" I respond genuinely.

She angles her head toward me, giving me a lazy smile. "You're a smooth talker. Has anyone ever told you that?"

Her comment makes me chuckle, but I don't say any-thing. "The first memory I remember—one that isn't from a story someone told me—is one of my mom and I. I remember she liked to play the radio while she cleaned, and she would use whatever cleaning utensil she was using as a microphone. So, for example, if she was doing dishes she would sing into a ladle, if she was sweeping she'd sing into the broom handle, if she was dusting, the end of the duster became her microphone. My mom wasn't the best singer, but she was very enthusiastic when she sang. It made her voice calming to listen to."

She pauses, lets out a small laugh, and shakes her head at the memory. "Well, anyway, I remember wanting to help her clean one day. So, as she was doing her thing, I grabbed a broom and started following her around. MC Hammer came on and she turned around so fast I'm surprised she didn't get whiplash. She picked me up and started dancing using my hand as a microphone." She starts dancing in her seat, bobbing her head to the music playing in her mind. "After the chorus played she put me down and started doing the dance from the music video. Meanwhile, I'm over there just spinning in circles because I don't know the moves. My dad comes in and immediately jumps in, breaking into the dance moves too." She starts laughing at whatever images are playing in her mind. "I can't tell you how old I was exactly, maybe four. It was a good day though."

I could listen to her talk all day. Her dulcet voice is like honey in my ears, so sweet and delectable. She looks over at me and smiles.

"You have a very nice voice," I blurt out without giving any thought to how it might sound.

Her cheeks turn a rosy pink as she blushes. "Thanks," she says as she pulls her blanket up higher on her body like she's trying to hide from my compliment.

We carry on our conversation for hours until my stomach starts to growl. I look at my phone to check to see what time it is and see that it's almost time for dinner. "I'm getting hungry. I bought some steaks, would you like me to grill them?" I ask, leaning forward in my chair.

She nods. "Oh yes! Anything I can help with in the kitchen?"

We both move to the kitchen, and while I prepare the steaks, she makes sides to go with them. Even though we've lived together for weeks, we've never cooked together. It feels so domestic—so right. I steal glances at her dancing to music only she can hear in her head, which makes me turn on music from my phone. I turn on "U Can't Touch This" and mimic what her mom did in her story by grabbing a spatula and singing into it. She turns to look at me and doubles over in laughter before grabbing a spoon and joining in.

After dinner we return to the fire pit. This time, instead of sitting on a chair, she lays her blanket out and lies down on it so she's staring up at the sky. I sat down in my chair before she was down, not knowing if she wanted me to join her, so I just stay in my seat.

Tessa puts her hands in her pocket and I see her hands fidget through the fabric of her hoodie. She takes a deep inhale then sighs as she turns her head toward me. "It's gorgeous out here. I could move here and be perfectly content." She smiles then turns her head back toward the sky.

The stars are starting to appear. With us being far away from the light pollution of a city, they are so much brighter than I'm used to. "It really is." I take a deep breath, sucking in the mountain air mixed with the smoky aroma coming from the fire.

"You can join me, you know. There's plenty of space on this blanket if you don't want to be too close." She looks at me coyly and bites her bottom lip.

She doesn't have to ask me twice. Plus, I'm still in my swim trunks and I'm getting a tad chilly, so snuggling up next to her will help warm me up.

As soon as I'm on the blanket next to her she lifts my arm and maneuvers it under her so she's cuddled into my shoulder. Her hand goes up to my chest and she starts running her fingers through my chest hair. The sensation sends a steady flow of blood to my cock, causing me to harden. Her leg folds on top of my thigh, making me harden even more.

"Are you okay that we didn't go do anything today? We leave tomorrow, so there's not much time for us to do much then either," I say, rubbing my hand up and down her arm.

She shifts her body slightly so she can look up at me. "Yeah. I had a really nice time. Maybe we can come again sometime. Then I can bring the proper attire for going on a hike." My heart swells at the idea that she'd like to come back here with me.

Tessa leans in and kisses me tenderly as she slowly moves herself into a position where she's leaning over me. "You should feel how wet you make me," she whispers in my ear, causing the semi I was sporting to stand at full attention.

My eyes widen and my breath catches. I pull back slightly to look in her eyes. She's got a shy smile on her face, watching me as she pulls her bottom lip between her teeth again. She sits up on her knees and grabs my hand. Ever so slowly she guides my fingers to her soaking wet pussy, causing a low growl to escape my throat. It also doesn't get past me that she's not wearing panties. Again.

"Fuck, Tessa," I say as I adjust my hand to a better position between her legs.

She widens her stance a little bit and wiggles her eyebrows at me. Then she steals a glance down at my tented swim trunks. "Maybe we should do something about this," she says with a husky voice as she runs her finger along the outside of my trunks.

I let out a sigh of regret as I realize where we are. "Hang on, I have to go get a condom." I move to get up when she puts one hand on my chest and shakes her head. She takes the hand that guided my hand to one of my favorite places and puts it in her pocket. When she pulls it back out she's holding a condom and giving me a seductive smile.

My dick pulses at the thought that she planned for this. Tessa intended for us to have sex out here. Just the thought of that makes me feel feral for her. She leans down, releasing my bulging cock from its prison, then bends her head down and licks the pre-cum from the tip. I watch as she opens the condom and slowly rolls it down my shaft. And fuck me, if that isn't one of the most alluring things I've ever seen.

I'm still massaging the inside of her pussy with my fingers as I watch her take control. She might not be one for dirty talk, but she sure knows how to make moves.

She suddenly stops me by pulling my hand out of her, then stands up and removes her pajama shorts. Leaving her hoodie on, she moves to where she's standing over me, one leg on each side of my hips.

I feel like I'm dreaming. I move my hand to my thigh and try to discreetly pinch myself. She lets out a soft chuckle, letting me know I wasn't as discreet as I'd hoped. Tessa looks so unhurried as she drops down to kneel above my aching cock. She grabs it in one hand, guiding it to her entrance. With her other hand, she uses her fingers to part her lips as she slowly lowers herself onto my cock.

I moan with pleasure as I feel the heat of her pussy as it slides over my dick.

"Fuck, yes. I love how you fill me up and stretch me out." Tessa moans unexpectedly, causing me to choke on a chuckle.

Her head whips up to my face at the sound of laughter escaping my chest, and her face reddens as I bite my lip. "Are you laughing?" she asks, biting back a laugh of her own.

"Nuh uh. Nope." I shake my head. "Why would I be laughing?" I ask. This time I do laugh.

She's fully seated on me, but instead of moving she shakes her head and sighs. "I knew the dirty talk was a bad idea."

I reach my hand up to cup her cheek, moving her face so she's looking at me. "Hey, you don't have to say anything if you're not comfortable. I will enjoy this even if we're both quiet." I think for a minute before adding, "Well, maybe I'd appreciate a few moans to stroke my ego and to let me know you're enjoying yourself." This makes her laugh again.

"No. I want to. But without going into details of my past, I've never done it before, so I'm worried it's going to come out weird and awkward," she says with a pout on her face.

I lean up and take her bottom lip into my mouth, giving it a suck before I softly bite it then release it just to give her a soft kiss. "Okay. Well, now that I know you want to try, I'll be encouraging. I'll say some things and you can respond however you feel best. And if at any point it feels weird, just say so." I search her eyes for any sign of agreement.

She nods her head, leans in for a kiss, then pushes my chest. "Now lie back down and let me ride you like I've been dreaming about," she says and then starts laughing, which makes me laugh. I love that she feels comfortable enough to laugh at herself.

She starts off slowly, moving her hips in circles, then she pulls up and slides back down. My hands move to her hips to help guide her as my body feels out the rhythm she's creating.

Once she's figured out her cadence, my hips join in, syncing up with her. "That's right. Ride my cock like the good girl you are," I say, testing out how she reacts to me giving her praise. She leans her head back and lets out a moan in response.

Then she slides one hand up under her hoodie and starts playing with her breast. The position I'm in would make it awkward to reach for the other one, so I continue to grip her hip with one hand and move the other between us to find her swollen clit. Once my thumb finds what it's looking for I start rubbing it in circles.

"Fuck! Yes! Keep doing that," she gasps out as she arches her back and keeps bouncing on my cock.

Tessa continues for a few more minutes before the walls of her pussy start squeezing my cock, letting me know she's close to the edge. I don't let up—my hips following her rhythm or my thumb with the massaging as her body finds its release.

Once her body relaxes and she comes back to the present I sit up, quickly switching positions so I'm on top. When her back is on the blanket I bend over and claim her mouth with a possessive kiss. While kissing her I pump my cock in and out of her wet pussy. Reaching my hand up her hoodie, I pull and twist at her nipple. The touch of my cold fingers makes her gasp.

I move my kisses down to her neck and she groans out, "Harder, Graham. I want you to fuck me harder." As soon as those words leave her mouth my thrusts get harder as the familiar tingle of my incoming orgasm starts to build. My balls tighten and my toes start to curl as I'm seconds away from coming. I give a final thrust before pulling out, coming hard and fast in the condom as my breaths come out as a pant.

I lean forward, placing my forehead against hers and closing my eyes as I breathe in the scent of the air around us. When I open my eyes, I see her staring at me with a sated smile on her face. She lifts her chin and gives me a gentle kiss before pulling her mouth back.

"You're incredible," I say, holding her stare. "I could easily get lost in you."

Chapter 53

Tessa

My heart started thumping faster in my chest at his admission.

"I could easily get lost in you."

I hold his gaze, afraid that if I look away he'll take the words back. He had the bravery to speak words that I feel so deeply in my being. Except, if I were being totally honest with myself, I've *found* myself in him. Instead of saying anything though, I lift my head up and kiss him again.

The sound of a twig snapping in the not-so-far distance causes us to break apart and look at the treeline. The only light on is the light from the moon and stars, the last of the kindling in the fire, and the glow of the kitchen light coming from inside the cabin. If it's more than an animal walking through the woods I wouldn't be able to see it.

After what feels like an eternity of squinting toward the treehouse, a large raccoon saunters into the glow of the light near the cabin. Graham and I both let out relieved laughs.

"On that note, maybe we should head inside and clean up," he says, pulling his trunks up and handing me my pajama shorts.

I slide the shorts on and grab his outstretched hand, letting him pull me up. I scrunch my toes around a bit of the blanket, and lift my leg to pull up the blanket. I lean over slightly to reach for the blanket, and once I've got it cuddled against my chest I look up and see Graham watching me with amusement on his face. "Did you just use your toes to pick up that blanket?" He chuckles.

I grin and nod. "Sure did. God gave me these long monkey toes, might as well take advantage of them," I say, looking down at my feet as I wiggle my toes.

He reaches for my hand and we walk toward the house, quietly trying not to scare the raccoon. When we get inside he spins me around and pulls me against him, causing me to release a squeal.

"So, do you want to shower first, or do you want me to shower first." He pauses and leans into my neck and whispers the next part into my ear. "Or we could shower together. Get a little more messy before we clean up."

My core tightens and wetness pools in between my legs. "Definitely the third option," I say in a breathy whisper.

He nods, grabs the blanket from my arm, and tosses it onto the table then leads me up the stairs to the bathroom. He somehow manages to lose his swim trunks along the way, so he's butt-ass naked by the time we get there. When he turns to look at me I'm greeted by a very hard cock.

I bring my hand to my mouth and bite my finger. "Oh," I gasp.

"Did you still want to practice dirty talk?" he asks in a husky voice.

Nodding my head I bite my lip and respond with a gulp. "Yes."

His pupils dilate with lust as he stares at me through hooded bedroom eyes. "Take off your clothes like a good girl," he orders.

I clumsily reach for the hem of my hoodie and pull it up, letting my tits bounce as I drop my arms by my side, leaving my curves on display. I swallow the saliva that is collecting in my mouth at the onslaught of arousal I feel as a result of seeing him standing fully naked and erect in front of me. My hands slide up my thighs and as they reach the waistband of my pajama bottoms, I stop and shake my head.

"I want you to do it. Get on your knees and finish undressing me," I manage to say with more confidence than I feel.

"As you wish." He falls to his knees and plants a kiss on the soft skin above my shorts. My thighs squeeze tightly of their own accord, trying to put pressure on my aching center. He drags his hands up my legs, starting at my calves. When he reaches the top of my shorts he ever so slowly pulls them down. As he lowers my shorts, he trails kisses down my legs, then he taps each foot to get me to step out of them.

He looks up at me expectantly when he's tossed my shorts behind him. I take a steadying breath as I gather my thoughts and channel my inner Rory from *Rekindling the Flame*. "I want you to tongue fuck my soaking pussy," I say, watching the fire in his eyes grow.

Graham looks at me and says, "You might want to lean back against the counter."

As soon as my ass is slightly pushed against the counter he hooks one arm around my knee and hikes it over his shoulder, opening me wide for him. He takes in a deep inhale that makes my cheeks grow hot knowing he's smelling my arousal. And before I have time to prepare myself he dives his tongue into my center, causing me to mewl. My grip on the counter tightens, causing my knuckles to turn white. My mind goes blank. I can't concentrate on anything but the feel of his mouth on me, his beard slightly scratching my upper thighs.

After a few moments, I remember I'm supposed to be practicing this dirty talk thing that he enjoys, so I let out a moan. "Graham, your tongue is pure magic in my pussy. Now add your fingers and make me come."

He responds by letting out a groan while sliding two fingers deep inside me. Once his fingers are inside he moves his mouth to focus on my clit. Within seconds I lose all control, scream out his name, and come all over his fingers and down his beard.

Graham leisurely lowers my leg, removes his fingers, and starts kissing up my body. As he stands he takes one nipple in his mouth, tugging and pulling on the other one. I let out another whimper as my legs start to give out on me.

When he pulls away he gives me a smirk before taking a few steps back to the shower and reaching in to turn on the faucet. "Fuck, Tessa, that was hot."

Once the water is a decent temperature we both get in. I wash my hair and then we take turns washing each other. When I'm done, I steal a few kisses before I step out to dry off.

After I'm out, I put on a pair of panties and climb into bed. Once he's finished he puts a pair of briefs on, then climbs in on the other side. Snaking his arm around my back, he pulls me in to cuddle him, leaning in the short distance and giving me a tender kiss on my forehead.

Graham takes in a deep breath that tells me he's about to say something so I sit patiently waiting. I scoot my body closer to him, trying to close any space there is between us. Finally, he asks, "What's going to happen when we get back home?" I can hear a tinge of concern in his voice.

I tilt my head so I can see his face. "What would you like to happen?" I'm worried about being the one to vocalize my desire to put a label on us. If it were up to me, he'd be my boyfriend and I'd be moving into his room when we got back. But I don't want to presume that's where his mind is at.

He takes me in. His hazel-green eyes look mossy as his eyes search mine for an answer I'm not wanting to voice. "I'd like you to be my girlfriend—if we aren't too old to use those terms. Boyfriend and girlfriend." His eyes take on a look of nervousness as he awaits my response.

I let out a girlish giggle, grabbing his face and pulling him into a kiss. "I'd love to be your girlfriend." My answer makes a smile spread across his face, causing wrinkles to form at the edges of his eyes.

He takes another steadying breath. "Okay. Great." He looks at me again, cautiously, before asking, "And are we the type of boyfriend and girlfriend who sleep in separate rooms? We already live together, but I'd like to know if I need to clear out some drawers and closet space when we get home." He arches a brow at me.

Another giggle bursts free. "Why, Graham Link, are you asking me if I want to share a bedroom with you?" I pull back slightly to give him what I hope is a flirtatious smile.

"Well, uh . . . ." he stammers and his nervousness is absolutely adorable. "I don't want to assume that because we're sharing a bed here that it means you don't want to have your own space at home."

The thoughtfulness behind his concern makes my heart melt. "If you don't mind sharing a bedroom with me, I'd love to move out of the guest room and into your room—*our* room," I say, leaning in for another kiss. He lets out a loud sigh of relief as I pull back.

We both scoot down into a lying position and I roll over to my side. He follows suit to spoon me. He kisses my cheek and whispers goodnight, but before I say goodnight back, I say, "Please wake me up for the sunrise if you're awake."

He nods into my neck and gives me another kiss. "As long as you promise not to chew my head off. Now, get some sleep, beautiful."

Chapter 54

Graham

The first thing I notice when I wake up is Tessa cuddled against my chest. The second thing I notice is that neither one of us woke up in time for her to see the sunrise. I kiss her forehead and look down at our bodies so I can assess the best way to untangle our limbs without waking her.

The second my feet hit the floor I hear a low grumble coming from behind me. "No. Come back to bed. Too early. Need sleep." Her comment makes me chuckle but when I glance at the clock I roll my eyes. She considers ten in the morning too early?

I walk around the bed to her side and lean down to kiss her again. "You can stay in bed. I'm going to go pee and then make some breakfast."

When I say the word *breakfast* she shoots up and cries. "We slept through the sunrise!" She throws the blanket aside and darts to the window yanking open the curtains. "We slept through the sunrise!" she cries again.

Walking up behind her, I wrap my arms around her waist and sink my face into her neck. I take a big inhale, feeling intoxicated by her scent. "It's okay. There will be more sunrises," I say as I kiss her neck.

She relaxes into my embrace and slumps her shoulders. "But it's our last morning here." She turns to look at me with her bottom lip sticking out in a pout.

"Well, this just gives us an excuse to come back," I respond before I suck her bottom lip into my mouth.

Tessa turns her body around in my arms so she can deepen the kiss. My morning wood becomes harder as she pushes her naked chest against mine. She pulls back lazily and smiles at me. "Did you say breakfast?"

Chuckling, I nod and bend down to give her a kiss on the cheek. "Yes I did. You can either crawl back into bed and sleep for a little bit longer and I can bring it up to you, or you can come down and sit in the kitchen as I cook."

"How about I cook for you? Breakfast is the one meal I'm good at." She looks up at me with a glint in her eyes.

"Sounds good to me." I smile back and give her ass a light smack causing her to jump and giggle at the same time. "Get to it then." I turn and head into the bathroom.

After I do my business and wash my hands, I walk downstairs to see Tessa bending down, looking in a bottom cabinet. I lean against the wall and stare shamelessly at her perfect ass in the leggings she put on. When she pops her head up and turns around she jumps at the sight of me.

"Holy shit you scared me. I didn't hear you come downstairs," she says, holding a pan in one hand and resting the other over her heart.

I put my hand over my own chest before I apologize. "I'm sorry. It's just the view; it was too good to not appreciate." This earns me an eye roll but I don't miss it as her cheeks turn a shade deeper.

I try to walk into the kitchen to help Tessa cook but she shoos me to the table. I'm not used to being kicked out of the kitchen, so I bounce my foot as I try to peek at what she's making. Once she's finished she beckons me back into the kitchen to help bring the plates to the table. When I come up next to her I see she made a feast for the two of us. There's pancakes, bacon, sausage, and scrambled eggs. She also sliced the fruit I bought but forgot about, and she added two slices of toast to both of our plates.

"I wasn't sure what you wanted and after looking in the fridge it looked like you bought the whole breakfast aisle for just a short weekend. I figured it needed to be cooked or it would get trashed." She gives me a nervous smile before adding, "We can bring home whatever we don't finish. I'll eat it on the way or for leftovers tomorrow morning."

"It's perfect." I close the distance between us, pull her in for a hug, and give her a kiss. Then I step back so I can grab the plates as she grabs the glasses of orange juice.

Instead of sitting outside by the fire pit, we opt to eat at the table facing the door to see the view from inside. Our conversation easily bounces between what our plans for the week are, the books we've been reading recently, the ideas she has for the memory book, and more about her best friend's upcoming wedding.

As we talk, my mind drifts to the future. I can see it so clearly—coming to this cabin a few times a year, going on vacations with her family, proposing with the ring Sherri gave me, starting a family of our own and creating family memories that she can add to those memory books for our children. I used to dream about marrying Tessa when I was a teenager, but when she moved away I thought I had to let go of that dream. Now that she's back and we've built a relationship stronger than what it was before she left, I can't help but allow those dreams to take root again. Of course it's too soon to propose now, but I can't imagine waiting a ridiculous amount of time.

Tessa's voice brings me back to the present. "What time did you want to leave?"

I look at my watch and consider her question. "Well, unfortunately, I have work tomorrow, so we should probably leave here no later than three. But I want to wash the bedding and towels before we go, so we can probably leave after that's done," I say, glancing around, making mental notes of everything I need to clean up. I don't want to leave Grant's cabin looking like a mess, even if he hires someone to come clean it.

She nods and looks around the room too. "How about you start the laundry, I'll clean up the kitchen, we can clean up the bathrooms together, and then go relax outside while the laundry is going," she says, pursing her lips and nodding as if she's agreeing to her own game plan.

Before we set to work on our chores I attach my music to the house speaker and hit shuffle on my playlist. "All the Small Things" blares through the house as we clean. I strip the bed and remake it with the extra bedding kept in the linen closet. I also grab the towels from the bathroom and bring them with me to the closet that houses the washer and dryer. By the time I've completed my chores and am heading to the bathroom to start straightening up, Tessa walks in the bathroom too and the music switches to "Forever Like That" by Ben Rector.

We both stand there in the bathroom, staring at each other, as the song plays around us, until I hold my hand out to her. She rests her hand in mine and I pull her to me, closing the gap between us. I position my other hand on her lower back, and she wraps her other arm around my shoulder and lays her head on my chest.

Chapter 55

Tessa

I'm in love with him. There's no other way to explain the feelings I have as we dance in the bathroom. We slow dance through the Ben Rector song and then through two other songs I don't know the names of. My brain is too busy repeating the words *I'm in love with Graham* over and over again to register what played.

We're in the car on the way back home after having made sure the cabin was spotless, Graham's hand resting on my thigh, his thumb drawing lazy circles on my skin as he drives. The music plays softly through the speakers while Graham hums along. I have my seat reclined so I can rest my eyes as my mind runs through all that happened this weekend.

We arrived as friends, and I can't decide if it was his initial hug goodnight or my kiss that set the rest into motion. Would I have been brave enough to make a move and make use of the condoms I brought if he hadn't pulled me in for that hug on Friday night? Would he have made a move on me if I didn't lean in and kiss him?

Taking a deep breath, I resolve to not let my questions consume me. I take my hand and place it on top of his, giving it a squeeze. He glances at me, smiles, and squeezes my leg and fingers.

"I thought you were sleeping," he says as he uses the volume controls on his steering wheel to turn the music down even lower.

"My mind won't stop moving a mile a minute."

"Want to talk about it?" He gives me another glance, his brows furrowing with concern.

I shake my head, even though his gaze has returned to the road. "Would this be this if I didn't kiss you?" I ask, moving my hand, gesturing between the two of us and looking at him with one eye open. Afraid to look at him, but also slightly afraid of not seeing his reaction.

He exhales and shrugs his shoulders. "I'd like to say definitively yes." He swallows then continues. "But I can't say for sure. Because I don't know if I was willing to risk our friendship if you rejected me. You're too important to me for me to lose what we had if coming on to you was unwanted." He looks at me for a beat longer than what is considered safe while driving.

Nodding my head, I respond, "I guess that makes sense. If I wouldn't have reciprocated your feelings you would have felt like I might want to move back with my dad. And you know I'm not quite ready to even visit the house yet." I look over at him and ask, "So, you were willing to continue to be unhappy just so I felt comfortable?"

"Tessa, I don't think you understand that I've liked you for a long time. My feelings for you go way beyond just having a crush. Just having you live with me as a friend made me happy," he answers, as if it was obvious. "I would have continued to lust from afar, as long as it meant you had a place to comfortably live. But even still, my attraction to you goes further than you living with me, it's about what makes you happy, even if I wasn't the one that was making you so. Tess, you deserve all the happiness in the world, and I will do whatever I can to make sure you can have that."

His response makes my eyes water. It's official, I am definitely in love with him.

"But, selfishly I'm thankful that you did kiss me, and even more thankful it led to more." His chuckle causes me to scrunch my nose in curiosity.

"Care to explain?" I inquire.

"You might think I'm a pig for this, but I was getting tired of taking care of myself in the shower. It's a bitch to have to clean the walls as often as I was." His admission has me snorting with laughter. "Plus," he adds, "the real thing is so much better than anything my mind was coming up with." He looks at me with lust in his eyes.

"Okay there, cowboy. Eyes on the road and mind out of the freshly-made memories until we're home safely." I laugh, guiding his face to look forward again.

He laughs too, but before he turns the music back up he says, in a serious tone, "But in all seriousness, I'm glad you made a move, because now I can concentrate on making sure you're happy and that you know that you're loved." He looks at me, the lust that was just in his eyes has turned to something akin to love. My cheeks flush and I squeeze his hand, unable to think of words to respond with.

After I've shared some of what's on my mind, I'm able to doze off, sleeping the remainder of the ride. Graham turning off the ignition after he parks in the driveway is what wakes me from my nap. I rub the sleep out of my eyes and sigh. I'm not ready to go back to reality yet. Once tomorrow rolls around I have to get back to work and try to move on from everything that happened before our trip to the mountains. But I'm thankful to have Graham here supporting me.

Graham grabs our bags from the backseat as I go to unlock the front door, but before I can turn the key the door opens. Grant's standing inside holding Catsby in his arms with a shit-eating grin on his face. He backs up and motions us inside as if this is his house.

"I was wondering when you would be getting in. Jay Catsby has been worried sick asking after you all weekend," he says, nuzzling into Catsby's neck.

Graham sets the bags down right inside the door and takes Catsby out of Grant's arms. "Thanks for stopping by and feeding him. I hope it was a lot of trouble and he shit on the floor so you had to clean it up." I gasp at him before he says, "I'm just kidding. We're grateful you offered us the cabin and to watch Catsby. Did Cori or Ethan come by at all?" He sets Catsby down who then saunters to me and rubs himself against my legs.

I sit down and rub Catsby's belly as I try not to listen to the brothers talk. They walk into the other room, making it easier on me to stop my eavesdropping. I take off my shoes, tossing them to the door and pick up Catsby, nuzzling my face into his black and white neck, causing him to purr. I consider getting up to take our bags to Graham's room but I don't know if Graham wants Grant to know about our change in relationship status yet. We didn't discuss when we would share the news with everyone.

They come back out of the kitchen and as I get a glimpse of them standing side by side I can't help but to think it's strange—they could be twins with their similarities. They have the same chocolate-brown hair, although Grant has some grays starting to peek through around the temples. They have the same stature and build, but Grant looks like he might hit the gym a little more than Graham. One of the only differences I see is that Grant has a clean-shaven face, while Graham keeps a neatly-trimmed beard. Thinking about Graham's beard and where it's been makes me blush a little as they continue their conversation. The two hug, Grant waves at me over his shoulder, and then he walks out the front door leaving Graham and I alone.

We look at each other for a moment before I stand up. I walk to my bag and start meandering toward the back bedroom. "You better have grabbed that bag because it holds the goods," Graham says from behind me.

"Maybe," I say, dropping the bag as I pull out the box of condoms and take off running to the room.

"Oh, girl, you better run!" Graham yells down the hall, causing me to squeak with laughter as he chases me.

I wake up and immediately look for the clock.

Two in the morning.

I glance over and see Graham's chest rising and falling as he breathes. As I carefully climb out of bed, I listen for the soft snores coming from him, indicating that he's still sleeping.

Once I've made it into the bathroom I sit on the toilet to relieve my bladder and my emotions catch up to me. My body shudders as a sob escapes my throat. I grab toilet paper and wipe before standing up and walking to the mirror.

Leaning against the double vanity, I stare at myself in the mirror. I watch as the tears slide down my face. My brown eyes—the eyes I got from my mom—glassy with emotion. How can I move this quickly with Graham? Who do I think I am, feeling this happy?

Chapter 56

Graham

Waking up to go to work this morning is difficult to do when I just want to roll over and continue pleasuring Tessa. Not to mention, football tryouts start this afternoon so I won't even be home at a decent time. If I wasn't the head coach I'd try to dip out early to get home quicker, but I have responsibilities.

The only thing that helps make it easy is Tessa waking up with me, so I'm not leaving her in bed. While I'm getting ready she moves from the bedroom to the kitchen with her laptop and tablet. She looks determined to get back to work this morning, so I make breakfast for us as she sits at her computer, checking and replying to emails. When breakfast is ready she sets aside her things and we talk about the upcoming events of the day.

"Remember, football tryouts start today, so I won't be home until closer to eight tonight. Maybe you can invite your dad over for dinner?" I say between bites of my pancakes.

She shakes her head. "He's on nights, remember? But I'll be okay eating by myself. Is there anything in particular you'd like to eat? I can try to make it and have your dinner set aside when you get home." The domesticity of our relationship feels natural and has me wondering if it's normal for it to feel this easy so quickly.

"Whatever you make will be fine, but don't worry about leaving any out. I don't mind reheating it if it's in the fridge." I pick up our plates and rinse them off before placing them in the dishwasher.

Tessa nods and takes her thumbnail into her mouth, a habit I haven't seen her do in a while. I grab my keys from the counter and walk toward her. I lean down to give her a kiss, but instead of kissing her lips, she tilts her head to give me her cheek.

"I'll see you after school. Have a good day. I—" I cut myself off before saying *I love you*, even though I feel it. I don't want to say it too soon and scare her off.

"Have a good day. Good luck with tryouts," she says, not looking up at me before pulling her work materials back in front of her. My eyebrows knit together. I know I have to go to work, but it feels like she's pushing me out the door.

The day feels longer than usual as I prepare my students for the state tests that will start later this week. We review all the skills we've learned throughout the year by playing a *Kahoot!,* and the kids surprise me with how well they're able to bounce from topic to topic during the game. I don't want to toot my own horn, but I feel pretty confident in my students' abilities as we prepare for the reading portion of the test.

Once the school day is over, I lock up my classroom and head over to the gym to meet Kyle Sydney, one of the gym teachers who helps me coach the football team.

"Hey, Graham, how was your weekend?" he greets me as I place my bag down next to his desk.

"It was good, nice and relaxing. I went up to the mountains for a little getaway." I don't mention going with Tessa. We went to high school with Kyle—he was a year behind us, but he knows Tessa. He's one of the lucky bastards who took her out on a few dates back then. Sherri got a kick out of him working here too, especially since she knew about my crush.

"Oh, I bet that was nice. Bring anyone special? Or did you go to hook up with the locals?" he asks, lifting his eyebrows at me.

I'm not about to feed into his need for details so I just look at him with a *wouldn't you like to know* smirk. Getting the hint that I'm not discussing it any further, he takes out a blank sheet of paper and starts writing down names as the boys start gathering outside of his office.

After we compare the list Kyle made with the list I have of completed parent consent forms, we take the boys out to the field. Once on the field, we run through stretches before breaking the boys up to run drills. The first day of tryouts actually runs smoother than I expect and pickup comes quicker than I anticipate. When the last of the boys are picked up Kyle and I say our goodbyes I head home with a smile on my face, thinking about how I get to go home to Tessa as my girlfriend and not just my roommate.

I pull into the driveway and notice the lights are off in the front of the house and I can't help but wonder if Tessa went to bed early. Walking into the house, I hear sniffling coming from the couch. I turn on the light and see Tessa curled up with a blanket pulled up to her chin. At first, I think she's watching a movie that's making her cry, but when I walk past the TV I see that it's not even on.

I move to the couch, and as I sit down, I lift her head into my lap. I run my fingers through her hair and whisper, "What's wrong, Tess?"

She sniffles again and rubs her hand under her nose, wiping away the snot that was collecting there. "I know we just agreed to be a couple, but I don't think we should do this."

My heart sinks as I register the words she just said.

I look at her, curled up and my mind flashes back to how she pulled into herself so deeply when she lost her mom. I blink a few times before I ask, "What makes you think that?" I try to keep the emotion from my voice, but I can hear the wobble.

Tessa pulls the blanket higher under her chin and shakes her head. I take a deep breath, trying to calm myself down. My anxiety is starting to spike because I don't understand where this is coming from. I thought we had a great weekend. Things were good when I left for work. What the hell happened to make her change her mind?

"Tessa, baby, talk to me. Please." This time I can hear the desperation in my voice.

She sits up, and instead of moving closer to my side, she pulls away, sitting on the opposite side of the couch. My heart starts to beat faster. "I just think this is a mistake." She won't even look at me as she talks. Instead, she focuses on the edge of the blanket as she plays with it.

My mind starts running through every single thing that happened this past weekend. I run through our morning, how happy she looked and seemed at breakfast, and then my mind catches on the memory of her being off when we said our goodbyes. "I'm very confused as to where this is coming from. I thought everything was going well," I admit, my tone is soft.

"My mother just died!" she yells, the sound startling me.

I nod my head, trying to piece together her train of thought. I'm painfully aware that Sherri died. She might not have been my mom, but she was the closest thing I had to one. I swallow a few times as I try to think of something—anything—to say. "I know," I say, reaching to touch her leg. I mentally slap myself on the head. Is that really the only thing I could think of?

She recoils from my touch. The movement hurts but I just bring my hand back to my lap. "Clearly not. If you truly understood that then you wouldn't think we should do this either. She *just* died." Her soft sniffles turn into full on sobs. "I shouldn't be this happy this soon," she whispers so softly I almost don't hear her.

Now I understand.

I slowly scoot toward her and gently pull her into my embrace. I run my hand up and down her arm as I kiss her forehead. "Tessa," I say softly, "your mom wouldn't want you to sit around being so sad that you can't find joy in life. She wouldn't want you to put off being happy because you think it's too soon." I continue to rub what I hope is a soothing motion on her arm.

Her sobs let up and turn into hiccups. "But, Graham, it's only been two weeks. How can I feel this happy already?" She takes in a deep breath but the hiccups continue. "It scares me with how happy you make me," she confesses in a whisper.

My heart swells with her admission, but I still feel crushed that she doesn't think she should be happy right now. "Do you think you need some time away from me?" I ask, then I hold my breath.

She shakes her head against my chest. "I don't know. I just miss her so much and I don't think I'm being fair to her." I squeeze her a little tighter. "It's too soon to be happy."

"How about you go take a shower and get in the bed. I'll sleep in one of the extra rooms—let you have some space until you decide what you want," I say as tears well in my eyes.

Tessa jerks her head away from me. "Is that what you want? To sleep away from me? You want space?" she yells, causing me to look at her with pure confusion on my face.

I hold my hands up and shake my head. "No. No, I don't want that. But it feels like it's what you might need." I take a breath and cautiously reach for her hand again. "Baby, I came home and you were crying, talking about how we can't do this. I don't want you to feel like I'm forcing you to do something if you don't feel like you're ready, even though I know in my heart that your mom would want you to be happy. Yes, even this soon. All I want is for you to be happy—I told you that yesterday. But if it's any consolation, I think your mom would be happy for us," I add the last bit thinking about the ring set I have in the room.

Tessa takes my hand and gives it a squeeze before nodding. Without saying anything she stands up and walks into my room—*our* room. She leaves the door open, but closes the bathroom door, leaving me out here in the living room with a growling stomach and an aching heart.

Chapter 57

Tessa

Once I get out of the shower I find the bedroom door is still open and the kitchen light is on. I crawl into bed, leaving the door open as an invite for Graham to join me if he wants. When I wake up in the morning the door is closed and Graham's not in bed next to me, nor does it look like his side of the bed was slept in. I look at the time and realize that even if he slept in here I wouldn't have seen him this morning. It's almost lunchtime so he's long gone to work.

I get out of bed and make my way to the kitchen where a note is lying by the coffee maker.

Tessa,

I'm not sure if you meant what you said last night about needing space, and I don't want to mess this thing up between us, so I slept in your old room last night. We still have tryouts this afternoon so I'll be at work late again, but please text or call if you need __anything__.

Yours,

Graham

Reading the note makes me irrationally angry. It makes me upset knowing he didn't come to bed last night. Even though the rational part of my brain knows he was just giving me the space I asked for. I toss the note in the trash and text my dad.

Me:

Hey daddy, want to go to Arlynes and grab some lunch?

Dad:

Sure, sweetie, I'll come pick you up in a few minutes.

Me:

Make it ten, I need to get dressed.

Dad:

Sounds good. See you then. I love you.

I set my phone down on the counter and make my way to the bedroom to get changed. It's almost May and the weather is finally starting to heat up so I dress in a pair of jean shorts and a T-shirt that my mom got me for my birthday last year. It has a picture of a sketchpad on it that says "I'm feeling a bit *sketchy* today." I put my hair in braided pigtails, slide on a pair of sandals, and walk out the front door.

I make it to my dad's truck just as he's walking out the front door. "Didn't I say I'd pick you up?" He pulls out his phone and checks his text messages.

"You did, but it didn't take me the full ten minutes so I figured I'd walk to you," I say as I open the front door and climb into the cab.

He gets in and puts his key in the ignition. Before turning it he looks at me and gives me a look of concern. "Everything okay, Bug? How was your weekend in the mountains?" he asks, giving me his full attention.

"It was good. We can talk about it at lunch. I'm starving," I respond, leaning over and starting the truck.

We drive the short distance to Arlynes with the only sounds being that of the wind coming through the open windows. Once we get to Arlynes we wave at the owner, Arlyne, who is behind the counter, as we pick a table near a window.

My dad and I look at our menus, more so out of formality, not really because we need it to see what we want. He orders the club sandwich with a lemonade and a side of fries. I order the Reuben, sweet tea, and a side salad. As we wait for our meals to arrive my dad stares at me with concern etched on his slowly-aging face.

"Okay, Bug, what's going on? Not that I'm not glad you asked me to lunch—I wasn't looking forward to heating up yet another casserole—but you look like something is eating you." He taps his fingers on the table in front of him.

I take in a deep breath and gnaw on the inside of my cheek. "I finally admitted my feelings for Graham this weekend." I let my confession sit in the air between us.

My dads face doesn't give away any sign of unease, but his words are laced with it. "And how did Graham respond?"

"He responded exactly like you expected he would—admitted that he's had a crush on me basically forever," I say, looking at the glass of tea that just arrived, running my finger through the condensation.

I hear my dad take a deep inhale. "So, why do you look down in the dumps? No offense, but shouldn't you be excited about that?"

Glancing up at him, I see his eyebrows are furrowed as he looks genuinely curious. "I am excited. But . . ." I pause as my emotions catch up to me and my voice starts to crack, "But Mom just died. I don't think it's okay for me to be happy so soon. Not this happy."

He reaches his hand across the table, palm up. I place my hand in his and he strokes the back of it. "Oh, Tessa. It's not too soon to feel happy. If I'm being honest, your mom would be thrilled to know that you and Graham finally admitted your feelings for each other. Your mom was very fond of him." He squeezes my hand to get my attention. "Losing your mom is not a good enough excuse for you to not find joy in your life. I know it's hard—believe me, I know. But she wouldn't want you to sit around being sad any longer than what you already did."

I sniffle, letting out a wet sigh. "But shouldn't it have taken me longer to be happy again?" I wipe my nose with a napkin off the table.

The waitress brings our food over and notices the sadness from our table and lets out a small whimper. My dad picks up a fry and eats it before responding to me. "Tessa, the grief of losing your mom hit you before she was even gone. Just because you don't feel like you've properly mourned her by feeding into this notion that sadness needs to last a certain amount of time, doesn't mean you won't still mourn her. You can grieve the loss of someone and still be happy." He's watching me intently.

"And where did you learn all this wisdom?" I ask with a weak smile on my face.

My dad shrugs his shoulders. "I started seeing a therapist when your mom got her diagnosis. The thought of losing my best friend, the person I've shared the best parts of my life with, almost killed me. I was in a dark place emotionally. Your mom told me I needed to see someone who could help me cope and come to terms with losing her." He takes in a steadying breath. "I'm still a ways from finding my own happiness with your mom gone—sadness comes and goes. You're feeling happy right now, but there will be days when the sadness sneaks up and you will feel as if you just lost her all over again. So, Bug, if you've found happiness, even the tiniest sliver, don't let the idea that you're letting her down by not feeling sad keep you from embracing it."

We eat the rest of our meal and talk about lighter topics, like Graham's idea for me to write a book of memories for my future children. The smile that crosses my dad's face when I speak about the book of memories is beautiful. Then we spend the car ride back to the house sharing memories of our vacations and different memories he thinks I should add.

He pulls the truck up the driveway and puts it in park as I unbuckle and climb out. He rolls the window down as I'm shutting the door and says, "Remember what I said. Your mom would want you to embrace your happiness. You can still mourn her without being sad. And when you are feeling sad, talk to Graham. I'm sure he'll be more than happy to sit and be sad about losing her too."

I thank him and then head inside.

I'm sitting on the floor, drawing a picture of my mom and I dancing in the living room when Graham comes home.

I look up at him and smile. "I missed you today," I say, causing him to let out a sigh of relief.

He drops his bag, tosses his keys on the coffee table and crosses the living room. Within seconds he's holding my face in his hands, searching my eyes with tears in his own. "I missed you t—"

I lean in and kiss him, cutting his words off.

Chapter 58

Graham

Hearing Tessa say she missed me today makes my body relax and release all the stress that has built up. I know I was worried about what she said last night, but I didn't realize just how much until I feel all the worry slip away as she pulls me in for a kiss. I drop to my knees in front of her and deepen the kiss. A soft moan escapes her mouth as her lips spread wider, letting my tongue sweep in.

She puts her hands on my chest and pushes me back a little, causing me to let out a groan of disappointment. "Your dinner is in the fridge. Go eat, then you can shower and we can go to bed. You've had a long day."

She's right. I know she's right, but I would rather go to the bedroom and not sleep.

I say as much, eliciting an eye roll.

"Graham, as much as I would love to have you buried deep inside me. You need to get some rest. It's almost nine and you have another long day tomorrow. We can fully make up this weekend," she says, eyeing me.

"Okay. Okay. I'll agree. But I don't like it." I pout as I stand up and make my way to the kitchen.

I open the fridge and see a plate of enchiladas covered in plastic wrap. I take it out and pop it into the microwave. As it's heating up I grab a glass out of the cabinet and fill it with water. I'm shuffling around the kitchen when Tessa comes in, carrying her sketchbook and tablet, setting them down on the island once she's seated.

She pushes the tablet closer to me so I can see what's on her screen. "What do you think?"

I pick it up so I can really look at it. Right away, I know what it's a picture of—it's Sherri and a young Tessa dancing in the living room. You can see the joy and love on both of their faces in this drawing. I look up at Tessa to find her looking at me with a hint of nervousness in her eyes.

"Tessa, this is beautiful." I look back down at the picture, really taking in all the details—the flowers on her dress, the crinkles at the edges of Sherri's eyes as she has her head tilted back, singing, and the curls framing both of their faces. Tessa's talent is truly remarkable.

"Thank you," she says, picking up the tablet and looking over the picture again.

She joins me at the island as I eat my dinner. She asks me about my day and how yesterday was with tryouts and everything. I tell her about preparing the kids for state testing and about the promise of those kids who have shown up for tryouts.

Once I share my day, I ask about hers. "So, besides working on your drawing, did you do anything fun today?"

Her cheeks turn a slight shade of pink, making me intrigued with what her answer might be.

"I did. I went to lunch with my dad." She glances at me through her eyelashes.

"Mm. How was that?" I ask as I take a sip of my water.

She bites her lip before she speaks again. "I told him about our weekend." I choke on my water. I know she was open about her sex life with her mom, but did she really tell her dad about us?

"And? What did he say?" I'm hesitant to know the answer.

"He's happy for us. He basically said *it's about time*." She picks up my water and takes a sip.

I look at her, confused. "Your dad said it's about time we hooked up?"

This time she chokes on the water. Maybe we shouldn't be having this conversation while either of us is drinking.

"What are you talking about? Why would he say that?" She looks at me like I grew three additional heads.

"You said you told him about our weekend and he said it was about time."

"I told him that we admitted our feelings for each other and that we hung out around the cabin talking, taking in the view of the mountains. I showed him some of the pictures I took. I said nothing about the sex. I don't need to give him a heart attack," she says, laughing.

I exhale, relieved to know it's still safe for me to show my face around Paul.

We talk a little more about her lunch with her dad and what she did when she got home as I finish eating.

As soon as I'm done I rinse my plate and put it in the dishwasher, along with my glass before pressing start.

Tessa holds her hand out to me. I take it and we walk hand in hand to the bedroom.

Climbing into bed after my shower, Tessa snuggles up to me. She places her arm across my chest and tangles her leg between my legs. I gently stroke my fingers up and down her shoulder as I feel her breath even out as she drifts off to sleep.

By the time the weekend's here I feel exhausted from staying late at work for tryouts, but I'm thankful that it's over and the team has been formed. Tessa and I agree we should have a relaxing Saturday and do something fun on Sunday.

Paul comes over Saturday night and we grill burgers, Tessa makes pasta salad, and I make an apple pie. We eat in the backyard, enjoying the early May evening. As I sit listening to Paul and Tessa talk, I start to try to mentally plan something special for the two of them for next weekend. It'll be their first Mother's Day without Sherri and I know it'll be hard on them both.

"I think my mom wants to do the Grand Canyon this summer." Paul's comment brings me back to the present.

"Oh, we haven't done that yet. Would she want to try to find somewhere to camp or stay in a hotel? What does Aunt Val think?" Tessa asks between bites of her burger.

"She and Dave seem to be for it. She wants to do the whole camping thing. But Val said if everyone is expected to actually camp then she doesn't think Lyla or Peter will come," he says.

I listen to them talk about their annual summer trip with ease. This will also be the first trip without Sherri, but it doesn't seem to have them in low spirits at the moment. "I went to the Grand Canyon for spring break with my roommate in college. It was gorgeous," I add to their conversation.

They both look at me, interested in my input. "Did you go camping, or get a hotel?" Tessa asks.

"We stayed in a hotel. My roommate wasn't a camper." I laugh. "But they have a ton of campsites, some even rent out tents and everything. I remember looking into it before he insisted we needed a hotel or he wasn't going."

"I think I'd want to camp—get the full experience." Tessa shakes her head and looks at her dad. "Screw Lyla and Peter; they don't have to come. It's not like they've gone every summer since we graduated high school anyway."

Paul snorts and admonishes Tessa. "Lyla and Peter have lives now that they're older. Lyla has that boyfriend she's been serious with, and Peter . . . Lord knows what he's busy with. But Val said Vince would still be cool with camping."

Tessa looks over at me and smiles. "You know, I would love it if you came with us this year." Her invitation makes my heart feel full with love. She's thinking enough ahead that she wants me to come on her family vacation with them.

"I would love to. As long as the dates don't interfere with football camp this summer," I say with a wide smile on my face.

Once dinner's over we say our goodbyes to Paul and Tessa turns on her music. We've started a tradition of playing music while we clean up the kitchen. I think it helps her feel closer to her mom. After we clean everything up, I grab her hand and spin her around, causing her to laugh. Then I bring her in close to me to slow dance, even though the song playing isn't a slow song. She lays her head on my chest and sways to the music.

I lean down and plant my lips to her forehead, mouthing into her hair, *I love you*, but I don't say it loud enough for her to hear. Instead I say, "Let's go to the bedroom," and I waggle my eyebrows, making her laugh again.

Chapter 59

Tessa

Tossing and turning in bed, I think about how I'm dreading tomorrow. It'll be my first Mother's Day without my mom and I don't know how my emotions are going to handle it. Earlier today, Graham told my dad and I that he has something planned for us and to be ready around ten, and to wear comfortable clothes. I roll over in bed and watch Graham as he sleeps on his back, his soft snores a comforting sound. I scoot over and snuggle against his chest, letting his snores drown out my racing thoughts and lull me to sleep.

I wake up when I feel the bed beside me sink down. I peek open one eye and see Graham sitting there holding a plate of scrambled eggs, bacon, and toast, with a mug of coffee. "Good morning, beautiful. I thought you might want to relax in bed for a bit before getting up to get ready for the day ahead."

I give him a sleepy smile, rubbing my eyes and letting out a yawn before I reach for the coffee. "You really are something special, do you know that?"

He leans down, giving me a kiss on the cheek before he sets the plate down on the nightstand. "Someone may have told me that a time or two," he says, winking at me.

I reach for my phone to check the time and see a text from Nell.

Nelly-Belly Peters:

*Thinking of you today, girl. Call me if you want to talk. *Heart emoji**

I quickly send her a response, thanking her and telling her to tell her mom "Happy Mother's Day" from me. Then I avert my gaze back to Graham, who has stripped down to his briefs to change into his clothes for the day. I grab a piece of bacon off the plate and eat it while I enjoy the view.

He glances over his shoulder and waggles his eyebrows at me. "Like what you see?"

"Definitely. Is my dad coming over soon, or is he coming over closer to us leaving?" I take a bite of toast, not taking my eyes off Graham and his mostly-naked body.

He looks at his watch before giving me an answer. "He said he'd be here around nine fifty."

Wanting to take my mind off what today is for a little longer, I set my coffee mug down and crawl across the bed toward him. "Then we have a little over an hour to kill before he gets here."

He takes a noticeable gulp then licks his lips as he nods his head.

"Have something in mind?" he asks, his voice husky with desire.

"I can think of a few things," I say, putting my finger on his chest and moving it down to the waistband of his briefs, keeping my brown eyes trained on his hazel ones.

I lower myself so I'm lying in front of him on the bed and I slide his briefs down over his hardening length. When he's fully exposed I roll over on my back, excited to try a position I read about in one of my books. I shimmy my way down so my head is dangling off the edge of the bed and I look up at Graham in time to see his eyes widen.

Taking his balls in my hand, I slowly massage and tug as I lick his shaft from base to tip. I gently kiss the tip before I say, "I want you to fuck my mouth, Graham."

Even from this far down I hear him suck in a deep breath. "Holy shit, Tessa. Are you sure?" Without saying anything I open my mouth wide, letting him know I'm waiting.

He grabs his cock and guides it into my mouth. I shift my body to make myself more comfortable now that he's in, and I adjust my hand on his balls and start massaging them as he slowly pulls back before he thrusts in. My other hand reaches up and grips his hips to encourage him to thrust faster and harder. He gets the hint and speeds up his pace, causing his cock to meet the back of my throat, making me gag.

At the sound of my gag he stops and looks at me. "Do I need to stop? Are you okay?"

I don't let him pull out of my mouth. Instead, I shake my head and talk around his shaft. "Keep fucking." I'm not sure if he heard the exact words I said because even to my ears they sounded garbled. But I do know he got the message because he picks the pace back up. I hollow my cheeks and use my tongue on the top of his shaft as the tip slams into my throat again. My eyes begin to water and I'm starting to drool.

From this position I'm unable to look up and see what his face looks like, but I hear him moan, "Fuck this feels incredible." I use my hand to slowly squeeze his balls. When I do that I feel his cock twitch in my mouth and his balls start to contract. "Tessa, I'm about to come. Should I pull out?"

I shake my head no and take my hand off his balls, gripping his hips with both hands, encouraging him to keep his rhythm going. Two more thrusts and he's filling my throat with his cum. When he's finished, I loosen my grip and he steps back. I slowly roll over on my stomach and make a show of taking a big swallow, even though I've already swallowed what he released in my mouth.

"Fucking hell, Tessa, that was so hot." He leans forward and kisses me. "Your turn," he says, moving towards my pajama shorts, but I stop him.

"No, sir. We don't have time for that, because I won't be satisfied with just your mouth," I say as I roll off the bed and grab my plate off the nightstand.

Graham groans as he throws his briefs back on and follows me out to the kitchen. "Now wait one minute. It's only fair that I get a taste too." He sticks out his lower lip causing me to laugh.

"And what would you like to tell my dad when he arrives and you're still balls deep in me? Because, like I said, I wouldn't be satisfied with just your mouth." I take a hearty bite of my now-cold scrambled eggs, as his face turns an adorable shade of red at the thought of my dad catching us. Instead of responding, he turns around and walks back to the room.

My dad arrives at exactly nine fifty like he told Graham he would. When I open the door to greet him I see he's wearing a pair of khaki cargo shorts, and a light purple polo shirt with black tennis shoes. He's dressed for comfort like Graham told us to be, and somehow we managed to match in a way. I'm wearing a light purple tank top, and black tennis shoes, but instead of khaki shorts like my dad, I'm wearing a pair of denim shorts.

He takes in my outfit and smiles. "Great minds."

I wrap him into a hug and bury my face in his chest. We both picked purple because it was my mom's favorite color, but neither one of us voices our reasoning out loud. "How're you holding up this morning, Bug?"

I pull back and lead him inside as I say, "I miss her, but I'm surprisingly doing okay so far. How about you?"

"About the same. But it's still relatively early," he says with a small smile.

After Graham walks out of the bedroom, we all load into his car. Graham is in the driver's seat because he's the only one who knows where we're going, and I let my dad take the passenger seat because he gets motion sickness in the back.

The first stop we make is too Zigglers for a to-go order that Graham had made ahead of time. Then we are on the road for about thirty minutes, headed in a direction that leaves me confused. I assumed he would take us to my mom's P.O. Box, but we're headed in the opposite direction.

"Where are we going?" I ask, leaning toward the front seat so my dad and Graham can hear me. I catch my dad smiling softly but he just shrugs his shoulders.

"It's a surprise," Graham says, taking a look at me through the rearview mirror.

I lean back in my seat and stare out the window, and my dad and Graham pick up where their conversation left off. I think about listening in, but I let my mind wander instead. I think about last Mother's Day, when my parents came to visit me in Richmond and I took them to the zoo. My mom loved all animals but her favorite were penguins, so we spent most of that afternoon watching the penguins swim around.

I'm pulled out of my thoughts as Graham puts the car in park. He gets out of the car and grabs a basket from the trunk. I stay in my seat, looking out the window bewildered until I see a glimpse of my dad's face in the mirror and see tears welling in his eyes.

"Where are we?" I ask my dad.

He turns to look at me with a sad smile and says, "Let's get out."

Still unsure, I unbuckle and climb out of the car. Graham has already set out a blanket, unpacked the food from Zigglers, and laid everything out. I walk down to where he is and I look around. We're at a lake that's surrounded by trees in bloom and flowers in the grass reaching towards the sun. Graham parked his car and set up our picnic in what looks to be one of the only clear areas. I watch my dad as he walks down to the water. He has a serene look on his face as he takes a deep breath.

"Graham, this place is beautiful and all, but what's so special about it?" I ask, trying not to sound rude. I really thought we'd be going to visit my mom. Somewhere we would be near her, even if she's not technically there. Instead, we're at a beautiful, but random, lake.

He pats the blanket next to him and says, "Sit and I'll tell you." So I sit down and look out at my dad who has taken a seat on a dock I hadn't noticed at first glance. "A few years back, I was having a particularly difficult time and decided to talk to your mom about it. You know that I'm not close with my parents, but at this particular time, I wasn't even in a good place with Grant. He and I rarely ever fight, so this was affecting me big time. Your mom told me about a lake that she liked to come to when she was struggling with things. I asked if I could come with her and she said no. She said it's a place you go by yourself to just reflect, but she did give me the address."

Graham pauses, looks around the clearing and then back at me. "This is the lake. She never told me the things she would come out here to reflect on. But she said she always felt at ease and clear-headed after an hour or so out here. So, I came out here after she told me about it. I was surprised to find that it helped me come to terms with where my relationship was with my brother. And ever since then, I come here when I need some clarity. It reminds me of your mom—more than anywhere else."

I take a deep breath in as a tear falls down my cheek. "I never knew she had a place where she came to be alone."

By the time I finish speaking, my dad is walking back to us and takes a seat on the blanket. "I didn't know about this place for years. One day, I got nosey after we had a particularly nasty disagreement. She left, saying she needed some time to think. I'm ashamed to say I got in my car and followed her," my dad says with a shaky breath. "I never thought she was sneaking around, so I wasn't following her to try to catch her in any act. I just wanted to know where she was going. And I followed her here. She got out of her car and went to sit on that dock out there. I sat in my car watching her as she watched the water for about twenty minutes before I decided to go home."

I swallow, trying to clear the lump of emotions forming in my throat. "When she got home an hour later she asked if I saw what I needed to see. I asked her what that place was, and she said it was a place that gave her peace when her mind couldn't find any. She apologized for leaving in the middle of the fight, but said she just needed to clear her head before she said something she couldn't take back." His tears fell freely down his cheeks as he continued. "After that fight, any time we argued or she was stressed about something, she told me she was going to find her peace, and I always knew she was coming here. This place held a lot of meaning for your mom." He looks at me and then he says to Graham, "Thank you for bringing us here. Sitting out on that dock . . . I felt her with me more than I have since she's been gone."

We each grab our food and sit in thoughtful silence as we eat. I fixate on Graham and am overcome with a strong feeling of love. He knew this place meant something to my mom and instead of keeping it between them, he shared it with me—with *us*. Even though my dad knew about this place, this visit seemed to have pushed the memory back into the forefront of his mind, and Graham was able to bring her back to him for a moment.

Graham stands up and reaches for my hand. I grab it so he can help me up. Holding hands, we walk along the water's edge. "I thought you should know this place exists. I think she would want you to be able to come here to get clarity when you feel lost."

I stop and look at Graham, take in a deep breath, and release it. I lean into him and wrap my arms around him tightly. "Thank you for bringing us here." Looking up at him I know this is the right moment. "I love you, Graham."

He takes in a breath, grasps the back of my neck, and pulls me in for a kiss. I relax in his embrace, melting into the kiss. Before he lets it get too R rated, with us being in public and my dad just down the lake, he pulls back and looks in my eyes. "I love you too, Tessa."

Chapter 60

Graham

Six months later

Sitting on the couch at Grant's holding my newest niece, Rosie, I look at my brother and say, "I'm doing it this weekend."

His face lights up as a smile spreads across face. "It's about damn time! What's your plan?" he asks, leaning forward, putting his elbows on his knees.

I look down at Rosie sleeping soundly against my chest, her perfect round cheeks tremble as she puckers her lips. "I took Friday off and Monday is a school holiday, so we're going to go to Baltimore for the weekend. I plan on taking her to the zoo, the museum, and the aquarium. My plan is to do it at the zoo the first day, but we'll see how it goes." I look up at my brother who is still smiling ear to ear. "What?" I ask him.

"I'm just so happy for the two of you." He leans back against the couch and then adds, "Do you know for a fact she's going to say yes?"

Swallowing back any doubt, I nod my head. "Yeah, we've been discussing the future for the past month and it's been made abundantly clear from many comments she's made that she's ready to get engaged." I give a sly smile. "She's even sent me links to rings she likes. But she has no idea that I've already got that taken care of."

He gives me a look of concern. "And you know she wants that ring? What if she really wants one of the ones she's sent you?"

I give his question a thought and tilt my head from side to side. "While she might like the rings she's sent me, I know she'll be more than thrilled with the one I have. It was her mom's, and honestly, it's very similar in style to the ones she's sent. But I don't think she thinks her mom's ring is a possibility."

Rosie begins to move around, letting out the cutest cry I've ever heard. At the sound, Lisa comes out of the room, freshly showered, with a smile on her face. "Thank you for holding her while I napped for a bit and took a shower. I'll take her now; she probably wants to nurse." She leans down gently, grabbing her newborn from my arms.

Grant looks over at me and then at Lisa. "You act like I don't take her for you to nap and shower every day," he says with mock outrage, causing Lisa to laugh.

"And you act like you didn't enjoy napping with me before I jumped in the shower." She arches an eyebrow at him. He lifts up his hands in surrender.

"Okay you two, I'm going to head home. I have to pack and get ready for this weekend." I bend down and give Lisa a kiss on the cheek. Then, I kiss my fingertips and place them on Rosie's head, knowing better than to kiss someone else's baby. My brother stands up, walking with me to the door.

"Good luck this weekend. I'm excited to have a sister," Grant says as he pulls me in for a hug.

"Thanks. I'll let you know how it goes," I say before stepping out of the door. As I get into my car, I take a minute to reflect, a smile breaking through my face as it hits me. I'm this much closer to having my own family, something I never let myself dream of.

Early Friday morning, I'm loading our bags into the trunk as Tessa sits in the front seat, playing with the music. She doesn't know where we're going, just knows that we're getting away for the weekend. I asked Paul two months ago for his blessing to ask Tessa to marry me. The tears in his eyes said more than his words ever could.

I double check my bag for the ring box before closing the trunk and heading to the driver's side.

"Everything ready?" Tessa asks, looking at me with a brilliant smile on her face. Her sunglasses hide her gorgeous brown eyes, but I just know they are gleaming too.

"Yep, everything's set. Are you ready? You don't need to do a tactical wee before we hit the road?" I ask, making her laugh.

She shakes her head. "Already went. Get in the car and let's go!" she says, unable to hide the excitement in her voice.

Two hours later, I'm pulling into our hotel, with Tessa passed out in the passenger seat. She fell asleep about forty minutes into the ride, which was okay with me, because it makes the arrival that much more of a surprise.

She blinks her eyes open as I put the car in park before sitting up and looking around, trying to see if she can tell where we are. "Do you want to wait in the car as I go check us in, or do you want to come with me?" I ask her as she lets out a yawn.

"I can come with you. Where are we?" she responds as she unbuckles her seatbelt and reaches down to put her shoes on. As I step out of the car, I look up at the sky. The clouds are threatening rain that the weather app did not forecast.

"You'll see." I walk around to her side to open her door for her. Hand in hand, we walk into the lobby of the hotel. I see Tessa look around, trying to see any signs of our location. She drops my hand when she sees the counter with the brochures on it.

I watch her for a moment as her face registers that we're in Baltimore before I walk up to the counter. "Good morning. Reservation for Graham Link," I say to the receptionist.

"Good morning, Mr. Link. Give me one moment," she says, typing something into the computer. "Thank you," she adds, then she reaches for the credit card and ID I placed on the counter for her. "You're in room two-eleven. The elevators are right that way and to the right. Please enjoy your stay," she says, placing my ID, credit card, and two room keys down on the counter.

"Thank you." I nod to her.

I walk over to Tessa, grabbing her hand, and we walk back out to the car to grab our bags.

"Why are we in Baltimore?" she asks, bouncing on the balls of her feet. She has told me time and again that she wants to go to an aquarium. So when the Internet told me this was one of the top three aquariums in the country, I knew I had to bring her.

I lean over giving her a quick kiss. "You'll just have to wait and see," I say, raising my eyebrows at her.

We got here a little past nine so the hotel is still serving their continental breakfast. We each grab a plate before heading to the elevator. When we get to our room, Tessa sets her plate down and falls backwards onto the king-sized bed that takes up most of the space in the room.

I sit on the couch by the window and start eating my breakfast as I watch her spread out on the bed. I pull out my phone and check the weather app. I have checked the weather religiously all week and never once did it predict rain. Looking at the app now, it says there is a ninety-nine percent chance of rain from ten thirty until three. I plop my phone down on the couch next to me. Looks like the zoo, and the proposal, will have to wait until tomorrow. Museum or aquarium it is.

Chapter 61

Tessa

I sit up from my spot on the most comfortable bed I've ever laid on and look over at Graham. He looks like he has a lot on his mind. I stand up and grab my plate, moving so I can sit next to him. I snuggle close but look out the window. The clouds looming in the sky look like they are going to open up any minute.

"What're you thinking about?" I ask before taking a bite of the blueberry muffin I grabbed.

He looks at me and smiles. "The weather is making me have to adjust some plans. So, I'm trying to decide what we should do today instead. Anything you want to do while we're here?" He holds my gaze as he waits for an answer.

I chew the inside of my cheek as I contemplate his question. "Considering I don't know what you have planned for the whole weekend, I'm not sure I should be the one picking," I say with a laugh. "I don't want to pick somewhere you had planned for tomorrow or Sunday."

He mulls over my answer then nods his head. "But this is your weekend too. If you pick something I had planned then we can just do it today, switching what I had planned for today on that day."

I smile at his answer. "How about we go to the art museum. I was reading about it in one of the brochures in the lobby."

A slow grin breaks out across his face. "That's actually what I was thinking. It opens at ten, so if we want to get there early we need to head out now. Or we can just arrive when we arrive." He's given it some thought, making me think that the museum was already on his list of things to do this weekend.

"Or, and hear me out, we could stay in the hotel today and explore the city tomorrow." I give him a seductive smile.

"And what would we possibly do in this hotel room to pass the day?" His voice matches my seductive smile.

I flutter my eyelashes and bite my lower lip as I lean over and press my mouth close to his ear. "We could give the neighbors reason to report a noise complaint." I stand up, grabbing his hand.

I walk us both over to the bed, pressing against his chest until he's sitting on the edge. When he's firmly seated, I walk to my bag and grab out a box of condoms and my bullet vibrator, not letting him see the items. I peek over my shoulder and see him trying to take a peek at what I'm grabbing.

I let out a soft chuckle, shaking my head. "Tsk tsk tsk. Be a good boy and wait until I'm ready for you to see." I turn my body while keeping the goodies on top of the bag behind my back. "However, what I have in mind requires a lot less . . ." I pause and take off my sweater, dropping it on the floor at my feet. "Clothes."

He sits on the bed, watching as I take off my clothes torturously slowly. When I'm fully nude, standing by the table where our bags are, I lower my hand to my center and rub my fingers through the wetness already gathering between my legs, keeping my eyes trained on Graham's face. I see him take in a sharp breath and swallow.

"Are you just going to sit there and let me have all the fun? Or are you going to strip too?" I ask, sliding my fingers in deeper, causing a slight moan to escape past my lips.

Graham kicks off his shoes and jumps up off the edge where he was sitting, unbuckling his belt and pants while his eyes never leave my body. Under his lustful eyes, I take my other hand and start massaging my breast as I continue pumping my fingers in and out of my soaking pussy.

Finally, his clothes are completely discarded and he starts to take a step towards me. "No, sir. Go lie down," I command.

He walks backwards, walking into the bed, shuffling himself backwards all while keeping eye contact. His hand moves towards his cock but he hesitates before grabbing it. "Can I?" he asks while giving himself a few slow strokes.

I bite my lip again and nod. Removing my hand from between my legs, I reach behind me and grab the items sitting atop my bag. While watching him stroke himself, I walk around to the side of the bed.

I set the unopened box of condoms on the bed. His eyes flick to it and he gets a sheepish smile. "Brand new box, huh? I'm pretty sure we still had some in the drawer."

I let out a throaty laugh. "Not nearly enough."

Joining him on the bed, I straddle his thighs. I move the vibrator from behind my back, clicking it on. Grabbing his cock in one hand I take over for him, rubbing my hand up and down as I lower the vibrator to the base of his cock—where his shaft meets his balls. He releases a guttural moan.

Once he comes close to finishing I stop and reach for the box of condoms. Taking my time opening the box, I watch as he throws his arm over his face. "You're gonna kill me, woman." He lets out a painful laugh.

"Oh, not for long." I unwrap the condom, rolling it down his length. When he's wrapped and back to watching what I'm doing, I turn myself around so I'm positioned with my ass toward him.

I grab his cock, positioning it at my entrance, then slowly lower myself down on him, causing us both to let out a moan of pleasure. Once I'm seated fully on him, I start to roll my hips, causing his toes to curl. I lean forward, resting my elbows on the bed as I continue to move my hips around. Graham's hands find my ass and he spreads my cheeks so he can watch as my pussy grinds against his cock. I move slightly, leaning on one elbow so I can reach my clit with my other hand. Using the vibrator, I put pressure on my clit, causing my orgasm to build quickly.

My body starts to tense, my pussy clenching around his cock as he yells. "Fuck! Tessa! Your pussy feels so good." His words send me over the edge.

I drop the vibrator as my body starts to give out.

Graham quickly sits up, putting his arms around my soft stomach. Without pulling out he switches us to the doggy position and starts pounding into me. "Holy—Shit—Graham—Fuck—Yes—" I choke out each word as my body is still trying to come down from my first orgasm. I quickly reach another as his thumb circles and massages my clit as he plunges into me from behind. Two more thrusts and he's pulling out, spilling into the condom. We both collapse—me on the bed, him on top of me.

"Holy shit, babe." He reaches up and moves the hair sticking to my sweaty face. All I'm able to do is nod and give a breathy laugh in return.

We spend the rest of the day finding new ways to bring that response from each other, stopping only to eat and recharge. For lunch we order sandwiches from room service and watch TV while we eat. For dinner we order a pizza, which we bring to the bathroom and eat in the bathtub, where I sit between his legs, resting my back against his chest.

We wake up the next morning to the sound of thunder clapping outside. A quick glance at the weather app has

Graham letting out a small groan. "Fuck. I guess there goes that plan," he says, barely loud enough for me to hear him.

"Excuse me?" I ask, leaning in closer. "I didn't hear you."

He turns his head to face me. "What I wanted to do—it's outside, so those plans have to change again. How about we go to the aquarium this morning? We can get there right when it opens. We can spend the morning walking around enjoying the sea animals," he says, making me smile.

I wiggle against him. "We get to go to the aquarium?" I practically squeal.

He nods his head and starts to sit up. "Yes, ma'am. But we have to get a move on. So get that gorgeous ass out of bed and get ready. We've got fish to see!"

We pull up to the aquarium and the rain is falling hard. Luckily, Graham keeps an umbrella in his car, so we're able to stand under it as we wait for the doors to unlock so we can get inside. We're one of the first people here and Graham takes my hand as we grab a map.

"How about we start out at the big viewing tank so we can actually have a good spot to watch the sharks and everything?" he asks, pointing to where it's located on the map.

I bounce on my toes and kiss him on the cheek. "Sounds perfect!" I sing as I head in the direction the map says to go.

Once we get there, we find we are the only ones there, so I drop Graham's hand and walk up to the tank. I'm mesmerized by the vastness capable of being inside a building. When I turn around to point out one of the sharks to Graham, I find him down on one knee, holding a ring box out. My eyes go wide and instantly fill with tears.

"Tessa Elaine," he starts as tears also begin to gather in his eyes. His mouth is moving, indicating that he's started on whatever beautiful speech he undoubtedly planned for months, but all I can focus on is the ring inside the box. I would know that ring anywhere. It's a simple gold band with a single round diamond. It's sitting alone in this box, but somewhere, I'm assuming at home, is the matching gold band that has small diamonds embedded within. Now tears are falling in earnest down my cheeks. He's not only proposing, but he's proposing with my mom's wedding ring. The ring I have wanted as my own for as long as I can remember.

It's when I finally look back at Graham's face that I realize he's stopped talking and is looking at me with hope-filled eyes, brimming with unshed tears as he awaits my response. I lower myself so I'm kneeling in front of him, cupping his face in my hands, and I pull him in for a kiss. "Of course I'll marry you. I love you."

He lets out a strangled sigh, takes the ring out of the box, and slips it on my finger. "I love you, too." He stands us both up and pulls me into a hug. The few people who have gathered in the viewing area clap at the sight of an accepted proposal.

I pull back and look down at my hand, at the ring he placed there. "How? When?" I ask, at a loss for words.

He smiles at me then looks at my hand. He twists the ring before answering. "Your mom gave it to me. She always believed in us."

I lean into his embrace, burying my head in his chest. I let the happy tears fall again.

Two weeks later, we are on our way to the cabin to celebrate Thanksgiving with my dad, Grant, Lisa, and the kids. Grant and his crew are meeting us there, but my dad is riding with us. I'm bouncing with excitement in the backseat at returning to where it became official for us.

I barely let Graham put the car in park before I throw open the door and run to hug Cori. She and I have created quite the bond in the past few months and I'm so excited she's going to be my niece.

"Are you ready to go inside?" she asks, pulling on my arm with the biggest smile on her face.

I laugh before responding. "Let me help my dad and Graham with the bags. Then we can head in."

I walk back to the car to see my efforts to help are wasted—they already have the bags in their hands. Graham looks at me with a mischievous smile on his face before leaning in to give me a kiss.

"You ready to head in?" he whispers into my ear.

"I've been ready to come back here since we pulled out of the driveway the last time." I turn to head to the door.

When we get to the porch, Graham opens the door and lets me step inside first. The moment my feet cross the threshold I'm met with a chorus of *"Congratulations,"* and a very distinct voice yelling, *"You're getting married!"* I look around and see my friends from Richmond inside, holding glasses of champagne with smiles glued on their faces.

I look back to Graham who's smiling from ear to ear and see Corinne jumping up and down next to him, clapping. "Happy engagement party, babe," he remarks before wrapping his arms around me to kiss me.

Epilogue

Graham

One year later

Two hours before "I Do"

There's a brief knock at the door as I'm adjusting my tie, so Grant answers it for me. Paul walks in with a smile on his face and glossy eyes filled with unshed tears. I look at him through the mirror and smile brightly.

"Looking good, son," he says, clapping my shoulder. "I can't be in here long because I've got to go see the bride, but I promised Sherri I would make sure you got this on your wedding day." He pulls out an envelope that has *For Graham* written across the front in Sherri's perfect handwriting.

I take it from him and look up trying to fight back my own tears. "What does it say?" I ask, choking back the emotions trying to fight through.

He shakes his head. "I don't know—I never read it. But I'll leave you alone to finish getting ready. I'll see you soon." Paul hugs me then turns to the door.

I look over at my brother and nephew who are sitting on a couch eating. Grant gives me a subtle nod, taps Ethan's leg and gestures for them to leave.

Once I'm alone, I take a small sip of the whiskey Grant poured for me as I take a seat before opening the letter.

Graham,

To you, on the day you marry Tessa. And if by some chance I was wrong and Tessa's not the one you're marrying today, I suppose I'm still happy for you, but a little sad for my girl.

I want to thank you for taking care of my Tessa for me. Her heart is so big, and she loves so deeply, that I know losing me was hard for her. I also know that losing me was hard on you. Maybe not as much as her, but you still lost me. And even though I'm sad to not be there today, I'm glad that you have each other, that you were able to fall apart together.

Continue to love and cherish our sweet girl as I know she will do the same to you. I'm sorry I'm not there to hug you and welcome you to the family, but I hope you know that I considered you my son long before today.

With all my love,

Sherri

I take a deep breath as a rogue tear falls on the letter. I knew Sherri thought of me as family, but to see it written in black and white has me fighting back more tears. I fold the letter back up and return it to its envelope, which I place in my jacket pocket. This will be how I bring Sherri with me today.

I check the time and see it's time I head out to the sanctuary. It's time to meet my bride.

I'm standing at the front of the church, the pastor on one side, my brother and nephew on the other. "I Will Always Love You" by Vitamin String Quartet begins to play signaling for Cori, Lisa—who is holding Rosie—and Nell, to walk down the aisle. Then, finally, Tessa and Paul. The crowd stands and turns to watch as Tessa and Paul stand at the open doors.

My breath catches in my throat and I feel like I'm floating. Tessa in her wedding dress is an absolute dream. I'm trying to ingrain this image into my brain so I can look back at it forever. She's got one arm looped with Paul's, the other holding a bouquet of red daisies, her head held high as they make their way down the aisle to me.

I lock eyes with her and can see my feelings reflected in her misty ones. Tears pool in the corners of my eyes, causing me to fight the urge to blink. I don't want to miss a second of Tessa, so I let my eyes sting. When she and Paul get to the bottom of the altar I step down, shake Paul's hand, and I loop Tessa's arm around mine as we make our way up the steps.

Tessa

Two hours before "I Do"

Nell insisted she be the one to bend down to tighten my shoe, claiming I shouldn't have to do any work on my special day. I don't argue with her, because I didn't let her do any work on her special day either. Once she's standing back up, we both stand in front of the mirror, staring at my reflection. My long, curly brown hair is pinned back, giving the illusion that I have a crown made of hair, with a veil pinned at the back of my head, and I'm wearing a sweetheart neckline and capped sleeves on my empire-style lace dress. I look at her reflection in the mirror and smile.

As she's reaching up to adjust a loose hair on my head, there's a knock at the door. "Come in," I call.

But before the door can open, Lisa steps in front of the door. "It could be Graham trying to sneak a peek," she says, looking at me before poking her head out the door. Once she sees it's not Graham, she steps aside. "Sorry, Mr. Gunter, I just needed to make sure Graham wasn't trying to catch a glimpse of Tessa." She giggles, walking back to the couch.

My dad stops in his tracks and takes in a deep inhale. A single tear falls down his cheek. "Oh, Bug, you look gorgeous." He walks over to me, pulling me in for a hug.

"Girls, can you give us a minute?" I say to Nell and Lisa. They nod, then Lisa picks up Rosie and motions for Corinne to follow as they step out of the room, leaving my dad and I alone.

I look at my dad and swallow before turning back to the mirror. "You think so?"

"The most beautiful bride I've ever seen. Your mom would be so happy for you." He kisses my forehead.

I suck in a breath at the same time I notice he does which makes me chuckle. "Dad," I say, turning around to look him in the eyes. "I hear music," I say as I watch his face light up with understanding.

His eyes frantically run over my face and down to my stomach then return to my face. "Are you saying . . . ? Are you—Are you pregnant?" All I can do to respond is smile and nod. His face lights up with excitement. "When did you find out?"

"I took a test this morning. I haven't even told Graham." I watch as he brings his hands to his face and wipes at his eyes.

"This is fantastic news, Tessa! You're going to be a phenomenal mother!" He pulls me in for a hug, but quickly pulls back. "Sorry, I don't want to ruin your look." He looks me over again and tilts his head down. "Right. I have something for you," he adds, reaching into his coat pocket, pulling out an envelope that says *For Tessa* on the front in my mom's familiar handwriting.

I stare at the envelope he's holding out to me, blinking. Too afraid to reach for it, scared it might disappear. He holds it up to me and says, "Your mom asked me to give this to you on your wedding day. She made me promise that you'd read it before you walked down the aisle." He takes a breath and then asks, "Would you like me to be in here while you read it?"

I bite the inside of my lip and shake my head. "No, thank you. I think I want to be alone with this." I hold it up as I walk to the couch that Lisa and Corinne were sitting on.

My dad nods. "I'll be right outside when you're ready."

Taking a deep breath to try to calm my shaking hands, I open the letter.

My sweet Tessa,

I wrote and rewrote this letter multiple times, each time feeling like I didn't say all that needs to be said. The first copy I wrote a week after my diagnosis. Now, this most recent copy. I'm writing about four weeks after that. I just got home from my weekly blood work.

You haven't been by to see me in a while and I know that you will beat yourself up over that for a long time. I want you to try to forgive yourself. Cancer is an ugly, horrible disease and it's hard to be around. I need you to know, I never held you staying away against you for one second.

I remember the day I found out I was pregnant with you like it was yesterday. I was being unbearably moody and I insisted your dad watch The Breakfast Club *with me. I ended up sobbing at the end when the letter was being read, even though I'd seen the movie a million times. Your dad just sat there staring at me, and then said, "Sher, I think we need to get you a pregnancy test." My immediate reaction was to shoot him the stink eye and say "fuck off." But I thought back to when I had my last period and realized he was right. I sent him to the store for a pregnancy test and a carton of ice cream. Twenty minutes later, we were hugging and crying because there were two lines on that little plastic stick confirming I was pregnant.*

Nine months passed so quickly and you were here, in my arms, staring up at me with your dark eyes. Looking at me in a way that told me you would always need me. In that moment, I promised you that I would always be there for you, and I would love you and keep you safe forever. And here I am, breaking that promise. I'm so sorry, Tessa. I'm sorry that I won't be there for you when you get that positive pregnancy test. Or when you get married. But this letter will find you on that special day. I made your dad promise me that. He said, "And what if she decides to never get married? When do you want her to get this?" I just looked at him and said that he would know.

This letter has been difficult for me to write, because it means I'm no longer with you. And that's a scary thing to process. Knowing there are so many things you will go through that I won't be there for. But I've come to terms with it and I pray to God each day that you have too.

How I wish I could be there with you today. There's no doubt in my mind that you are the most beautiful bride, and Graham is going to be so lucky to have you as his wife. And if by chance I'm wrong, and you aren't about to marry Graham, my apologies, and I hope this other man treats you right.

Tessa, you were my greatest accomplishment out of life, and being your mom was my favorite thing in the world. I hate that I got sick and it took away my opportunity to watch you become a mom and experience the greatest gift life has to offer, because you're going to be the best mom to ever exist. I'd wager even better than me.

I'm so proud of the woman you have become. You have always made me and your father proud and I know you will continue to do so.

Even though I rewrote this letter so many times, I still feel like I'm leaving so much out. Lean on your father, help him move on and even lean on any future woman he might bring into his life. You deserve to have the best life possible. Don't let losing me dampen your shine.

I love you always,

Mom

I blink to try to stop the tears from falling. Reading my mom's words after she's gone has my emotions running rampant. I run my finger down the edge of the page, recognizing this from the journal I purchased her before her first round of chemo. I grab the water sitting on the table in front of me and take a rather large sip to help swallow down the lump growing in my throat. I fold the letter and put it back in the envelope, placing it with my things on the table. Standing up, I walk to the mirror to make sure my make-up isn't too smudged from crying.

"I did it, Mom. I found the happiness you knew I could find. I just wish you could be here physically, but I know you're here in spirit. I love you," I say as I look up to the ceiling.

Once I've gathered myself, I open the door to find m dad sitting on a chair just outside. He looks up at me and smiles. "Are you ready to go get married?"

I nod, pulling him into a hug as he stands up.

Nell, Lisa, Corinne, and Rosie weren't too far from the room, heard my dad talking, and joined us.

"Let's go get you fucking married!" Nell basically screams. "Oh shit, young ears. Sorry," she says, looking over at Corinne and Rosie, then covers her mouth when she realizes she said another cuss word when apologizing.

We get to the doors of the sanctuary, and when they open up I hear "I Will Always Love You" playing over the speakers. Corinne walks in first, followed by Lisa holding a freshly-turned one-year-old Rosie. After a count of ten, Nell looks back at me, smiles, then takes her turn.

I loop my right arm with my dad's left and he squeezes my arm with his right hand. "Like Nell said, let's go get you fucking married."

I let out a laugh, then take in a deep breath.

Taking a step into the sanctuary, I don't look around at all my friends and family in attendance. Instead, my eyes instantly find Graham, and I can't help as my smile widens across my whole face. My eyes start to gloss over as the tears sting, but I keep my eyes locked on my groom.

My dad squeezes my arm again. "We're almost there, Bug," he whispers, making a small laugh escape my mouth. I feel like running down the aisle to Graham, but I'm pretty sure that wouldn't be ladylike.

When we get to the altar, Graham takes a few steps down to meet us. He shakes my dad's hand, then takes my arm from my dad, looping it in his. Together, we take the steps back up to the altar. I hand my bouquet to Nell before turning back to Graham.

I reach my other hand out and grab his. As we stand there, holding hands, he mouths "I love you" and I whisper it back. I quickly look down at my stomach and back up at him and give him a brief nod. The smile on his face gets even brighter as the realization of what that simple gesture means. I hold his gaze for a moment more before we turn to face the pastor who has begun the wedding ceremony.

The End

Bonus Chapter
Paul

Five and a half weeks after diagnosis

We just got back from what was supposed to be Sherri's third chemotherapy treatment. Instead, it ended up being an appointment with her oncologist that had us both in tears. Her lab work from yesterday showed that the treatments aren't working like they should and her levels are climbing at a rate that would endanger her more if they continue to pump her body full of any more medicine. I wish I could say that the news came as a surprise, but honestly, with how fast I've watched her health decline, I unfortunately saw those precious, promised months, quickly turn into not nearly enough weeks.

Now, I'm sitting here with my laptop open on a TV dinner tray, researching the differences between home hospice and a hospice facility, as Sherri rests on her recliner. Her doctor gave us the number of a woman who works at the hospice center close by so we could set up an appointment, but I'd like to do some research before we make that meeting.

From what I'm seeing, the differences are that at home, a nurse comes, at most, a couple times a day and, at least, a couple times a week with the family doing most of the care. At a facility, the nurses are there around the clock to take care of her needs, so there isn't any added stress or responsibility placed on the family. Another difference is where she would be most comfortable. At home, she doesn't have to go anywhere and will be able to pass in the comfort of the home we built together the past thirty-four years. Otherwise, she can pass in a facility where nothing is familiar. I know what I'd prefer. I'd prefer her to pick at-home care, but in the end it's up to her. Wherever she'll feel the most comfortable.

We tried to call Tessa on the way home from Sherri's appointment, but her phone didn't even ring, it went straight to voicemail. Sherri texted Graham and asked if he could have Tessa call us when he got home. We would like to share this news with her in person, but Sherri says she understands if Tessa still isn't ready to come back over here.

I put my face in my hands and let out a shaky breath. I can't believe I'm losing my best friend in a matter of days. A week or two, if we're lucky. I sit up and look at Sherri asleep on her recliner, and suddenly I'm back in our high school library. I'm a stocky sixteen-year-old, failing English, sitting across from this beautiful fifteen-year-old, who is calmly explaining the story that our teacher expected us to read. I remember being instantly infatuated with her and not caring that my failing is what brought her into my life. I *needed* her to be part of my life.

I blink and I'm a slightly less stocky nineteen-year-old, standing at the front of a small church, watching my future bride walk down the aisle with her arm linked with her dad's. Her long, white lace dress with puffy sleeves over her shoulders, and long lace running down her arms, holding a bouquet of lilies and the biggest smile on her face. I wipe at the tears sliding down my cheeks. Next thing I see is my best friend, now twenty years old, lying in a hospital bed with messy brown hair and twinkling brown eyes, looking down at our precious, brand new little baby girl, wearing an even bigger smile on her face than she had on our wedding day.

I stand up and step out of the room to get some air. This is not how I envisioned my future with Sherri when we were just teenagers falling in love. Sure, I knew there would be sickness throughout our lives together. But I anticipated us turning gray together and watching our grandkids play in the yard. I used to tell Sherri that when we got old and gray I would be the one to die first, because I couldn't imagine what even one day on this planet without her would be like. Who knew I would be finding out the answer to that, and a lot sooner than either of us could have expected.

Stay tuned for a novella featuring Paul.

Acknowledgements

First I'd like to thank my husband, Mr. J.B. Lee, for supporting my dream of writing a book. He didn't question it when I told him about the idea I had, he just encouraged me to do the thing. He is the backbone of our family, working hard so I can be home with our daughter and fulfill this dream of mine to become a published author. He's my very own Graham mixed with Paul and I couldn't write a better MMC for myself if I tried.

Thank you to my friends and the select few family members who actually know that I wrote and published a book. Your support and belief in me means more than you could possibly imagine.

To my alpha readers, Kelly, Natalie, Michelle, Megan, Nikki, and Caitlin. You girls read this book when it was unedited, raw, and in its early early stages and saw the potential those bones had. You gave me your honest feedback which helped me fix it to become the version my beta readers got to see.

Which leads me to my beta readers, Vanessa Ratiu, Kelli Cooke, Emma Kate, Mary DiMarzo, @annalees_reading, Sam Schreiber, and @goodgirlsbookshelf. You ladies took my work and helped me polish it to a point where I believe, with the help of my editor, it will be perfect. You left your honest feedback along with all the messages of your feelings while reading, and I absolutely loved every bit of it.

To Caitlin Lengerich, my incredible editor (no, she didn't edit the acknowledgements, so if there are errors it's all on me and the fact that I'm human.) You took my baby and helped me turn it into what it is today, for that I am forever thankful.

Thank you to Kelli Cooke, Emma Kate, Michelle Naomi Mosley, Ellie K Drake, Katelyn Snyder, Madison Myers, Cassandra Moll. and Dee Jordan for being such amazing, supportive indie authors who helped me navigate the scary world of self-publishing. You all gave me advice at some point during this journey that encouraged me to keep going. Without fellow authors like you, *Falling Apart Together* would still be a Google doc sitting in my drive looking for its way in this world.

Thank you to Lauren Gnapi with Elemental Opal for my beautiful cover art. You read my book, came up with concepts and took my ideas and created this beautiful art that depicts the mood of the book and is absolutely stunning to boot!

Thank you to Snigdha from Beyond the Books PR for helping me promote this book so that way it was able to reach a larger audience. Your support through this process has been an extreme comfort. I'm looking forward to working with you again in the future!

Lastly, to you, my readers. Whether you loved this book and felt the heartbreak, grief, and healing I put into these words, or if you hated it and never want to read another book by me again, thank you. You picked up this book and gave it a chance, and for that I am grateful for you.

About the author

Image drawn by @junidr
aws.ca

    J.B. Lee was born and raised in Florida but life brought her to Virginia where she has spent the last decade of her life. J.B. is a wife and mother. When she's not spending time with her husband and daughter she is reading or writing. She started writing in March 2023 when the same scene kept playing out in her mind until she put it down in her notes app. She has since added many story ideas to her notes app in hopes of bringing these characters to life. J.B. has a degree in elementary education and spent six years in the classroom and has hopes to one day return, but for now she enjoys creating stories that will pull at your heartstrings while also giving you a happily ever after.

9 798218 686482